THINGS WORTH REMEMBERING

THINGS *worth* remembering

JACKINA STARK

BETHANYHOUSE
Minneapolis, Minnesota

Published by Bethany House Publishers
11400 Hampshire Avenue South
Bloomington, Minnesota 55438

Bethany House Publishers is a division of
Baker Publishing Group, Grand Rapids, Michigan.

Printed in the United States of America

Library of Congress Cataloging-in-Publication Data

Stark, Jackina.
　　Things worth remembering / Jackina Stark.
　　　　p.　cm.
　　ISBN 978-0-7642-0711-2 (pbk.)
　　1.　Mothers and daughters—Fiction.　I. Title.

PS3619.T3736T48　2009
813'.6—dc22

2009025125

For my daughters, Stacey and Leanne.
You delight your dad and me.
You are our beloveds.

MONDAY

CHAPTER ONE

Kendy

I finish emptying the dishwasher and snap the door into place, contemplating only one glorious thought: The third Monday of July has finally arrived. For months now, that date has been circled on the colorful rooster calendar hanging in the laundry room. I've anticipated it almost as much as I've anticipated next Saturday, the day our only child is to be married.

Maisey and our future son-in-law should be here by six, ready to sit around the kitchen table, enjoying good food and the rest that comes from being in the presence of those we love.

I'm setting veggies on the counter when Luke, most

helpful of husbands, comes in with the lettuce I forgot when I bought out the store this morning. He's talking on his cell phone but manages a smile as he hands me the plastic sack.

Is that sympathy I see in his warm brown eyes?

My heart braces itself.

"Well, be safe," he says, "and we'll just see you when you get here, then."

He disconnects and shoves his phone into his pocket. "Best laid plans. They're getting a late start. Apparently Maisey didn't get away from work as soon as she intended."

"I didn't think she was going in today."

"Something came up, I guess. I doubt they'll be here before ten."

I gather the little troop of green onions, carrots, radishes, celery, and tomatoes that I've just deposited on the counter and return them to the refrigerator. "We can save the salad for tomorrow," I say. "The pie's made; maybe they'll want a snack when they get here."

How's that for a semblance of cheerful acceptance?

Luke smiles again as though he has read my mind.

As a rule, I've become pretty good at acceptance—it's called self-preservation. It's also an answer to one of my frequently borrowed prayers: "Help me accept the things I cannot change." Despite the fact that Niebuhr's entire Serenity Prayer is hanging on my bedroom wall, I'm not sure I'll be able to attain acceptance on such short notice, not this particular afternoon.

Luke has bounced back nicely, though. He says the delay will give him time to clean up his desk properly, and before I've shut the refrigerator door, he's heading for his home office.

I have things to do too, good things, but I'm just not very eager to do them—I'm in a fixing-a-family-dinner mode.

Well, regroup, Kendy.

Two hours later I have done just that. When Luke comes into our bedroom, where I'm stretched out on the chaise longue, I have read five of the children's books from the stack I'm reviewing before school starts and finished next week's Bible study lesson.

"Done," he says.

"Me too," I say, putting my Bible and workbook on the round table beside the chaise. I love the table, a fantastic find in an out-of-the-way antique shop years ago. It's a small oak dining room pedestal table, cut down to the right height for my chaise and big enough for all the things I like to have at my disposal when I sit here.

"Scoot," Luke says, and I make room for him.

He stretches out beside me and pulls me into his arms. This simple act makes acceptance—a translucent thing hovering in the distance—seem slightly more accessible. Or is it a mirage?

"Are you okay?" he asks.

"Actually, I've been fairly productive," I say, sounding more matter-of-fact than I feel.

"That's good."

He says we should run into town to get something to eat. I don't really want to go, but I say okay.

I know he wants to keep me busy. Chances are he'll find a movie he's been dying to see. *What,* I'll say, *have they released* Godfather IV?

He pats my shoulder, pleased, no doubt, that he has gotten such an agreeable response from me. "Then we'll come home," he says, "spray ourselves with mosquito repellant, and wait on the porch for the kids."

"Good plan," I say, and then I kiss him—a long, ten-second kiss—because he has come to rescue me.

Maisey

I put down my briefcase and the sackful of best wishes so that I can rummage in my purse for the keys to the front door. Before I can find them, the door flies open. The cause, I'm happy to see, is not magic or mayhem but Marcus.

"Well, my goodness, you're here already," I say.

He grabs my briefcase and steps back to let me in.

"I thought I was supposed to call you when I got home," I say, giving him a quick kiss.

"You took too long. I decided to come on over and find a place for the stuff I picked up while we were at my parents'. Dad and I spent most of Saturday in the garage. If you had come out there at almost any given time, you would have heard me saying, 'You don't need this, do you?' "

"And I *might* have come out there if your mother hadn't kept me busy most of the day copying your favorite recipes into a little ringed notebook she had proudly labeled *From the Blair Kitchen*. You haven't really had a good look at that thing yet. I am truly finding it hard to believe one of your favorite dishes is Yankee Red-Flannel Hash."

"As a matter of fact, feel free to tear that sucker out of your notebook, but don't tell Mom."

"Not to worry."

"You should have told her to pull up a chair. *You* have a few recipes *she* might want."

Marcus puts my briefcase on the bar and comes over to the sofa, where I've plopped with my sack. "What's that?" he asks.

"This," I say, holding up the sack with one hand and patting the cushion next to me with the other, "is a great idea. They had a surprise shower for me at work. That's why Gram asked me what time we were heading to Indiana today. She said she'd like to take me to lunch before we get away. Only lunch wasn't at her favorite restaurant like I thought it would be; it was in the *board* room, which amazingly enough, my grandmother can actually reserve. It was a luncheon shower. Wasn't *that* a nice surprise?"

"Your grandmother was cutting it close."

"Well, that's true, but she wanted two girls who've been on vacation to be there."

"But, Maisey, it's almost five. The shower couldn't have lasted that long."

"True. I ended up writing an article for next month's newsletter. Someone else was going to do it for me, but I was right there. I had done the research, and I really wanted to do it myself. I called Dad this afternoon. It's cool."

I walk into the kitchen to get a bottle of water and some granola bars out of the pantry. "We can eat snacks on the way." I unscrew the cap and chug half the bottle before I come up for air. "So, guess what's in the sack."

"There's no time for guessing."

"I'm almost packed," I say, returning to the couch to pick up the sack.

"Almost! Maisey, we should have left hours ago."

"I told you. I've talked to my parents. It's no big deal, Marcus."

He says nothing. Translation—it's a big deal to him.

Oh brother.

With a huff, I toss the sack on the coffee table and take my terribly tardy self into the master bathroom to collect toiletries to put in my overnight bag. Marcus follows me as far as the bedroom, holding the sack I no longer wish to discuss.

"So, what's in here?"

"It doesn't matter," I say, tossing my hair dryer and straightening iron into the suitcase.

He takes out the tissue paper and looks inside. "Cards?"

I come over and take the sack out of his hand and put it on the dresser. "They're *gift* cards."

"Why are you so ticked?" he asks.

"You're the one who was ticked. I just wanted to show you what we got at the shower, but you act like not getting to my parents' house exactly when we planned is the crime of the century."

I sidestep him and rush into the bathroom, grab the cosmetic bag from the linen closet, and empty the contents of my makeup drawer into it. All the while, I carefully avoid eye contact with Marcus, even though he has followed me and is standing in the doorway.

"Okay," he says, coming in to stand behind me. I don't look into the mirror, but I know we are reflected there, his hands rubbing gentle circles on my upper arms, his eyes—the rich brown of Dad's eyes—penetrating. "What's going on here?"

He turns me around and waits for me to look at him. I don't want to, but I do, quite sure he can outwait me.

"I just don't like you griping at me when I have something neat to tell you." I go into the bedroom to retrieve the sack, and he follows me. "Look," I say, "we have at least twelve gift cards or certificates for some of our favorite restaurants. The president of the company even gave us one!"

"You're kidding."

"He sent it with Gram."

I pull out the cards and certificates and spread them on the bed. "Wasn't this a cool idea? We can have a great date once a month with no hit whatsoever to our budget."

"That's very cool," he says, giving them a quick look. "But we really do need to go."

I stuff everything back in the sack. "I know." I point at suitcases standing by the armoire. "You can take those two out. I really am almost ready."

Marcus takes the suitcases down to the car, and I finish packing the overnight bag and change into something comfortable. Then, wanting everything in its place, I remove the gift cards from the sack I brought them home in, put the sack in a plastic container for such things, and take our future dining dates into the living room and put them in the top drawer of the desk.

"Ready?" Marcus asks when he comes back in. "It wasn't easy, but I got everything into the trunk."

I head for the thermostat. "I've turned it up already," he says, "and I've locked the patio door. Everything's good."

I stand in the middle of the living area and look around. I smile at Marcus, who's standing in the doorway, clearly anxious to leave.

"Come here," I say.

I can tell by the look on his face that I'm holding him up. He's a man with a mission, and he will not be satisfied until we have accomplished it. I know he wishes we were in Indiana now, getting out of the car in time for dinner and greeting his future in-laws, Luke and Kennedy Laswell—or to his way of thinking, a second set of parents. He is far more eager to arrive than I am.

Still he comes to me.

I put my arms around his waist and look up at him. "The next time we're in this apartment, we'll be Marcus and Maisey Blair. I think that calls for a serious kiss, even if we *are* getting a late start."

He kisses me sweetly, and I can't help wishing it were possible to fast-forward my life just this once, and *voilà*, it's not Monday evening with a long week ahead of us, but it's Saturday night, and Marcus and I—standing before a profusion of white flowers and flickering candles—have just been pronounced man and wife.

Kendy

Luke and I are sitting on the front porch in comfortable wicker chairs, drinking unsweetened tea and reviewing a movie that was far more entertaining than I expected it to be. It is too late on a Monday night for there to be much traffic on the state highway that runs in front of our house. We have been peering into the darkness for quite some time, and finally bright headlights illuminate the night and a car turns into the driveway. *Driveway* is something of a misnomer; the house is set at least fifty yards from the road.

"False alarm," Luke says as the car backs out and heads in the direction it came. It isn't rational, but I'm rather irritated at the car and its unidentified driver. Those headlights significantly elevated my heart rate. Maisey called when she and Marcus crossed the Indiana line, and I was sure that had to be them.

I'm about to go inside and refill our glasses when Luke says, "More lights." And this time a car turns in and makes it all the way up the drive.

Hallelujah!

Luke and I walk out to meet the kids.

"Finally," Marcus says, getting out of the car and stretching. Luke and I give him a hug. We've made that drive many times and know exactly how he feels.

Then there is Maisey—her blue eyes bright in the porch light; her brown hair, strikingly streaked with natural highlights, pulled into a ponytail. She looks fit and adorable in layered tank tops and rolled-up sweat pants. She comes around the front of her car and gives her dad and me a quick hug. "Sorry we're late," she says.

"What happened, honey?" I ask, the four of us walking to the back of the car. Marcus pops the trunk, and the men begin to unload the luggage.

"Since we weren't leaving until this afternoon, Gram asked if I'd come in so she could take me to lunch."

"We were leaving at one," Marcus said.

"*Tentatively,*" Maisey countered. "I thought we were just going out to lunch, but instead she had a surprise shower for me. Wasn't that a nice thing for Gram to do?"

It was an *unbelievable* thing for my mother to do.

"It was very nice," I say, recovering from the incredible.

"I told Maisey her grandmother was cutting it close," Marcus said.

All of us tromp into the house with our share of luggage. There's a lot. They have packed for this week and for their honeymoon as well, since they are flying out of Indianapolis.

"Maybe she *was* cutting it close," Maisey says, "but it was still nice."

All of us are standing in the entry, looking at Maisey as though she must have more to say. I grab the duffle bag sliding off her shoulder.

"Actually, I'm the one who made us late," she says, taking the bag from me. "Since I was at the office, I wanted to finish an article for next month's newsletter instead of letting someone else do it. I'm sorry if I messed up dinner or anything."

"Well, there's pie," I say, "in case you're hungry."

"I'm starved!" Marcus says.

"Oh, guys," Maisey says, wilting before our eyes. "I'm so tired and not in the least bit hungry. Do you mind if I crash?"

Her question is rhetorical.

She's looking at Luke—of the three of us, the one most likely to support this relinquishing of our time together. Even he seems surprised, though.

"Well, sure," he says. "Go to bed if you're tired—we have all week."

Marcus helps Maisey lug their things from the entry hall up to their rooms, and then he hurries back downstairs for pie and conversation. A more affable young man I have not met, and Luke and I must look something like his parents would look sitting here, filled with pride and love, watching him eat with gusto and listening to him talk about life since he last saw us.

After Marcus finishes two pieces of pie, he insists on rinsing his own dishes and putting them in the dishwasher before he borrows a book Luke has been telling him about and heads to his room.

As we part at the bottom of the stairs, Marcus says, "Maisey and I will be down for breakfast bright and early tomorrow morning!"

This sounds like sweet reassurance rather than a statement of intention.

Does Marcus sense my disappointment?

I like to think myself capable of concealing or, better yet, dismissing disappointment. But it's hard. First we forfeited the anticipated evening, and then the night. If only Maisey had been hungry rather than exhausted—hungry to sit awhile, to eat and talk and laugh. The third Monday in July is here, and it turns out that so many components of contentment still lie beyond my reach.

These thoughts accompany me as I head into our bathroom and put on my gown and robe to begin my nightly ritual. Mother used to say you age a year every night you neglect taking off your makeup. She read that somewhere. I doubt she believes it, and I surely don't, but along with brushing my teeth and taking my calcium and multivitamin pills, I seldom overlook my three-step routine: clean, exfoliate, and moisturize.

Luke's already asleep when I turn out the bathroom light and walk into our room. Doubting I can sleep just yet, I confiscate my Bible from the oak table and start into the living room so I won't disturb Luke.

"Read here," he says.

"Oh, I thought you were asleep."

"Almost," he says. "But you won't bother me."

"I thought this might help," I say, holding up my Bible.

He doesn't seem surprised that I need a little help.

"Try Psalm 37," he suggests.

I sit down, put my feet up on the chaise, adjust my robe,

and turn to the Psalms. I have had occasion to practically memorize a few of them, but not this one.

"Psalm 37?" I ask.

He nods.

I turn to it and begin reading. " 'Do not fret,' " I read aloud.

I look at Luke. He smiles before he closes his eyes, unable to keep them open any longer.

Silently and slowly I read the first eleven verses of Psalm 37 and find wise words that are not altogether unfamiliar: *Trust God, delight in him, wait on him.*

I return my Bible to its place on the table and turn out the light. I know I could not have received better advice, and I plan to heed it, but I can't suppress a sigh as I carefully make my way across the room in the dark and slip into bed beside my husband.

TUESDAY

CHAPTER TWO

Kendy

I open my eyes and can hardly discern the dresser six feet from my face.

Not good.

I had wanted to sleep until the sun filtered through the white slats of the plantation shutters to grace the bedroom with warm and reassuring light. I turn the digital clock with its brightly lit numbers toward me, and I groan ever so slightly.

I'm quite sure this day will require more than five hours' sleep.

Luke is still sleeping peacefully. I nudge him over on his side and snuggle up behind him. I may be awake, but I don't have to get up. I have never slept until noon, but today I would like to try.

I'm pretty sure Maisey would appreciate it.

Will I ever quit longing for the Maisey who was once mine?

She was thirteen when a vein of irritation and a strange sadness began to run through our relationship. Make that a pulmonary artery of irritation. No book, workshop, or Mom's Night Out prepared me for it. Can puberty possibly effect such a vast and enduring change? Can a mother's crisis?

I would have thought our closeness, the envy of all my friends, immovable.

But *immovable* is a God word.

I'm so glad Marcus calls her Maisey. I wondered if she'd give up her nickname when she went away to college. She might prefer Mother to Mom now, but I have not switched from Maisey to Maize, though I chose the name Maize with love before she was born. When they placed her in my waiting arms and she looked up at me with such interest, the warmth of a summer afternoon filled me, and I knew the name fit. But Maize became Maisey in no time.

"My sweet girl Maisey," I used to sing as we rocked and rocked, "is more darling than a daisy." When I took down the teddy bear border from her pink little-girl room, I painted the room yellow (Maize Yellow—think silk tassels in an endless field of ripened corn, delight of my eyes, nourishment for the world) before I stenciled daisies around her wide white window frames.

When Maisey was younger, Luke tended to use her proper name and liked to tousle her hair and declare, "Maize is amazing!" Sometimes he'd just look at her—over the breakfast table, for instance—and shorten it: "A-*maz*-ing." Though she must have heard it hundreds of times, she never failed to smile when he said it. Who wouldn't?

After I finally got in bed last night, I lay here over an hour wishing, wishing I could sleep. But my mind would not settle down to rest; it *insisted* on thinking.

About the irony for one thing—the wedding irony.

I was quite old enough to plan my own wedding twenty-four years ago, but I couldn't help being disappointed that Mother didn't make time to help for the sheer pleasure of it. Maybe, as she said, she didn't *have* the time; after all, I had given her only three months' notice. But I've always thought her involvement would have made it easier to walk down the aisle without a father by my side.

There was nothing atypical about my mother's choice; I should have expected it. But her abdication of even this unique opportunity struck me as sad well before I had a daughter of my own and found Mother's choice unfathomable. Long before Maisey held out her hand and showed us her engagement ring, I began anticipating the days we would spend together preparing for her wedding.

But she has not wanted any help, or at least she has not wanted *my* help. She has taken care of everything. When people ask me for details about the wedding, I smile and say, "It's a surprise."

Irony upon irony.

Dwelling on irony is as unproductive as wishing for sleep.

Clearly, I was fretting—big time.

Recalling the alternatives from Psalm 37, I did the one thing that can always calm my restless soul. I turned my worries and sorrows into prayers. I had only two petitions as I lay there. I asked God to supernaturally intervene so that Maisey's wedding will be as wonderful as we imagined it would be when she was a child. And I asked him to please help me sleep.

And he did. Five hours is better than none.

Do I hear six?

I throw my arm over Luke, yawn deeply, and close my eyes.

Maisey

I open my eyes and see the daisies.

They have danced around my window frames since I was twelve years old.

One week before I turned fourteen, I announced that all I wanted for my birthday was to have my yellow room painted lavender. Dad lowered his paper and said, "You're kidding. Why would you want that? You love your room."

Loved, Dad, *loved*. I had loved it a lot.

I just shrugged my shoulders. I had a reason, that's for sure, but I would never have told him what it was, not in a million years.

Mom stopped sweeping the kitchen and looked horrified. "I'm sorry, honey," she finally said, "but we already have your present."

They said we could talk about lavender later, but I'm twenty-two and getting married in five days, and here I am in my yellow room staring at the happy little daisies. I'm sure they're here to stay.

I hear a tap on the door and am relieved to hear Marcus whispering, "Maisey!"

I sit up and finger comb my hair, hoping to look at least decent.

"Come in!" I call, so ready to see him.

When he opens the door and stands there in his T-shirt and cargo shorts, his dark hair still damp from a shower, I am struck by his beauty—even two years and four months after I first laid eyes on him.

He leaves the door ajar and walks across the room. Pulling up my bedspread, he places the extra pillow vertically against the headboard and leans against it. He stretches out his long legs and crosses them at the ankles, and I notice once again what nice feet he has.

"Good morning," he says, leaning over to kiss me.

I turn so that his kiss lands on my cheek. Covering my mouth, I warn, "Morning breath."

Fearless, he moves my hand, gives me a quick kiss on my mouth, leans back, and smiles.

"Up and at 'em," he says. "Your folks will have breakfast ready soon."

"I'm not hungry."

"You should be. You had a granola bar for dinner."

"I had *two*. Maybe I'm just too excited to eat. And I want to fit into my wedding dress. It's soooo beautiful!"

"So you've said. Let's see it."

"Like that's going to happen. Saturday's coming. Besides, even if I wanted to show it to you, which I most certainly do not, I couldn't. Gram's bringing it with her on Friday."

"She's coming that early, huh? I figured she'd swoop in around six on Saturday, drive straight to the church."

"Well, you were wrong, weren't you?"

"Maybe, but I'm not wrong about breakfast. You need to eat, so would you please get in the shower?"

"I thought we were supposed to have some lazy days before the craziness begins."

"You're awake. What's the problem? Come on. I'll wait for you on the patio. It's a perfect day. In fact, we should have gone for a swim this morning before I cleaned up."

I'm not at all ready for him to go when he jumps up and takes off with one more "Come on!" I hear him very nearly running down the stairs, and I know I should get going.

If he hadn't come home with me, I might have slept all morning, but Marcus, like Dad, is a morning person. Actually, he has many of Dad's traits. I noticed that right away.

We met in a way I'd recommend to anyone who wants to know what someone is really like. Our campus houses joined forces to build a house in Mexico the spring break of my sophomore year, and we ended up riding in the same van, though I sat in the front, and he and his buddies sat in the back. We exchanged smiles and little else on the way down, except for somewhere in west Texas, when he asked me if I wanted a drink of his Dr Pepper. On the way back, it was a different story. We sat side by side in the middle of the van and talked about life as the youngest of five children and as an only child. Most of the time, though, he loaned me his shoulder, and we took long naps resting our heads on either side of a shared pillow.

We were exhausted from mixing concrete, hauling lumber, nailing up chicken wire, troweling on stucco, and doing anything else that putting up a two-room house required. It wasn't much of a home, we thought, standing back and looking at what we had accomplished when our workweek came to a close. But the family we built it for had been living in a cardboard hovel, and they seemed to think it was a palace. It was during this week that I saw how dependable and hardworking Marcus is. He is also pleasant and kind. Unlike a few on the team, he ate any meal the host family generously and sacrificially prepared for us, and he always cleaned up the work site and then himself, never complaining about the trickle of cold water that passed as a shower or the truly disgusting bathroom conditions. These qualities drew me to him more than his incredibly good looks.

I was so hooked.

He was too, though. He said he began falling for me when he saw me—sweat dripping, hair tied back in a bandanna—patiently showing the ragged children who had congregated around me how to mix concrete. He said he was "irrevocably" in love with me when, after a day of hard work, I brought out the Play-Doh I had packed and let the kids make colorful houses of their own, constructing a whole village before they were done. When they showed us their masterpiece, we clapped as if they had just unveiled Michelangelo's *David*.

Returning to the university after that exhausting and exhilarating nine days, we unfolded ourselves from our middle seat, limped off the van, and exchanged bandannas and phone numbers.

We were a done deal.

Kendy

"Are you going to sleep all morning?" Luke asks, wearing nothing but his black boxer briefs.

I glance at the clock that now reads 7:46. "That was my fervent prayer."

He walks to his closet, takes a pair of jeans off a shelf, and pulls them on. "I'll start breakfast. That boy has an appetite, doesn't he?"

"He does," I say, throwing back the covers. I get up and stretch. "Isn't that nice?"

Luke pulls a black T-shirt over his head. I love him to wear black anything, from T-shirt to tux to boxers.

I head for the bathroom but stop to give him some advice. "Listen, if the kids aren't downstairs, slow yourself down and read your paper before you start breakfast. Okay?"

"Okay, but hurry."

Luke is obviously ecstatic a new day has dawned. He is the ultimate morning person; if there were a club for such people, he would be the logical choice for president.

"Don't bother with your hair," he says. "Leave it natural."

"Oh, Luke."

"I mean it," he calls from the living area on his way to the kitchen. "I like it that way."

Actually, he likes my hair any way I wear it. My hair—"the color of roasted coffee beans," Luke noted on our first date— is one thing he consistently compliments me on, whether it's curly, straightened, or pulled up. He also said early on, maybe on that same date, that he hadn't expected someone with such dark hair to have sky-blue eyes. I told him I hadn't expected someone with light brown hair, very nearly blond, to have such warm brown eyes. A little flirting going on, for sure—we were both quite pleased with what we saw. Aging, I'm happy to say, has not changed that.

He is back with a glass of orange juice just as I am wrapping myself in a towel and stepping out of the shower, steam hovering. The juice isn't a bribe; he brings it most mornings, but this consideration puts me in the mood for compromise.

He leaves as quickly as he came, and I sit at my vanity, applying gel to my hair and scrunching it, encouraging curls, even though I'll be pulling the mess into a loose sort of bun after I put on my makeup and get dressed. Opening the top drawer on my right, I set out the items that will transform my face into all it can be. At forty-nine and forty-seven, Luke and I look pretty good, and we feel even better.

I am blessed. *Extravagantly* blessed.

After the Lord God himself, Luke and Maisey top my list of blessings. Marcus has slipped into the slot for blessing number four. How grateful I am for him! Few things could be more wonderful than a daughter marrying such a good man, though I doubt my mother has ever had the ability to appreciate such a boon. But I was thrilled when Maisey brought Marcus Blair home, relieved she had chosen so well after one Blah and two Disasters. Marcus makes her smile.

Please, God, let her be happy.

She surely seemed happy when she showed us her ring at Christmas. She seemed happy when she called and told us she had found her wedding dress—or more precisely, told her father.

Several things have hurt me in this life; not being with her when she found her dress five hours from home is on the list somewhere. Maisey had asked for a bride doll the Christmas she was five, mesmerized by her aunt's wedding the fall before. Since then I've been dreaming of the day, or days, we would shop for her wedding dress. What can I say? A mother helping her daughter to find just the right creation for that momentous walk down the aisle strikes me as one of life's happiest endeavors. The night she called to tell us about buying her "dream of a gown," in part to prepare her father for the credit card bill, I sat beside Luke on the couch, a striking contrast to Maisey's exuberance.

My dejection seemed a tad inappropriate. "Being hurt because I wasn't included is silly, isn't it?" I asked afterward.

"Not so silly," he said.

But she loves the dress; that's the most important thing.

Mother was with Maisey when she selected the dress. This was difficult to process, since Mother had allowed someone else to help me choose my wedding gown. One Saturday after going with Maisey for one of her fittings, Mother called on the way to her office in downtown St. Louis. "Maize looks like a princess in her dress," she said. "No, let me amend that. She looks much more sophisticated than a princess. She looks like a queen, confident in her ability to lead and thrilled at the prospect." Natural image for my CFO mother to conjure, though she actually laughed at her own excess.

I couldn't bring myself to ask Mother what the dress looked like. I did ask Maisey when she and Marcus came home for a few days at the end of their spring break.

"It's white," she said.

I managed to suppress a *No kidding*. (To be fair, I suppose she did have a range of options—there's ivory, for instance.)

Then Maisey, unable to squelch the excitement welling up from her heart, let details escape: The dress was strapless and straight—fitted but not too tight—the back of it falling into a short oval train. "Elegant," she said in the end. "You'll think it's elegant, Mom."

I turned so she wouldn't see the tears spring to my eyes. Not because I was so pleased to finally hear about the dress, but because she had called me Mom.

CHAPTER THREE

Maisey

"Stay awhile, Dad," I say as he stands up and collects his juice glass and the papers scattered on the patio table.

"I've stalled long enough," he says, tucking his reading glasses into the pocket of his T-shirt. "Time to start breakfast."

He waves at Marcus, who is making a turn at the shallow end of the pool, ready for another lap. Shower or no shower, Marcus decided this gorgeous morning called for a swim.

"It's not so hot yet," Dad says. "I think we'll have breakfast out here."

He kisses the top of my head on his way inside. I want to jump up and hug him and say, *Really, Dad, stay with me awhile.*

I've been missing him. He's been my go-to guy for almost a decade now.

"Come on in," Marcus calls, treading water under the diving board.

He makes it look tempting, but my resolve is strong. "No way; I've had my shower. You practically insisted, if I recall."

"I've had mine too."

"But I've done my hair. Save your breath. It's not happenin'."

"The water's great. How can you resist?"

I get up, walk to the edge of the pool, and dip my toes into the water, strawberry pink polish glimmering in the morning light. "I'll sit here, but don't get my hair wet. I mean it. Remember, the girls are giving me a shower this afternoon. A *personal* shower."

He swims over and holds on to my feet, pretending he is going to pull me in, but I know he won't.

"How personal?" he asks.

"That will depend on who's giving the gift."

I hear the French door open. Marcus says, "Good morning, Kennedy."

"Good morning," Mother says. She walks over to where I'm sitting and combs her fingers through the hair I spent way too long straightening. "Did you rest well, honey?"

"Yes," I say.

"Your hair looks pretty."

"Thanks."

"So, are you two ready to eat?"

"I am," Marcus says.

"Sure," I say.

"I'm taking orders. Do you want waffles or pancakes?"

"Pancakes," Marcus answers.

"Pancakes are fine," I say.

"Do you like pecans, Marcus?"

"Love 'em!"

"Okay, then. We'll be out in a few minutes."

Marcus pulls himself out of the pool and grabs his towel off the lounger. "I'm starving!"

"You're always starving," I say and smile, because I like his enthusiasm for good food. His enthusiasm for many good things is another of his excellent qualities.

"Your mom's very pretty, isn't she?" Marcus says, his eyes having followed her retreat into the house.

"I guess."

"The first time I saw her, I knew you'd be gorgeous for a lo-o-o-ong time. My friends and I have been known to check mothers out for that very reason."

"Oh, you have? Well, Dad made a contribution too, you know."

"I don't think of your dad as pretty."

"Well, he is," I say. "You two have that in common." I cup water in my hand and toss it at him before getting up from the warm tiles and pulling a chair out from the table.

Mother returns carrying a large pewter tray with glasses, pitchers of milk and juice, butter, and syrup. "We're almost ready!"

Marcus jumps up. "That looks heavy," he says, taking the tray from her and setting it on the cart by the table.

"Thanks. It's *very* heavy. Apparently I'll do anything to save an extra trip."

"Is there anything else I can do to help? Besides swimming laps and relaxing on the lounger, that is."

"You can help next time. We like company in the kitchen. But this morning, we've got it covered," she says, smiling at him. She has an endless supply of smiles.

Marcus can't help himself—he has to smile back. He likes her.

Most people do.

All my friends love her, for goodness' sake. They have since we started kindergarten; Jackie, since preschool. We were six the first time Jackie came to the house, but instead of playing with our baby dolls as we had planned, we spent most of the time in the kitchen with Mom, helping her make peanut butter cookies. I'm sure Jackie had started loving her when she was four years old and Mother volunteered at our preschool, but she fell head over heels that day in the kitchen. Mom told her she had been born during the Kennedy presidency. "If there was ever a man your gram loved, it was President John F. Kennedy," she said, smiling at me while I pressed the cookies with the tines of the fork like she had shown me.

"Thus," she said, turning her smile on Jackie, "she named me, her only child, Kennedy." Then Mom leaned on the counter, face-to-face with Jackie, who sat perched on a stool across the bar from her. "And you, little miss, could be named after his First Lady, Jackie Kennedy. I've seen hundreds of pictures of her, and she was very classy." Jackie looked at me, and I looked at her, like we had just learned the most glorious thing.

Jackie still loves Mom. She'd like to stay over here until the wedding—"all the better," she said, "to do my maid-of-honor duties."

"Sorry, girlfriend," I told her, "we've got a full house." And with Marcus here, it really is.

"What are you thinking about?" Marcus asks.

"About Gram naming Mother after John Kennedy. She loved him, you know. Someone's probably naming a son or daughter Barack as we speak."

"Was your mom's dad a Kennedy fan too?"

"I wouldn't know. He's never been in the picture. He's the great anti-father."

"When did her parents get divorced?"

Have I not told him this?

"They didn't," I say. "They never got married. We don't discuss him. Really, he's a nonentity."

I hope that puts a period on the topic, at least for now, because my parents are coming through the doorway, laughing about something, happy as the daisies upstairs "gracing my windows," as Mother used to say. Dad's carrying a platter of bacon and another platter of steaming pancakes. Mother's carrying a stack of plates with napkins and silverware stacked on top.

The topic of her miserable father seems to be blessedly forgotten when Marcus looks up and sees my parents and the platters of food.

Kendy

"Please say you'll come to the shower early," Jackie says when I pick up the kitchen phone. "Really, we could use your help. No one here can do bows."

I hesitate, hardly knowing what to say.

Finally I sputter, "What do you mean, honey?"

Now Jackie seems to hesitate. "Maisey *did* invite you when she was home during spring break, didn't she?"

"She must have forgotten. She had a caterer, a florist, and a photographer to worry about, if you recall."

"Well, that is absolutely no excuse."

I laugh and tell her that a personal shower seldom needs a mother present and that I'll see her soon.

"Not soon enough!" she says.

We don't stay on the phone long, and I take myself back into the living room, where I left the newspaper I had just started perusing. I open it randomly, and unfortunately, to the obituary section. I skim it and hope, given the way things are going, I'll find no one I know there. I had been aiming for the opinion page, thinking it might be good this morning to invest a few minutes in someone else's concerns.

Maisey has been home only twice since spring break, once for her graduation reception in May and once for her church wedding shower the second weekend of June. She did not mention the shower the girls are giving her today until we were eating breakfast this morning.

Luke and Marcus had left for the golf course right before Jackie called, and I can't imagine a nicer way to spend the afternoon than attending the shower Jackie and Heidi are giving Maisey. I hear Maisey's door click shut and her footsteps on the stairs. I look up and see her holding her car keys, looking absolutely beautiful in white linen cropped pants and a pink cotton sweater.

"I'll be back in a few hours," she says, hair swinging as she heads for the door.

I fold the paper, slide it into the magazine holder next to my chair, and stand up. "Jackie called to ask if I could come to the shower early," I say.

Maisey stops and begins riffling through her purse for something.

What I've said is remarkable. Ordinarily I would have let it go. I have come to cherish equilibrium.

"I thought it was a girl thing," she says, still digging in her purse.

"She said you were supposed to invite me when you were home for spring break."

"Oh, really? I don't remember that. Do you want to go?"

Her question strikes me as far more complicated than it sounds, certainly more complicated than she intended. And poignant.

I stand looking at her, trying hard not to cry, not to look like I *want* to cry. I've had some practice in this area.

I wish I didn't care about any perceived slight. I wish I didn't want so much to share this unique time with girls I have loved since most of them were five years old, seventeen years now. I wish my daughter and I were laughing our way to her car, hoping she wasn't about to unwrap a lacy red thong. I wish she were warning me on the drive over to Jackie's *not* to call my flip-flops *thongs*.

Maisey has finally located a package of gum in her purse and is opening it. She looks in my direction and asks again, "So, do you want to go?"

The answer comes to me effortlessly, in the form of another question: *Don't you want me to go, Maisey?* But that is too honest, and honesty would make her uncomfortable—and late, and she should be neither when she walks into Jackie's apartment for her personal shower.

"Sort of," I say with a laugh. "But I'm not ready, and I have plenty to do here."

The chicken enchilada casserole, already prepared, is sitting in the refrigerator awaiting dinner tonight. But, hey, I've got a book that needs reading around here somewhere.

"Tell the girls I'll see them at the rehearsal Friday," I say.

"They're coming over to swim tomorrow morning, remember?"

Did I know that?

"Dad's grilling hamburgers for lunch."

"Is he? Well, that's good," I say.

She stands there as if needing to be dismissed.

"Well, have a good time. I hope you get six bottles of Happy." She loves that fragrance. "And a red lace thong," I add.

"Oh, Mother."

And with that she rushes out the door to the apple green Jetta we bought her in May, when she graduated from college.

So anxious to leave.

Free at last.

I watch until Maisey has turned her car onto the highway before confiscating a book from the bedroom and heading to the patio. But I find myself staring at an empty pool, completely ignoring the book in my lap. Not having purchased a great book to have on hand this week turns out to be a grave oversight. On the other hand, I doubt the best book ever written could compete with my musings today.

Maisey's tenth Christmas has come to mind, antithesis to her flight to Jackie's. Actually it is Christmas Eve that shines so brightly in my memory.

Luke had driven into Indy to work, though Maisey and I pleaded with him not to. Christmas Eve was one of the company's best paid holidays as far as I was concerned. "Luke," I had asked, hardly hiding my disgust, "how many others are working on Christmas Eve?"

He had answered with a question of his own. "How many others are going to be a partner by the time they're forty?" I walked off without another word. I had wanted to push it, though. It was snowing, and we could have gone sledding if he had been home to make it happen; he would have had as much fun as Maisey and I.

But not to worry, we girls had grown used to such defections and had learned to embrace satisfying alternatives. I put on Christmas music, and Maisey and I made cookies and candy as the snow fell in enormous fairy-tale flakes outside the kitchen windows. We ate warm cookies and drank cold milk while sitting at the kitchen table, watching the heavens pile snow on the covered pool, the fenced yard, the field, and the woods beyond it.

"I don't want to be a teenager, Mom," she announced out of the blue.

"Well, my goodness, sweetie, why wouldn't you want to be such a glorious thing?"

"I don't want to not like you!"

I laughed at that.

She laughed too.

"But, Mom," she said. "You should hear how some of the older kids talk about their parents!"

Part of me wished I could keep Maisey in the fifth grade forever.

"I wouldn't worry about it, honey. Not liking each other just isn't possible. Of this I am sure."

"Did you ever not like Gram?"

"Well, that's a different story, dear."

"What do you mean?"

Luke called then, allowing me to postpone an explanation of my childhood, one quite different from Maisey's. I was so glad for the interruption that I was only upset, not livid, when he said he'd be late for dinner, even though I could not fathom what could be so important on Christmas Eve.

"The roads must be getting worse by the minute," I said. He told me not to worry—he wouldn't be much longer and he had arranged for someone to put chains on his tires.

That evening, pleased that he was finally home and that we were going to have a spectacular white Christmas, the three of us ate chili in front of the fireplace, the ottoman our table, the finest the maitre d' had to offer. Afterward we once again watched Jimmy Stewart's epiphany in *It's a Wonderful Life*, and then each of us opened one present, saving the rest for morning, a Laswell tradition. We had only one more day before I put the Christmas CDs away, so we turned out all the lights except for those twinkling on the tree and ended the evening by listening to the music we loved.

It was bedtime—in fact, Luke had fallen asleep on the couch—but Maisey and I hated to leave the fire, the tree, the moon shining on the snow heaped outside the windows, and the promise and peace of "O Holy Night."

That refusal to give up the night provided me one of my sweetest memories. I sat snuggled with a soft throw in Luke's big leather rocking recliner, and Maisey, a tiny thing even at ten, lay on the floor watching the fire. Looking over at me, she smiled, got up, climbed into my lap, and put her head on my shoulder. We didn't say anything for the half hour we sat rocking, holding each other close.

There are some things for which there are no words.

CHAPTER FOUR

Maisey

I find a parking place and take a minute to observe the apartment complex where Jackie and Heidi have lived for a month now. It looks nice, quite nice.

Well, I'm here, Jackie, I think as I get out of the car and lock it. *On Tuesday, just like you wanted.* I had wanted the shower to be later in the week, but that didn't suit her at all. Her text message made that clear: *Good grief, so when do you plan to come home?!*

She doesn't think I'm home enough, and Marcus tends to agree. Ever since his boss gave him two weeks off, he's been all about spending as much time here as possible before the wedding, but goodness, five days is a long time. Of course

Sarah, the sole college representative in the wedding party, will arrive from Florida on Friday morning, and the Blair gang will arrive Friday afternoon. That leaves just two days to kill. The girls will take up most of the day tomorrow, and maybe I can talk Marcus into going to Indy on Thursday.

I arrive at the door of my friends' apartment and ring the bell.

The door flies open, and Jackie shouts, "Get in here!" She must have taken lessons from Marcus.

"My goodness," I say as she pulls me into their living room, "I do believe I've materialized in Pier 1 Imports."

"All but," Jackie says, taking my purse and throwing it in the coat closet. "Did the giraffe give it away?"

"He's quite chic," I say, looking with approval in his direction.

"It's pretty much all Pier 1, at least in the living area and kitchen. Our parents bought Heidi and me dishes, a lamp, several throw pillows, and a few indispensable accessories for graduation—not a cute little car, Spoiley Girl." Heidi has walked into the living room while Jackie is carrying on and is nodding her head in agreement.

They are so exaggerating. Their apartment is too cute, thanks to the collaborative efforts of their generous parents.

"I wish you guys could see the place Gram found Marcus and me," I say. "I'm going for the Pottery Barn look—the real thing if my parents and grandparents are buying, a knockoff otherwise."

"Didn't we tell you? We're coming to see it the minute you get back from your honeymoon," Jackie says. "Hey," she adds, as though she's just thought of something far more important than apartments and upcoming visits, "I thought I told you to invite your mom to this little party!"

"Sorry," I say, placating her as best I can with a shrug and a smile. "I guess I forgot."

Jackie is not placated. "I should have called myself."

"You can see her tomorrow."

"Yes, I can. Meanwhile, tell her I love her so much, I'm going to gobble her up. Can you remember that?"

Oh brother. With that comment, I ask her to point me in the direction of a bathroom.

Jackie was referring to one of Mother's and her oldest sayings, dating back to preschool. On the days Mother volunteered, she read to us while we ate the cookies she had brought, and then she did anything else our teacher wanted her to do. And our teacher wanted most of all for Mother to monitor our fifteen-minute recess.

We were running to the merry-go-round one spring morning when Mother shouted to Jackie, "I love you so much, I'm going to gobble you up!"

Jackie screamed and ran faster, yelling, "I'll beat you off with a *stick*!"

No chance of that, of course. Most of the class would not be sitting on a colorful slice of merry-go-round, holding on to a handle for dear life, if my mother hadn't been out there pushing it.

"Harder, harder!" the kids called.

And she pushed harder, but not much. We were only four, and she would never have put us in danger, which was considerate for a child-eater.

As I walk back down the hall, hoping the subject of Mother is dropped, the doorbell begins to ring nonstop, and the apartment quickly fills up with girls whom I'm so excited to see.

We spend the first hour chatting and eating and drinking, and then I open presents from friends who have been extremely generous. There are three bottles of Happy and several ooh-la-la things from Victoria's Secret. When everything is unwrapped and stacked neatly on the side-by-side cubes Jackie uses as a coffee table, I hear yet another reference to my mother.

"Your mom would be so proud of us," Heidi says.

"She most certainly would be!" Jackie said.

For a minute I think someone might ask for a moment of silence.

Yet it's true; Mother probably would be proud. Except for one outrageous exception, good taste ruled. Mother will be glad to know I received several bottles of Happy, forever my favorite fragrance. I've splashed it on even when the name on the bottle was just wishful thinking.

I wait around until everyone is gone before I thank Jackie and Heidi for the third or fourth time and rush to the car to begin my double-checking, which I've scheduled for after the shower. I stop by the caterer's and the photographer's and then drive to the florist's. I'm listening to tunes, rather glad I chose a florist so far away; I'm counting on Dad and Marcus being back from their golf game before I return to the house.

When I leave the flower shop, I sit in the car, admiring the arrangements in the display windows and making calls. I check on the cake, the band for the reception, and the bridesmaids' dresses. *Check, check, check.* Everything is so under control.

With all my tasks complete, I head the car toward home, thinking how good it is to get things done. It was also good to see my friends. Mother would say that seeing them "refreshed my heart."

It will be nice to see my grandparents too. They're driving over from Indy for dinner tonight. Marcus admires Miller and Anne Laswell almost as much as he does my parents, and I doubt we'll get a chance to spend any real quality time with them at Friday's rehearsal and dinner.

I pull into the driveway and see Dad and Marcus getting their golf clubs out of the back of Dad's SUV. Sometimes things just work out.

Mom's on the porch, welcome all over her face. I get out of the car, give the guys a hug, and ask Marcus to help me carry in my loot.

"*Our* loot really," I say, pointing at satin peeking from one of the sacks I hand him.

We're walking up the stairs to the porch, and I think to tell Mother I got three bottles of Happy.

She smiles.

"Oh, and, Mother," I add, as the four of us walk into the house, "Jackie said to tell you she loves you so much, she's going to gobble you up."

"That's sweet," she says.

And it *is* sweet.

But Jackie might not love her so much if she had a few more facts. She needs to get herself a copy of *Kennedy Marie Laswell: The Unabridged Version.*

Kendy

One could say Maisey was merely delivering a message from Jackie. I don't believe Luke caught the irony; I'm the great irony detector. He's not oblivious to the tension that sometimes surfaces, but the irony he can miss. Or maybe our daughter's telling me that her *friend* loves me wasn't ironic at all.

I am so sorry to doubt that.

The last nine years with Maisey have not been miserable, except in stark contrast to the thirteen years of utter joy before them. I try very hard not to think about the differentiation, but that has been impossible today. I'm beginning to think it might be impossible this entire wedding week.

We have almost two hours before a dinner that is already prepared, so Luke showers, dresses in crisp khaki Dockers and a black polo shirt, and heads into his office to deal with today's e-mails. Maisey and Marcus, glad to see each other after so many hours apart, go upstairs to look at her gifts and to discuss her personal shower and his golf game. And here I sit, stretched out on the chaise longue in Luke's and my room, covered with a throw to protect me from the chill of the ceiling fan that quietly stirs the air from the first of May until the end of September.

I have found my book to be an asset after all. Voracious reader that I am, it is on my lap, answer for what I'm doing if anyone should ask. However, I've had it with me all afternoon, and my bookmark is sandwiched between pages ten and eleven—no offense to the author.

Margaret would not be fooled by the book in my lap. I find myself missing her today. Isn't that odd? She's been gone almost twenty years now, but today I long to see her, long to hear her voice. She'd walk in, slide my legs over, and sit down by me on the chaise. *What's wrong with my girl?* she'd ask.

I'd say, *I'm missing you, Margaret.*

What's this you're reading? she'd ask, picking up my book and looking it over.

I can't recall, I'd say.

She'd take it from me and put it on the table. *Talk to me, honey.*

I look across the room at my dresser, where among the framed pictures is one of Margaret holding eighteen-month-old Maisey in her lap. Maisey has on a red-checked sundress and a matching floppy hat, and she's looking up at Margaret, laughing. Margaret died shortly before Maisey's third birthday. If the house were going up in flames, I'd risk my life to rescue Luke, Maisey, and that picture.

I've always believed God in his mercy sent Margaret to me. What would I have done without her?

Mother moved us into a tenth-floor condominium with its view of the Gateway Arch standing distinct and proud in front of the mighty Mississippi River. It would have been unbearable except Margaret and Hugh lived across the hall. Just retired from teaching sixth graders, Margaret was thrilled to find a girl moving in who had just graduated from that very grade. She called me the best retirement gift God could have given her. I was sad she and Hugh couldn't have children of their own but so happy to become their surrogate daughter. Margaret and Hugh were the best stand-in parents a girl could have. They taught me most everything I know about nurturing.

I was so blessed neither of them enjoyed traveling. Except for one three-month experiment with living in Florida for the winter, the only trips they took were to see Margaret's sister and her husband in Indiana, and most of the time they took me with them, sitting in the back seat with my tape player and books. They enjoyed each other, their friends, their church, plays and concerts, and me. They helped me with my home-work, played a million card games with me, took me with them most places they went, and made dinner for me most nights, sending a plate to Mother when she got home from the office she revered and loved.

I became a teacher because of Margaret. Mother wasn't happy when I told her what I wanted to do. "That is just *stupid*, Kennedy, choosing to work yourself silly without compensa-tion. You'd better hope you marry someone who can support you, like Hugh supported Margaret!"

She had that weapon in her arsenal because, one night while Mother ate the lasagna Margaret had sent her, I told her that Hugh had been a vice-president of the company he worked for. That had impressed her.

What impressed *me* was that Hugh had an imaginary friend named Jahooty, who hid gum for me in an eight-foot ornamen-tal tree that stood by their living room windows. Every day when I came into their apartment, Hugh watched with a smile on his face as I walked over to the tree and searched among the glossy leaves until I found my stick of gum, unwrapped it, and popped it into my mouth.

"That crazy Jahooty," he'd say, shaking his head, white hair gleaming.

"I *love* him!" I'd say, giving Hugh a side hug on my way to find Margaret.

I knew without being told that Hugh's identity was not wrapped up in the position he had once held. His joy lay elsewhere too. He died between my junior and senior years of high school, sitting on their balcony, relishing the morn-ing sun. The day after his funeral I spent the afternoon with

Margaret and her sister and discovered that Jahooty had left me one last piece of gum.

I have kept it in my memory box, which sits high on the top shelf of my closet. Every now and then, usually with no forethought, I take down the box, open it and, seeing the stick of gum lying on top of other keepsakes, press my nose against the red wrapper, always believing the smell of cinnamon still faintly lingers there.

I think of doing it now, but Luke peeks in the door. "What are you doing?"

I hold up my book. "Reading. Sort of."

"Calm before the storm?"

"How about another figure of speech?"

He laughs. "Well, the calm part works. You look peaceful. You must not be reading a thriller."

"No," I said, "this is no thriller. Leviticus might be a faster read."

"Mom and Dad should be here in an hour," he says.

"Good."

I love Luke's parents. I could not have ordered better in-laws than Miller and Anne Laswell. They helped fill the void left by Margaret and Hugh.

"I set the timer before I came in here," I say. "The casserole should be baking as we speak. Check to make sure before you go back to your office, okay? Everything else is ready."

"Okay." He turns to leave and then stops, looking as though he almost forgot to tell me something, an important something. "I beat the boy by two strokes, you know." He smiles and gives me a thumbs-up.

Luke's pleasure in winning a round of golf makes me smile. "You wake up expecting a good day, and what do you know, you get one," I say, placing my paperback prop on the table next to me.

"I don't know about that."

"It's true. You're quite the positive one. What a blessing that is."

He laughs as he shuts the door, like I'm kidding. But I'm not. I'm really not.

Maisey

Marcus approves of everything I show him, except for the red see-through baby-doll pajamas trimmed in black faux fur. Something about the net fabric rather repulses both of us. As I gingerly fold the two pieces and put them back in the pink-striped sack to return, Marcus says, "I will say I sort of like the fur around the edges."

"You're kidding."

"It's soft. But it can't make up for the red net."

"A girl who wore flannel pajamas to every sleepover we ever had gave it to me. All of us turned and looked at her, trying to tell if her gift was a joke or a breakthrough."

"Well, most of this stuff is great," he says.

"Don't you wish men had personal showers?" I ask.

"If men gave one another showers, we'd buy tools, hand them over without wrapping them, and pass out beef jerky for refreshments."

"You're funny. How about this? You can have any Sears or Wal-Mart gift cards we get to buy tools."

"It's a deal."

"Why don't we go into Indy Thursday so I can take this red-and-black monstrosity back and get something we like?"

"Do you want to take time for that?"

"I thought that's why we came home all week, to have a little time to relax and goof off. I've been busy beyond belief today."

"I thought we came to have time with your folks."

"We've had time."

"I had a few hours with your dad this afternoon, but neither of us has had much time with your mom."

"We spent the morning with her."

"An hour max at breakfast. By the way, wouldn't she like to see this stuff?"

"She can see it sometime. I haven't seen you all day either, you know."

"You're going to see me nonstop soon."

I place the gift I'm returning on my dresser and take the rest of my stash into the closet to pack later. I don't know why Marcus is so worried about my mother. She's fine. Getting ready, I'm sure, for dinner with Grandpa and Grandma.

"I'm glad my grandparents are coming for dinner, aren't you?" I call from the back of my walk-in closet.

"I'm always glad to see them. We're spending a week in Hawaii instead of Pocahontas, Illinois, thanks to them."

"Do you love me or their travel agency?" I ask as I emerge from the closet and find Marcus kneeling beside my bookcase.

"Both," he says, looking up at me.

"What are you looking at?"

"You have C. S. Lewis's Narnia books. How many are there?" he asks, counting. "Seven?"

"Yes, I have the set."

He's reading titles. "Pardon me—I didn't have a *set*. But I read some of these when I was a kid."

"But did you read them three times? We read all of them at least three times. *The Lion, the Witch, and the Wardrobe* maybe more. It was my favorite book."

"So you sat up here reading when you could have been outside playing?"

"Not really. Mother read to me at bedtime. It was the first thing we did in our nightly routine."

"Sounds nice."

"You mean your mom didn't tuck you in?"

"No, she just told me to get my Star Wars stuff put up and get in bed."

"Well, Mother made quite a production of it."

The memory is suddenly vivid. Terribly vivid.

"I must have missed out when Mom yelled from the front of the house, 'Are you in bed yet, or do I have to come back there!' "

I laugh at Marcus's perfect imitation of Dottie Blair, especially since I know how much he appreciates the practical and hardworking mother who took excellent care of him. She will come rushing in Friday afternoon, toting four or five of her grandkids, a list of things to double-check before the rehearsal dinner that night, and confirmation numbers for the rooms she has reserved for the whole Blair clan, which includes five sons. Marcus is the youngest.

"What's the second thing?" Marcus asks.

"Second thing?"

"You said reading was the *first* thing you did every night."

"Oh, prayers and stuff like that. Hey, I'd like to rest awhile before I get ready for the big dinner. Give me a few minutes, okay?"

Marcus isn't offended by my request. In fact, I should be

offended by how quickly he jumps up and takes off. He leaves my room with the C. S. Lewis classic in his hand and says he'll see me downstairs.

I'm glad for a little time to myself. I turn on my ceiling fan, pull back my bedspread, pull it back over me, and sink into my pillow. Talking about my childhood bedtime took me to a place I haven't been in a long time.

Mother tucked me in for the first thirteen years of my life. There were exceptions but not many. She would make no apologies, she said, for starting me to bed an hour early so we'd have our special time together. We read a book the first half hour or so, and then she'd snuggle in beside me to tell a story of her own, sometimes made up, sometimes real, although she said occasionally the real ones were "embellished."

"What's *embellished*?" I asked her.

"Details, usually imagined," she said, "which are added to improve the story ever so slightly." Then she'd laugh.

Eventually I told her stories too. She could always tell when I threw in a detail for added interest. "You're embellishing, aren't you?" she'd ask, and I'd smile in reply.

One night she fell out of my bed while laughing at a story that hadn't needed a single embellishment. It was about the day Jackie crawled under a stall I was occupying in the girls' bathroom at school and asked what was taking so long.

Mom climbed back into my bed that night and said I was her funny girl. "Actually," I said, "Jackie's the funny one." I loved it when Mom laughed at my stories.

After the story exchange, we settled down for prayers. I'd pray first because I was younger, then Mom would pray. Her voice soothed me. I always thought God must be glad to hear the sound of her voice too. Any fears I had disappeared when she prayed.

The last step before turning out the light was pulling up my covers to my chin and working her way around my face with kisses—forehead, cheek, chin, and finally a peck on my nose. Actually, a face full of kisses was *almost* the last step. Most nights Mom paused as she turned out the light and said, "Good night, sleep tight, don't let the bedbugs bite."

I always came back with some comment from the bugs like, "Hey, Mom, the bugs say they aren't biters!" So the final thing I heard each night was her laugh.

Well, that was a long time ago.

I suddenly feel sick to my stomach, agitated rather than rested. I've sent Marcus away for nothing. Instead of chilling before dinner, I may throw up before dinner. Or maybe *during* dinner, right on my plate, making Grandma and Grandpa so glad they drove over from Indianapolis.

Taking a trip down memory lane is not what the doctor ordered. I jump up and smooth the bedspread, take a deep breath, and walk into my bathroom to get a drink, a long one. Maybe the doctor ordered hydration.

The bugs say they doubt it.

CHAPTER FIVE

Kendy

"Everything's fine," I say.

Dead silence on the line. I've sent everyone else out to the patio, and I'm rinsing dishes, balancing the phone between my ear and my shoulder. I begin to wonder if the connection has been broken.

"Hello?"

"I'm here," Paula says. "I just wish I believed you."

"Would I lie to the best friend a woman could possibly have?"

The compliment does not pacify her. "Withhold, maybe." She knows me well.

"I'm not withholding. We had a wonderful dinner, Miller's

favorite. And Miller and Anne really seem to like Marcus—who wouldn't, I'd like to know—and of course they are so happy to have some private time with Maisey, relatively speaking. The last time I peeked outside to see if anyone needed refills, Maisey was trying to talk her grandfather into a swim."

"Hmm," I hear, or something of that nature, enough response for me to continue chattering. It's true: I am chattering.

"She knows better than to bother asking her grandma, who has refused to be seen in a bathing suit since she turned sixty-five, though I should just have her thin little legs. But Anne says she's done with bathing suits. It's another spin on retirement. Get it? She hasn't retired from the travel agency, not completely anyway, but she did retire her bathing suits, or retire from wearing them. On trips, however, she feels required to wear a bathing suit now and then to be sociable, but not without one of her darling cover-ups.

"They're selling the business next year. Did I tell you that?"

Silence.

"Hello?"

"Do you want to go to lunch tomorrow?" Paula asks.

"I would, but the girls are coming over tomorrow morning to swim. I'm eager to see everyone. Luke's grilling hamburgers for them—the return of a summer tradition. Why don't you come here?"

"I might drop by. I need to see that you're fine."

"I am."

"Maybe."

Mercy, she's unrelenting.

"You're sweet," I say. "I love you. I'll see you tomorrow."

I hang up, put the last of the dishes I've virtually washed

into the dishwasher, run a clean paper towel under hot water, and look for lurking spots on granite counters that could conceal not only a crumb or a spatter but a squadron of flies.

For some reason, I seem intent on leaving the kitchen spotless before I sit with the others on the patio. I'll only mess it up again if and when I can interest anyone in dessert. The upside is I can clean it again. I find great satisfaction in that.

My thoughts return to Paula. I'm so grateful for her. I hope she knows that.

Of course she knows that.

She came into my life because of Margaret, another reason to thank God for her. Paula is the granddaughter of Margaret's sister. We met when Margaret and I visited her sister the summer before Paula and I began the ninth grade. Up to that point, I had not known a happier week.

I had friends in St. Louis, at school anyway. But Mother didn't encourage friendships. I wouldn't say she intentionally discouraged friendships—she just didn't like the idea of people coming over to our place, and she didn't much want me going anywhere else either. After all, she didn't know "those people," and for some reason I accepted this, instead of saying, "Well, how *would* you, Mother?" Sarcasm wasn't in me then, nor was pleading, arguing, or even calm reasoning, the one exception being repeated inquiries about my father. The ability to confront when necessary is a quality I have developed as an adult.

Margaret must have noticed that she and Hugh passed for best friends as well as surrogate parents. I'm sure she arranged for me to spend time with Paula. Margaret admitted it pleased her no end to see Paula and I enjoying each other so much the summer we met—laughing together on a porch swing, where we outdid each other with tales of junior-high angst; and rushing from the car when Margaret let us out at the mall to shop and see a movie. Being with Paula became a summer tradition. When Margaret and I went to visit her sister, Paula would meet us there, and after a few days, I'd pack my things to spend a few days at Paula's house, playing tennis in the park (a short-lived pursuit) and swimming at the municipal pool, sunning on our beach towels while chatting with Paula's school friends.

Through the years, the drive to Paula's reinforced my love for fields ripe with soybeans and corn. When we were seniors in high school and she had her own car, the Happy Honda, I sat in the passenger seat, studying the Indiana countryside, and made an announcement: "When I have a child and if it's a girl, I'm going to name her Maize."

"No," Paula said, "you're not."

"Oh, but I am. I love these fields. Love them!"

"Love them all you want, but name your daughter Jill—or Sue."

"I've made up my mind. I actually studied the etymology of the words *corn* and *maize* for a paper I wrote last year."

"You did a paper on maize?"

"And corn—'often used synonymously.' I made an *A* on that paper, if you'd like to know. The word *maize* has always struck me as quite romantic."

"Well, Miss Maize better get ready for the jokes," she said.

"She'll think it's worth it."

When I graduated from high school, I traveled across Illinois and into Indiana to attend Butler University with Paula, and when she was invited to join one sorority and I another, we decided to stay together in the dorms and later in an apartment near campus rather than be separated. We knew the time might come when once again we would have to be long-distance friends, but we were putting it off as long as possible. And then, gift of grace, we both got jobs in the same elementary school, not far from where Paula grew up.

"Hey," Luke says now.

I look up and see him standing in the open doorway. "Hey, yourself."

"Are you about done?"

"Just finished," I say, pulling the trash drawer open and tossing the paper towel into it. The front sack is nearly full, but I resist the impulse to replace it. "I'm on my way out."

I grab a pitcher of peach tea and ask Luke to get the ice bucket.

"I think the kids are going to swim. Want to join them?" he asks.

"I don't think so. Your folks are still here, aren't they?"

"Of course. Dad's not budging until he's had the cobbler and ice cream."

"I thought so."

We head outside, Luke pulling the door shut behind us.

"Miller," I say, setting the pitcher on the table, "are you ready for dessert?"

"Soon," he says, pulling out the chair next to him. "Take a load off, girl."

I pat my father-in-law's hand and sit down beside him. "That sounds lovely."

Maisey

"Come on," I beg, trying to pull Marcus to his feet.

"Your mom just got out here," Marcus says. "And what

about dessert?" he asks, as though we haven't been talking about going for a swim for the last thirty minutes.

"It will be much better after a little exercise. Let's go change. Pleeease."

"You might as well get going, Marcus," Grandpa says. "The sooner you swim with our girl, the sooner you can eat some cobbler with us."

This advice motivates Marcus. He lets me pull him out of his chair, and I wave at the grandparents as we head into the house.

"Two minutes," he says before we go our separate ways at the top of the stairs.

"I'm not moving that fast. I'll just meet you downstairs. I'll bring towels."

I shut my door behind me, comfortable in the darkness. Leaving the lights off, I walk across the room to look out the windows unobserved. On the patio below, the four older Laswells sit around the table, talking. Actually, it looks like Grandma is doing the talking, using her hands as expressively as an orchestra conductor. Whatever she's saying is making them laugh.

The pool is beautiful at night, the water glimmering in the moonlight. I've always enjoyed swimming under the stars. Well, not *always*. I started my solitary night swims the summer I was thirteen—a teenager finally. Oh, how I had dreaded that. I remember telling Mother the Christmas before I started middle school that I didn't want to become a teenager. Sometimes when I sit near a window watching it snow, I recall her laugh as she assured me we could *never* not like each other.

I believed her.

A couple years later I could have stayed in the pool twenty-four hours a day and my parents wouldn't have noticed. They were certainly too preoccupied to notice my slipping into the pool most evenings, with only the moon and stars for company.

Unfortunately, the summer after that, when this practice had become a consoling habit, they had begun to see me again.

The night Mother came out and found me floating facedown in the water, they laid down the no-swimming-alone law. She so overreacted. She dove into the water, flipped me over, cupped her hand under my chin, and swam me to the stairs on the side of the pool. I was too shocked to protest.

"What were you thinking, Maisey?" she said, holding on to the side of the pool, trying to get her breath.

"Mother! What were *you* thinking? That's the question!" I grabbed the hand bars and pulled myself up the steps. "Are you practicing to be a lifeguard or what?"

"Stop right there, Maisey," she said, climbing out of the pool behind me.

I grabbed the towel I'd thrown on the table and wrapped it around myself. Mom stood dripping in the shorts and T-shirt that clung to her body. She walked across the patio, opened the door, and called for Dad to bring her a towel and robe. I wanted nothing more than to go to my room, but I was pretty sure I had better not move.

When she came back to the table where I stood frozen in place, tears were streaming down her face. "I thought you were *dead*, Maisey! You *looked* dead, floating in the water like that! I thought you had hit your head or something."

She covered her face with her hands and shook with sobs.

I looked at her in amazement, trying to understand why, since I was perfectly fine, she would be crying hysterically.

Dad came out then, bringing a towel and her terry cloth robe, asking what was going on.

Mother took off her shorts and shirt, just letting them splat on the patio, grabbed the towel from Dad, and rubbed down her arms and legs. When she had dried as much as she had patience for, Dad helped her on with her robe, and she collapsed in a chair.

"I thought she was dead, Luke."

"I was only seeing how long I could hold my breath," I said. "I counted to sixty."

"She was floating facedown in the water!"

Hysterical—she was hysterical.

"Maize," Dad said, "go get ready for bed. We'll talk about this later."

For the first time in a year, Mom came in with Dad to kiss me good-night. Dad had taken over bedtime duties when she had dropped out of life the summer before. When she finally felt better and wanted to take over again, I begged Dad to continue our new tradition. He seemed to like the idea, and I guess Mother thought he deserved to share this time with me, since she had hoarded it for thirteen years. But according to Dad she agreed "reluctantly." And she did seem sad, but she had been sad for months. Dad tucked me in efficiently, fifteen minutes max, after we decided I was old enough to read to myself and to say prayers on my own. Mother said the transition had been too abrupt. And most nights she'd peek in and blow a kiss or say, "Sleep tight." I always said, "Good night," but the bugs never had anything to say.

"I'm sorry," Mother said, sitting beside me on my bed the

night of the "rescue" and fight. "It was a misunderstanding. But, Maisey, no more swimming alone."

"Mother!"

Dad, standing beside the bed, laid a finger on my lips, forbidding another word. "It's not safe, Maize. We should never have allowed it. It's a rule now. Break it and you'll be grounded from the pool. We love you too much to risk an accident."

"Do you guys get to swim alone?"

"We guys are grown, Maize," he said. "But generally speaking, we won't be swimming alone either."

They kissed me then and left the room, but not before looking back as though to make sure I was still there, tucked safely into bed. As soon as they shut the door, I got out of bed and stood at these windows, looking at the pool, wishing they hadn't messed with something I had grown to love. Gliding alone through the water, pretending I didn't have a care in the world, didn't make that last year go away, but for a few brief moments, it had helped.

Why did Mother have to come out there and ruin everything?

Kendy

We're watching Maisey and Marcus swimming laps. It's a freestyle race really, and since Maisey is behind with no hope of gaining the lead, she grabs Marcus's feet and holds him in place. A skirmish ensues, and the race has become a water wrestling match. It's fun to watch them have fun.

Shortly after the kids jumped into the pool, Miller told us he had asked Clay and Rebecca to stop by to pick up some material and to sign papers for a trip the four of them are taking in September. Clayton Laswell is Luke's uncle, Miller's younger brother—seven years younger.

Clay and Rebecca must have heard Maisey and Marcus carrying on in the pool, because they have come around to the back of the house and are joining us on the patio.

"I can't believe we're crashing the party," Rebecca says.

"We won't be long," Clay adds.

I'm mortified.

Residue—the word *residue* comes to mind.

"Well, you need to be long enough to have some cobbler and ice cream with us," Luke says.

"We're glad you're here," I say, moving to make room for Rebecca between Anne and me before going into the kitchen with Luke to get what we'll need for the dessert Miller has been waiting for.

The six of us sit amicably around the table, eating and talking, and after some coaxing, Maisey and Marcus get out of the pool, put a towel around their shoulders, and eat their dessert sitting shoulder to shoulder on a nearby lounger.

Marcus has never met Clay and Rebecca, though he's been here five or six times in the last two years. Miller tells him that Clay retired in June, and Marcus seems to be genuinely impressed that Clay served one school district for forty years, over twenty of them as superintendent of schools. When Marcus asks him the secret to such a long tenure, Clay gives his standard answer: "Good teachers." Marcus says it must be good administrating too, and after a rather thorough question-and-answer session, Marcus congratulates him on his years of service and his retirement.

I can't help myself. I lean over and hug Marcus.

"What accounts for your impeccable manners in a day

marked by so much crudeness and self-absorption?" I ask, more of a compliment than a question.

"That's easy," he says, "a drill sergeant disguised as my mother."

Maisey, disinterested in the lively conversation Marcus has been having with Clay, has pulled up a chair behind and between Anne and Rebecca. She asks Rebecca about her job. There are always stories, remarkable stories.

Rebecca, the most reserved of the Laswell clan, has been the director of a shelter for battered women for the last nineteen or twenty years. Most people would say Clay is dedicated to his job; those who know Rebecca, however, would say she is fiercely committed. Clay always said it was too bad she was salaried, because she'd be rich if she had been paid by the hour. Rebecca, focused and no-nonsense, would respond that they were already rich by anyone's standards, whereas the people she worked to help were needy in every way.

"So," Maisey says, "are you retiring too?"

"As a matter of fact," she says, "Friday is my last day—as director anyway."

"I can't imagine that, Rebecca," I say.

"I know. It was a hard decision, very hard. But I'll be assisting the new director part-time next year. And after that I may volunteer some. We'll see," she says, patting Maisey's bare leg.

At one time, until she was in middle school and her friends became preeminent, Maisey had been as much Clay and Rebecca's girl as she was Miller and Anne's. Before we put the pool in, Maisey spent most summer days in their pool. Clay had the whole month of July off, and it was he who taught Maisey to swim, turning her into an expert at every stroke except the butterfly, which she hated, as did Clay. She wasn't in the first grade before she jumped from the diving board and swam into his safe arms. And Rebecca, though often at work when we were there, equipped the pool with any kind of apparatus she thought Maisey would enjoy. For years Maisey was the sole Laswell grandchild, and Clay and Rebecca agreed with Luke: Maize was a-*maz*-ing.

Jackie doesn't call her Spoiley Girl for nothing. I doubt anyone on this earth has been loved more than my daughter.

Clay and Rebecca take off soon after the cobbler has been eaten and properly appreciated, and not long after that, Miller and Anne get up, stretch, and say they have to be going too. "We've stayed up *way* past our bedtime and still have a drive ahead of us," Miller says, glancing at his watch.

Luke and I walk his parents to their car, but as soon as Miller turns on the ignition, Luke heads back to the patio to be with the kids. I stay and wave my in-laws out of the long drive and onto the highway until their car becomes only the two tiny red dots of their taillights. As I turn, intending to join the others on the patio, the wide stairs of the front porch seem to call my name, inviting me to stay awhile.

So I plop here and stare at the lawn stretching luxuriously to the highway lying beyond it in the darkness. I almost always sit out back, but this is nice too. I have chosen steps over the chairs that Luke and I sat in last night, waiting for the kids. A chair would be too intentional, like I needed to be alone, needed to step away from *trying*, even if for just a moment.

I didn't dream Miller and Anne would stay until eleven. They probably wouldn't have if Clay and Rebecca hadn't stopped by.

Clay.

Well, one thing has not changed: I will never stop being thankful to him for introducing me to his handsome nephew. But I have more than Luke to thank him for. Six or seven months before that introduction, I had welled up with gratitude when he gave me my first teaching job. I actually sent him a thank-you note, although Paula had said that was over the top. To her thinking, my verbal thank-you had been very nearly effusive.

I couldn't help it. I've always loved this area of Indiana, one county over from where Paula grew up, and I couldn't believe it when Dr. Clayton Laswell offered me a fourth-grade classroom, the desire of my heart. Nor could I believe he hired Paula as well to teach another fourth-grade class in the same elementary school.

Paula and I were impressed with Clay Laswell from the moment we met him. After our interviews with the building principal and the hiring committee, I waited in his secretary's office while Paula had her interview. When she came out of Dr. Laswell's office, she waved a folded sheet of paper in front of her like she needed to cool off and said, "Whoa." Passing her on the way to his office for my interview, I laughed.

But when I walked in and he stepped around his impressive mahogany desk to shake my hand, I understood what she meant. Clayton Laswell was Robert Redford handsome. Well, that's what he is now. Then he was Brad Pitt handsome. He was the thirty-eight-year-old brand-new superintendent of schools, offered the position, according to the scuttlebutt, because of his excellent record as assistant superintendent and his ability to work amicably with everyone: teachers, staff, students, and parents.

But what impressed us besides his relative youth and his

good looks was his enthusiasm and philosophy of leadership. He believed in giving classroom teachers as much autonomy as possible, but at the same time, he didn't leave them, especially new teachers, to live "lives of quiet desperation." His teachers could count on guidance and impressive resources. Listening to him talk that day, I felt like jumping up and waving pompons.

Clay Laswell was also a good listener. He seemed to want to know everything about me as a person, as well as a potential teacher. He thought it was quite interesting that I left St. Louis to come to Indiana to college and that I wanted to stay here and teach, preferring the countryside to the glories of the city. He seemed even more interested in my thoughts on teaching, nodding with approval when I explained, among other things, my desire to provide a "positive zone" in my classroom. Some people would have laughed, calling such a thing the idealism of a teacher who has never taught, but Clay Laswell seemed to believe it was an exciting possibility.

I hoped he wasn't just being nice until he could get the crazy girl out of his office.

"He's with it!" Paula said as we drove out of the parking lot that afternoon. "How cool would it be if we got those two openings?" she asked.

The fact that we didn't make it into the same sorority four years earlier flashed into my mind, but I didn't mention it to Paula. No jinx thinking. I didn't doubt we'd get jobs for the fall, but I wanted so much for us to get *these* jobs.

Two days later, while eating cereal in our apartment before heading off to practice teach (a week left and counting), we got a call from Dr. Laswell's ancient but efficient secretary. She was pleased to inform both of us that we had received board approval and asked if we could come by that afternoon to sign our contracts. We gave each other high fives and danced a boogie in the living room before we threw on our clothes and ran out the door, planning to meet back home at three-thirty for the forty-five-minute drive to sign on the blessed dotted line. Our future had arrived.

And now, twenty-five years of that future have unfolded—a quarter of a century. They have been good years, but sitting here tonight, I'm acutely aware they could have been better. Wounds have marred my world, some of them self-inflicted. I have found those hardest to bear.

I stand up, brush off the seat of my shorts, and walk back to the patio, back to those who might be waiting for me there.

CHAPTER SIX

Maisey

"Kennedy, you look tired," Marcus says when Mother returns to the patio.

"You know, Marcus, I do believe I am."

Dad pushes back his chair and says, "Well, it's late. I think we should all hit the hay." He stands up and stretches. "What time are the girls coming tomorrow?"

"Around ten. And, Dad, don't fix a big breakfast."

"Fine. We'll fend for ourselves in the morning. Marcus, you know where the cereal is."

"I do, sir."

Mother comes up behind Dad, slips her arms around his

waist, and leans her head against his shoulder. Marcus is right; she does look tired.

"Are you asleep?" Dad asks her.

"Just about," she says.

They go inside then, saying they'll see us in the morning. And just when I think we'll have some time alone, Marcus decides we should turn in too.

"You don't want to watch a movie or something?" I ask.

"It's midnight, Maize. Let's call it a night."

"I'm pretty wired," I say. "Are you sure you don't want to at least get in the hot tub before we go to bed?"

"No way. I'm waterlogged already. And beat."

"Okay," I say. "Let's go, then, party pooper."

On the way to our rooms, he says how much he enjoyed my grandparents and how nice it was to meet Clay and Rebecca. "Your great-uncle is pretty impressive, isn't he?"

"What do you mean?"

"I mean, working for the same district for forty years and becoming the superintendent of schools before he was forty— that's something."

"Rebecca has run a homeless shelter for years. It's a really hard job."

"I'm sure. You know, I don't remember you ever mention-ing them."

"Maybe not. We don't see them all that much anymore."

"It sounds like they live close."

"A few miles from here."

"Any kids?"

"Three. They were quite a bit younger than Dad."

Suddenly I am as anxious as Marcus and my parents to turn in. The family tree is not my favorite subject. I kiss Marcus good-night at the top of the stairs. "I cannot wait until Saturday night," I say. "I want you with me tonight. I'm questioning my values."

He smiles sympathetically. "Four more nights, babe, and I'll love you and hold you all night long."

"I don't know if the Queen of Self-Control can wait." I kiss him again.

"You'll be asleep in no time."

"No, *you'll* be asleep in no time!" I kiss him one last time, a quick giving-up kiss, and drag myself to my room. "Good night," I say before clicking the door shut behind me.

I make it to bed in record time, but here I am, wide awake. I hate that. My mind won't shut up. I wish we kept sleep aids in this house. Honestly, I'm getting some tomorrow.

If he hadn't been so tired, I could have told Marcus a lot of things he might have found interesting—like why Dr. Clayton Laswell disgusts me.

But of course I wouldn't go there.

There are quite a few other things I haven't told Marcus that wouldn't make me sick to discuss. Have I ever completely explained to him that if you live in this county, it's a big deal to be a Laswell? My great-grandfather once farmed thousands of acres around here. When he realized Grandpa and Clay didn't want to farm, he sold off most of his land and gave a ton of his money to missions and charities. He called it feeding the hungry in a different way. I never met him, but I have loved him for that.

Jackie has always said I'm more than lucky to be a Laswell. I think that had as much to do with Clay Laswell's reputation and influence and infectious personality as my great-grandfather's acres and money. It's generally agreed that Clay is the very definition of leader. Everyone knows him. Or thinks they do. And based on what they know, everyone admires him. And he loves it, I'm sure.

But he isn't the only respected Laswell.

One day a policeman stopped me for speeding, took one look at my driver's license, and said, "Laswell, huh." I thought good ol' Uncle Clay might get me out of a ticket, but it turned out Dad did. "He's a fine man, your dad," the police officer said. "He's taken good care of a lot of people around here, including my folks."

"He's great," I said, and I meant it.

Maybe the officer could see that. Maybe that's why he let me off with a warning. Jackie sat in the passenger seat, accumulating more data for her favorite assertion. She shook her head, stuck my insurance card back in the glove compartment, and said, "It's a perk! How many times have I told you that being a Laswell is a stinking perk?"

"Being a Laswell isn't problem free," I said.

This, she ignored.

"Do you think my folks will let me change my last name to Laswell?" she asked. "Really, it just makes sense."

"We'll ask them," I said.

Dad was made a partner in a national accounting firm based in Indianapolis before he turned forty. I should tell Marcus that. Dad's the impressive one, not his uncle. After Dad became a partner, he had more say about things, and the fall I started eighth grade, he began working from his office at home, only going in to the Indy office once or twice a week. That was so nice.

What would I have done otherwise?

Kendy

Finished with my nightly routine, I walk into the bedroom and slip between the crisp white sheets. Luke marks his book and puts it on his bedside table.

As he switches off his lamp, I get a look at the clock. "Oh my, it's almost *one*!"

"It's late," he says, "but it was a nice evening. I'm glad Clay and Rebecca stopped by. Dad and Mom enjoyed visiting with them."

"Everything went very well. I'm quite relieved."

I roll over and face the wall, and Luke snuggles up behind me. I love it when he does this. Nothing makes me feel better than lying here with his arm thrown across me, claiming me. I back farther into him so he'll know how glad I am he's there, and in response his arm draws me even closer to him. We do this on nights we don't make love, and I can't say which is more pleasurable.

He is asleep before either of us has the energy to say anything else.

Luke's hand is warm in mine.

I've been holding that hand a very long time now. We were married twenty-four years ago in June, only a few months after Clay introduced us.

Each year Clay and Rebecca hosted a series of Christmas parties or receptions for the schools in the district. The Friday night of the elementary party, they invited Luke. Luke was twenty-four and, having earned an MBA, just beginning his job with an accounting firm in Indianapolis.

Clay invited his nephew for two primary reasons. One, his boys, fourteen and thirteen, were tired of smiling at hundreds of teachers and administrators but thought they might endure one more party if their hero, Luke, would come and play pool with them. Two, Clay wanted Luke to meet me. He said later that Luke had been too busy too long to nurture a serious relationship, but now that school and job hunting were behind him, he should have time to think of matters of the heart.

I had come to the party with Paula and her fiancé, but somehow they disappeared while I was putting away my coat. I had just stepped into the beautifully decorated living room, about to join the two rowdy male sixth-grade teachers standing in the far corner of the room, laughing about something, when Clay called my name.

"Kennedy," he said, "I'm glad you're here."

"I'm glad to be here," I said, giving him my aren't-you-glad-you-hired-me smile.

"I've sent my daughter to the basement to rescue my nephew. My sons think he is their personal property, but they're going to have to share him a few minutes, because I intend for him to meet you."

I could hardly believe Dr. Laswell was taking time away from rooms full of guests to focus on me at all, much less to say such a thing. He wanted *his* nephew to meet *me?*

And then the nephew appeared, as handsome as Clay Laswell, but younger—fourteen years younger, I later learned. It would be an understatement to say the introduction was awkward. I felt like everyone in the room had stopped what they were doing and saying to look at us. But when Luke Laswell shook my hand, it was warm and unaccountably comfortable, and I was happy I had worn the black velvet dress Paula coveted, and I was more than a little disappointed when two boys came up from the basement to drag Luke back to their lair.

Later that evening, after I had been as outgoing and gracious as I could stand, I felt the need to escape the crowd, and I stepped into the study off the main hallway. I was drawn to the quiet of an empty room and the warmth of a four-log fire. I stood watching the flames, glad to be out of the fray momentarily, when I heard, "There you are."

I turned and saw Luke standing in the doorway.

"You caught me," I said.

"I've interrupted your peace."

"Are *you* in need of peace? Come in. This room is lovely. I haven't had the nerve to go down to the basement. I've wondered if it's reserved for family, off limits to guests."

"As a matter of fact, several of your peers have made their way down there. That's how I managed to make my getaway. The boys are beating their former sixth-grade teachers at pool."

"Well, now I *know* I'm not going down there."

It was clear that neither of us wanted to be anywhere but where we were. We sat on the sofa and began to really introduce ourselves. When people came to the doorway and peeked into the room, they saw us talking quietly but intently, and they invariably chose to go away. We were invariably glad.

Before Luke was discovered by one of the boys and dragged away again and before I found my coat and thanked the Laswells for a wonderful evening, Luke and I had made plans for the following night. We spent every weekend together after that, and he proposed to me the week of spring break, the middle of March.

After dating six months, we were married in June, and after dating her boyfriend for three years, Paula married in August. "Who would have thought you'd be married before me?" Paula said when I showed her my engagement ring and told her the wedding date we had chosen.

Mother was horrified, naturally. "Good grief, Kennedy!" she said. "You hardly know the man."

"You know what, Mother, that's just not true. I know Luke very well. You should be *thrilled* I'm going to marry such a good man. One who can supplement my teaching habit, by the way." *And almost as ambitious as you*, I could have added—but I didn't know that yet.

She turned around and walked into the other room that day, and I stood there wondering why I had expected anything different. It occurred to me that after so many years, she still thought "good man" was an oxymoron, at least on a personal level. She always seemed to get along with the male species at work.

If I were fair, I'd have to admit Luke's and my courtship was a bit of a whirlwind. But sometimes, and it is wonderful when it happens, things are very clear.

Other times, of course, they are not.

But by God's grace, and to my mother's utter amazement, Luke and I are still married.

I squeeze my husband's hand, and though I know very well he is sound asleep, he squeezes my hand in return.

WEDNESDAY

CHAPTER SEVEN

Kendy

I walk into the kitchen and find Marcus pouring Raisin Bran into a serving bowl—a *serving* bowl! The word *chipper* comes to mind while watching him happily fending for himself. I do believe we're going to have another morning person in the family.

"Have some cereal, Marcus," I say with a smile.

He looks up and smiles too. He has a gorgeous smile. "Good morning, Kennedy."

"It's time you call me Kendy, Marcus. No one calls me Kennedy except Mother and my dentist."

"I'd like that."

"So," I say, pointing at the cereal box, "is there any left for me?"

He shakes it. "Plenty. And I saw another box in the pantry."

"Okay, then. I love Raisin Bran. I have since I was a little girl. This made breakfast a snap, which pleased my mother no end."

Marcus laughs.

What does he know?

Marcus chooses a chair at the round table by the windows instead of a barstool, and I come over and join him.

"Luke says he's going to mow before the pool party," he says, nodding toward the outbuilding where Luke keeps the tractor. "I told him I'd come out and do the trimming if he trusts me with his weed eater."

Marcus looks as if that would be as exciting as exploring Mars. I have a constant urge to hug the boy. I tell him I'm glad he had the time to come here for the week, and he says his boss gave him two weeks off with pay as a wedding gift.

"I should write him a thank-you note," I say, sort of meaning it. Time to spend with the man who loves my daughter is invaluable to me.

"So," I ask, "do you like having so many siblings?" It rather fascinates me that he has four brothers, all with names beginning with *M*. I try to keep them straight.

"I do," he says.

"And you're the youngest, right?"

"I'm the baby boy, five years behind the others," he says. "I've been called the Caboose, the Afterthought, the Crowning Glory, and Oops. Mom says all the monikers are appropriate."

"I like Crowning Glory."

"Mom would appreciate that. Even though I was their little surprise, she and Dad plugged away at my formation until the day I left for college. They say they went into the house when I drove off, put their feet up, and said, 'Whew! We're done!' "

"What was one of their important lessons?"

"Frugality," he says with no hesitation.

The mother of the bride is comforted to hear it. "So," I say, "Benjamin Franklin would have been proud to know your parents?"

"He would have *loved* them. They did their best to teach my brothers and me financial responsibility. An allowance did not come without strings attached: They taught us to tithe ten percent, to consider giving an offering on top of that, and to save at least twenty percent, and then we could decide what we should do with the rest. I was unanimously voted the best saver of us all. The story goes that I still have all the money I put in my piggy bank before I started school."

"You're kidding."

"That's the story. But no one can find the bank to prove it. My theory is they made it up at some point and now believe it to be true."

"An embellishment gone awry," I say.

"Exactly."

"Well, I'm sure your brothers will be delightful escorts for Maisey's friends." I get up and bring the carton of orange juice back to the table. "A big family sounds like fun," I say.

"It is."

"It also sounds boisterous."

"That's for sure. And if five boys weren't enough, we always had a dog or two—house dogs—and a cat that died just a few months ago at the impressive age of twenty-one."

I have to laugh. "I have absolutely no frame of reference for so much activity. Like Maisey, I was an only child, and to make matters worse, I lived in a condo, my only companion a goldfish incapable of making a ruckus."

"Did you like being an only child?"

"It was okay."

He looks at me as though I should have more to say.

"There really isn't much to tell, but I'll try to come up with a detail or two for you one of these days."

"I'll hold you to that," he says, jumping up, rinsing his bowl, and heading out in search of a weed eater.

I put our bowls into the dishwasher, get the ground beef out of the refrigerator, and begin to make hamburger patties for the cookout, thinking about how differently Marcus and Maisey grew up.

She, like I, grew up as an only child, though Jackie practically lived here during middle school and high school. Like Marcus, Jackie was one of five children, and her mother never seemed to mind loaning her out, at least to us. I did not want Maisey to be an only child. Oh, how I had wanted another! But my doctor was amazed I ever became pregnant at all, and even then, getting Maisey to term required spending most of the last three months of that pregnancy in bed. I'm blessed to have even one child, and I know it.

Mother, on the other hand, didn't want *me*, much less another child. I'm sure of it, although when I finally exploded one day in high school and accused her of that, she slapped me. She slapped me hard—I couldn't have been more shocked. She had never spanked me or hit me in any other way until then, and for that isolated incident, she did not apologize. Looking back on it, I suppose what I said was unfair. She could have ended her pregnancy, illegal at the time but still an option; she could have put me up for adoption; she could have sent me off to boarding school. And she was merely grateful for Margaret and Hugh's presence in our lives; she did not hire them to be my surrogate parents. She does not know I have called them that.

Truthfully, and I imagine it was because of Margaret and Hugh and Paula, there were times I didn't mind living in a home populated by only two quiet souls and one very nearly comatose fish, even when Mother was gone so much of the time. They say there are two kinds of people in this world: those energized by people and those energized by solitude. I'm sure I'm the latter. I need alone time. It keeps me relatively sane. But there's a difference between solitude and loneliness. I know this, for I have been both alone and lonely.

Lonely, I hated.

And listening to Marcus, I realize I have no stories I want to tell, no tales from the condominium.

I do have one especially lovely memory I cling to with a tenacity that puzzles me. I was in the ninth grade when a blizzard trapped Mother and me in our condo. Everything was shut down for three whole days, including the company Mother worked for. That was the one year Margaret and Hugh tried the snowbird thing, spending the three months of winter in Florida, where some of their oldest friends had retired. So Mother and I hung out together while the snow swirled in the lights of the city, massive mounds of it building up on the sidewalks and streets, making them utterly impassable.

We scrounged up stuff to eat, pulling cookbooks from a top shelf to see what we could make with the ingredients we had on hand, and we watched a lot of old movies, chatting almost like girl friends during commercial breaks. I asked her questions about work, and during several commercials she regaled me with stories about some of the people she worked with.

Those were enchanted days as far as I was concerned. We stayed up late, never consulting the clock, and two of the three mornings we were snowed in, we didn't even get dressed. We stayed in our flannel pajamas and robes and cooked and watched television and played Scrabble and gin rummy. Mother said I was good company.

I remember wishing it would snow forever.

Maisey

Considering how late it was when I finally got to sleep, I'd say I'm up pretty early. I pull on a T-shirt, a pair of shorts, and tennis shoes, and tap on Marcus's door. I can't believe he's gone already. When I get to the bottom of the stairs, I hear Marcus and Mother talking in the kitchen. She is saying something about Benjamin Franklin, and he is saying something about financial responsibility.

Is that crazy or what?

That's a conversation I don't want to interrupt—or join. I hear the familiar and somehow comforting hum of Dad's mower and look out the front door to see him beginning the first long swipe down the front yard.

I remember all the times he mowed with me sitting on his lap. I remember him teaching me how to mow with that rider when I was older, turning expertly around the trees like he does. I remember meeting each other in the garage when we were through with the yard, giving each other high fives, toasting each other with bottles of water from the fridge we keep out there.

He's reached the end of the first row, hugging the long driveway, and is coming back toward the house now. I slip out the front door and run toward him. He must see me waving my arms, because he has stopped and is idling the motor, waiting for me.

"You want to do this?" he asks.

"I will," I say, "but I really want you to take a break and play a game of Horse with me."

"I've just started, honey."

"Please," I plead. "We might not have time later."

I know he wants to get the yard done, but I see in his face that he also wants to play ball with me. We've played together since the summer before I started the eighth grade. We were sitting alone at the dinner table one evening in July when I asked him if he could get me ready to try out for the basketball team that fall. "Sure," he said, and in less than a week the mini-court was poured, the goal set, appropriate tennis shoes purchased, and we began my foray into "the thrill of victory and the agony of defeat." We'd play until we were hot beyond endurance and then we'd hit the pool. When winter drove us inside, we moved from the court—that is, the cement pad off the driveway—to the church gym. I think of the year it began as Mr. Dickens's "the worst of times," except for this sliver of happiness.

I learned stamina, teamwork, and overall technique in long hours of practice at school, but I learned how to shoot from Dad. I made more three pointers than any other girl on our high school team, and we won state my junior and senior years. Everyone said I looked like a cheerleader instead of a basketball player, but I was devoted to the game. Basketball came along just when I needed it. I believe my sudden desire to play was sent from God to help Dad and me survive a house that had become too gloomy to bear. I know basketball, among other things, transformed our relationship. Starting that summer, I became a daddy's girl, and I hoped somehow that would be enough to make up for the son he would not have.

"Just one game," I plead, holding on to the steering wheel, determined, it seems, to rescue him from the tyranny of prudence. "It's *tradition*."

"Tradition, huh?"

I guess that does it for him. I'm happily victorious now that he has turned off the motor. "I'll get the ball," he says. "One game!"

I hug him. "Thanks, Dad."

I watch him stride across the lawn toward the garage, and though I now have a communications degree, I love him beyond what I could possibly express.

Kendy

The hamburger patties are in the refrigerator, and I'm putting potatoes on to boil when Marcus reappears.

"Taking a break so soon?" I ask.

"Haven't started," he said. "Apparently Maisey talked Luke into playing a game of Horse before he mows."

"My goodness. I thought I heard the mower."

"He started but didn't get very far."

"Well, they love to play."

"I've been watching them. They played ten minutes before Luke finally got an *H*."

"It will be a battle. They're very good. Both of them were starters in high school. Didn't they ask you to play? Three can play."

"Yes, but they're out of my league. I'm going to have to challenge your daughter to a game of football and see if I can put her in her place."

"Or soccer. She can dribble a ball far better than she can kick it. She gave soccer up before she really got started. I thought sports were a lost cause. But four years after she walked off the soccer field for the last time, she picked up a basketball and became a star."

"She didn't play at all in college."

"No, and that surprised us. But she still seems to love it. She and Luke usually play when she comes home."

"She volunteers as a coach at the Boys and Girls Club. The kids adore her."

Marcus suddenly seems to recall why he is here and asks for some granola bars for Maisey. When he retrieves her breakfast and returns to the game, I get out what I'll need to make the potato salad, wishing I had time to watch Luke and Maisey do their thing.

I missed most of her eighth-grade year, when she and Jackie decided to take up basketball, but from the first game of her ninth-grade season until the last game of her senior year, neither Luke nor I missed one of her games, even the ones played out of town. She was joyful on the floor and a joy to watch. Jackie complimented her one night after a particularly hard-won game by saying she was no Spoiley Girl when it came to basketball. Although the girls tended to pass Maisey the ball as often as possible, she was not a ball hog. She was a team player who praised and encouraged everyone else.

I saved all the newspaper clippings from her high school basketball career and made her an album. Each year several newspaper articles, complete with pictures, featured her. I always told her she didn't take a bad picture even when she was going up for a basket. The album was a love gift, something I worked on secretly for four years, thinking she'd be thrilled to have it. She did thank me, and she and Jackie sat down at the kitchen table and looked through it together the Monday after all the graduation festivities. But I didn't get the impression she was thrilled. Jackie seemed more excited than Maisey, though pictures and comments about her were scarcer by far. The day we returned from taking Maisey to college, I found the album lying on the bottom shelf of a side table in the living room. I put it in the cabinet with all the other albums, thinking some day she might want it.

It could happen, as Paula likes to say about things that are quite unlikely.

Maisey had loved her baby album. She was in the third grade the first time she saw it. I thought I'd show it to her when she was a little older, but we were snowed in for days and had run out of fun things to do. Luke had stayed in Indy with his parents, not willing to risk getting stuck here, unable to get to the office. Digging out the album had kept me from being furious about that decision. The label *baby album* isn't really adequate. If it is an album, it is one unlike any I've ever seen. It's a journal, really, containing anecdotes of delightful things Maisey did and said from the time she was born until she started preschool four years later. I suppose I called it an album because many entries are illustrated with pictures. Not working the six years until she started first grade allowed for this, as well as other such extravagances.

I began the album the day Maisey was born. Her birth was an emotional experience for everyone; even my doctor had tears in his eyes when he handed her to me that morning.

In a checkup I had shortly after Luke and I became engaged, my gynecologist warned me that, because of an abnormally small uterus, I might never conceive a child. For some reason, this didn't bother Luke or me all that much. We were happy and busy with careers we loved, and we simply agreed that we'd look into adoption if I hadn't become pregnant by the time I turned thirty.

It didn't make sense, then, when hardly a year after Luke and I were married, I developed a chronic case of morning nausea. I didn't call the doctor until I had missed two periods and taken two home pregnancy tests, both of them positive. Though I considered them only tentative proof, I put the wands in the passenger seat the day I went to the doctor, testimony that I had several good reasons to bother him.

Luke had intended to go with me, but something "critical" had come up at the office. I cried most of the way to the doctor's office, partly because now that there was a chance, I wanted very badly to be pregnant, and partly because my husband had allowed something, however urgent, to keep him from what might possibly be one of our most extraordinary moments.

I still remember lying on the examination table behind the tent of a modesty sheet and hearing the excitement in my doctor's voice when he shouted, "Confirmed!" I hadn't trusted the pregnancy test, but that simple word finally convinced me.

And thrilled me.

I was so happy that my irritation and disappointment with Luke abated. In fact, I almost didn't mind that he wasn't there. I could savor this inconceivably good news before I shared it with anyone but God himself. Luke called me at home later and asked about the verdict he had been expecting. (He had had complete faith in the plus signs.)

"Well?" he asked.

In response, I chose to echo my doctor's life-changing word. But instead of shouting it, I whispered it: "*Confirmed*. The pregnancy's confirmed, Luke."

But the pregnancy was far from easy. I began spotting in my sixth month, and I was told that, unfortunately, along with a small uterus, I have an abnormally small cervix. Miscarriage was very likely. I went straight to bed and spent over two months there reading and praying and gently rubbing my stomach, reassuring my little girl that everything would be all right.

Luke was there the morning our miracle child made it safely into this world, and we held her and kissed her and thanked God for her. When the nurse took Maisey away for a while, I asked Luke to bring me the little notebook and pen in my purse. He helped me sit up as comfortably as I could in the hospital bed, and I wrote the first entry for the baby album. I still recall how it began: *You came to us today, eyes wide with curiosity, and you snuggled into our hearts and filled them with a joy we didn't know existed.*

In the album are pictures of Maisey smiling, revealing her first shiny tooth; her face covered with a good portion of her first birthday cake; her sucking on her binky as though it were the source of oxygen; her holding Jackie's hand in front of the Christmas tree in her preschool classroom. And there must be an even million pictures of her sleeping in glorious peace. For each of these pictures there are stories, and there are more stories without pictures. I had left my camera at Miller and Anne's the day I walked into Maisey's bedroom and found her putting Vaseline all over the back half of her rocking horse. "There," she said, looking up at me, goop all over her fingers, "he feel better."

She was a happy and hilarious child, and I wanted a record of it so that I would never forget those incredible moments of grace.

Maisey loved the baby album. During the blizzard the year she was eight, we sat together on the sofa, the album open between us, and laughed and cried at the wonder of Maisey's first four years. We read it twice during those snowbound days—the second time with Clay after he had plowed our driveway—and then I put it away. But we read it again at least once every winter after that—until the year I skipped fall and winter altogether.

CHAPTER EIGHT

Maisey

Dad didn't go down without a fight. The swim party will begin in a couple of hours, but a long shower is now imperative. First I want to call Jackie. I grab my cell phone from the dresser, lie across my unmade bed, and press five on my speed dial.

"What are you doing?" I ask when she finally answers.

"Well, let me see. Oh, that's right. I just got up, and I'm trying to get ready to come to your house!"

"No need for sarcasm, sweetie."

"That's not sarcasm—that's stating the obvious. Sorry. If you'll give me a second, I'll see if I can find my sensitive side."

A few moments of silence, something we've observed for years. It usually takes a while for Jackie to find her sensitive side.

"Oh, there you are," she finally says, though not to me. And then after another practiced pause, her sensitive side takes the phone from Miss Brusque and says, "Okay, let's begin again. Is there something I can do for you?"

"So nice of you to ask, but no."

"Are you quite sure?"

"I just thought you might want to come over before ten. Like now would be good. I've been playing basketball with Dad, and I'm hyped up, ready to 'move it, move it.' I'm getting in the shower, and by the time I'm out and in one of my darling new bathing suits, you could be here! I'd really love that. Don't you want to come early and beat the crowd?"

"Listen, I could be there right now if you had let me stay there this week like I wanted."

With no warning whatsoever, Miss Brusque grabs the phone from Jackie's sensitive side.

"I'm pretty sure I even begged," she continues. "I could have used a break from Heidi, you know. Of course you know. Plus, you're going to live in St. Louis for who knows how long."

"I would love for you to be staying here, but Marcus is staying in your room. I told you that."

"And I told *you* I could stay in your room with you. For that matter, Marcus could have stayed with you, and I could have had my room. I miss it."

"Marcus and I don't sleep together, Jackie."

"Fine. We're back where we started, then—I could have shared your room with you."

"Okay, big mistake. I'm sorry. But come over as soon as you can."

"I'm trying to get Heidi up, which, as you well know, is not so easy to do. If you're in such a hurry, you can skip your shower and come drag her out of bed yourself!"

"Just let her come over when she decides to get up."

"You need to chill, girl. We'll both be there by ten, just like we planned."

We disconnect, and I seem held to the bed by an unseen weight. The impulse to "move it" has disappeared as quickly as Jackie's sensitive side. Actually, Jackie's finding her sensitive side is our little joke. I accuse her of being brusque, but she's everything a best friend should be, including supportive. She has supported anything I've thought I should do, though I'm guessing she'd draw the line at mass murder. She didn't even carry on all that much when I decided to go to college in St. Louis instead of going with her and Heidi to Purdue.

"I just need to get away," I said.

"Purdue is away," she said.

"Farther," I said.

She ended up saying she didn't get it, but at least I wasn't going to Stanford. I told her thanks for thinking I could get in.

She's generally curt with her support, of course. But the bulk of her curtness is a persona and one of the things I love about her. I'm lucky that Miss Brusque has been Spoiley Girl's best friend since we were four.

What she said on the phone just now is yet another example of her support: "Fine."

That was her typically understated nice. I appreciate her response to my continued and not-so-easy commitment to abstinence. I've seen one too many talk-show hosts lately who are not so accepting. Incredulity is the popular media's typical response. A college graduate, even a high school graduate, who chooses abstinence until marriage is no longer weird but stupid or perhaps flawed. I should have written a research paper on the growing prejudice before I graduated. Except I'm too young to be a curmudgeon. Besides, the consensus would probably be that I need sex.

I know for a fact that Jackie hasn't had sex yet either; at least she hadn't the last time we talked about it. But I don't think it's so much a spiritual conviction or a considered commitment to self-control as it is a lack of interest in any one person for any length of time. When we were juniors in high school, Caitlin, our fourth musketeer, confessed she had been having sex with a boyfriend who dumped her, the first time having been after she had way too much to drink at a party she wished she hadn't attended.

I told Jackie later that would never happen to me. She said I shouldn't be so sure about that.

"Hey, you should know by now that if I put my mind to something, I do it," I had said, sitting on this very bed. "Anyway, it seems to me that those who practice self-control *before* marriage have a better chance of practicing it *after* marriage."

"Probably so," Jackie said.

"And with a little self-control," I added, "maybe people wouldn't louse up their perfectly lovely lives."

"*Lovely* is a Kendy word," Jackie said.

I faux glared.

She hopped right back on the subject. "Well, I'm sure you're right—a little self-control is good for the body and soul."

I must have glared again.

"A *lot* of self-control?"

This called for a smile.

"So," she said, "do you want to go downstairs and make some nachos?"

That ridiculous question made me laugh. It still makes me laugh. It's become a saying we use to conclude any heavy discussion: *So, you want to make some nachos?*

I love Jackie.

I know I should shower and get downstairs, but I decide to call Gram and check on my dress. I never, *ever*, call her office phone, but I can call her cell. If she's doing something ultra important, she always switches it off.

I'm surprised when she answers. She's surprised to hear from me this early on a Wednesday morning.

"Have you picked up my dress yet?" I ask.

"Not yet. You'll be glad to know that I'm picking it up on my lunch hour."

"Great!"

"I'll call you this afternoon to assure you it's safe in my coat closet."

I disconnect after thanking her for taking the time to pick it up for me.

I really wish my dress had been ready before Marcus and I left on Monday. Gram said it would be her pleasure to pick it up, and she sounded like she meant it, but I'd feel better if it were hanging in *my* closet right now. I can't wait for Saturday, when I get to put it on and wear it for hours. (The incredulous will be glad to know I'm equally eager to take it off.)

Gram has great taste. I'm so glad she made time to shop with me. Of course, since I interned in the Communications Department of her company last semester, she saw me most days. She actually made appointments at several boutiques, which according to her would help enormously. I would not have had the nerve to walk into a couple of the places she took me, including the shop where we discovered my dress. She told me not to worry, that she'd cover anything over what Dad was willing to pay. Of course that wasn't necessary.

I must have tried on thirty dresses, five in the shop where I finally found the dress I wanted. It needed altering, but the minute I tried it on, we knew this was what I'd been look-ing for.

"Oh!" Gram said, standing in the large dressing area, staring at me in the mirror. "It's the perfect dress, Kennedy."

She didn't even notice she had called me by Mother's name. I started to say something, but it really didn't matter. What mattered was that the dress was perfect.

Kendy

I'm sitting here in a wrought-iron swivel rocker watching the kids play their version of water volleyball. Marcus and Maisey are challenging Jackie, Heidi, and Caitlin. Luke is lying nearby on a lounger, refusing to budge until he has to grill the hamburgers. I gave up my lounger an hour back when I kept getting up to chase any ball that escaped the boundaries of the pool. Well, exercise is exercise.

Marcus said I should come be on their team and make the sides equal, but Maisey said it wasn't necessary since Mar-cus was such a big guy and had the skill and determination of two.

I could hardly argue with that.

They've called a halt to the game to take a drink break.

Jackie and Maisey have taken orders and are coming from the kitchen with bottles of water and two diet colas.

Jackie keeps one of the colas and hands the other to me. "Let everyone else be healthy," she says, dragging up a chair to sit beside me. When the others return to the pool, she tells me she's going to mutiny.

"I'm sitting this one out," she calls to them.

They return to their game, and she squeezes my hand and says in a conspiratorial tone, "What I want is time to chat with you. I've been missing you!"

"I've missed you too, sweetheart. But you're home now, and I expect to see you more often."

"Don't worry. I know where my room is. It's only on loan to Marcus. I plan to spend the night here now and then, you know."

"I'd love it. I wish Maisey were going to live closer."

"Hasn't she told you? She was saying before you came out that when Marcus graduates from law school, he's going to try to get a job in Indy."

No, she hasn't told me, but I don't tell Jackie that. She may be able to detect it, however, because I can hardly process such good news. The very thought of their living nearby makes me wildly happy.

"That's a ways off," I finally say, "but it would be wonderful, wouldn't it?"

"It would be great."

Maisey is as lucky to have Jackie in her life as I am to have Paula. I've told Jackie that on numerous occasions.

"I have big news too," Jackie says. "I haven't even told Maisey."

When she says Maisey's name, we almost involuntarily

turn toward the pool to look at her. She is looking at us as well, though I don't think she could have heard Jackie say her name. As we watch, the beach ball lands on Maisey's shoulder, and Marcus tells her to get her head in the game.

I turn my attention back to Jackie. I'm more than curious. "What news?" I prod. "And why haven't you told Maisey?"

"Oh, it's so fresh off the presses. And I don't know what will come of it. Plus, this is Maisey's weekend. I just feel like giving you an exclusive."

"Well, how nice. Let's hear it."

"I think I'm in love."

This revelation strikes me as stupendous. "Is that a fact?"

"I believe it is."

"And do I by any chance know the lucky fellow?"

"As a matter of fact you do."

"Spill it," I say, sounding like Jackie.

"Well, you haven't seen him for a long time. When he was in grade school, his family moved from here to Ohio. He came back to Indiana to go to college at Purdue, but we didn't run into each other there until this year. We started dating seriously after spring break."

"And where is he now?"

"Here! Or near here. He got a job in Indy. He's coming to the wedding."

"Well, that's exciting, isn't it?"

"Ask me why he's coming—besides the fact that I really want him to."

"Why is he coming?"

"He wants to see *you*!"

"My goodness. Who *is* he?"

"Okay, enough suspense. *He* is Sam Meyers."

"Sam Meyers? Do I know a Sam Meyers?"

"Think kindergarten. Think a little boy saying, 'I'm stwong!' and tipping over the teacher's desk to prove it. He said he just meant to lift it a little bit."

"Sammy? Little Sammy?"

Oh yes, I remember him. And I remember it taking us a while to put that desk back together, but Sammy was one of several reasons I thoroughly enjoyed volunteering for Maisey's kindergarten class.

"When Sam comes to the wedding," Jackie says, "he wants to bring you a toy John Deere tractor."

This makes me laugh.

When Sammy was five, he was the cutest little boy in the world, but he did have a destructive streak. The day I brought a toy John Deere tractor to class for show-and-tell, Sammy asked if he could see it, and in no time at all, he was standing before me with tears brimming in his huge blue eyes, holding the green tractor in his open hand.

I knelt to his height and said, "My goodness, what's wrong, sweetie?"

He opened his other fist to reveal one of the tires from Luke's tractor. This particular toy was an antique and not cheap. What had I been thinking to bring it?

"Oh dear," I said.

"Don't wowwy," he said, sniffling, tears spilling over. "My dad's a good fixer."

I stood up, tousled his mass of blond hair, and told *him* not to worry because my husband was a good fixer too.

I had been teaching fourth grade again for more than a year when Maisey and Jackie and Sammy were in the second grade, and I brought cupcakes for his going-away party. Tears spilled from my eyes when I gave him a big hug and he walked out of our lives, never to return.

Until now, that is.

"Oh, Jackie, I can't wait to see him!"

"I knew you'd love it. He's just as sweet as he was then, Kendy, but now he can say his *Rs*, and he doesn't seem to tear stuff up."

"Jackie!" Maisey calls, floating on an air mattress with the others, except for Marcus, who seems to have disappeared. "Hellooo! This is a *swim* party. Get in here!"

"Your daughter can be so demanding," Jackie says, getting out of her chair. "I've been telling her all morning she needs a chill pill. A thousand milligrams should do it."

"Well, humor her. We'll be eating before long."

"Okay," she says, "but remember—until the weekend is over, Sam is our secret."

Maisey

I always make my bed. Mother ingrained that habit in me before I started school. But it's just as well I never got it done this morning, because Caitlin and Heidi are stretched out across it. Jackie is slouched in the chair by the windows, and I'm sitting next to her on the ottoman.

We were going to do this decently and in order. Everyone was going to take her shower, and after we were cleaned up, we were going to meet here so I could give them their gifts. But running up the stairs, they persuaded me to scrap my plan. I can't believe I've kept these presents from them this long. I'm eager to see the gifts again myself. I had the gold and silver bracelets with the girls' names inscribed on them wrapped when I bought them, and I haven't seen them since. They are beautiful. Mom and Dad gave me permission to buy them something this nice; they love my friends too.

"Hand them over," Jackie says, nodding at the presents sticking out of the sack sitting beside me.

I make something of a production of it, pulling out one at a time, reading the label, and handing the gold-wrapped gift to each of them. "Wait," I say when I hand the first one to Heidi. "Open them together."

When they are all distributed, they tear into the paper, open the boxes, and stare at their bracelets. The looks on their faces tells me I have made a good choice.

"Whoa," Jackie says.

"No kidding," Heidi says.

Caitlin runs her finger across her name. "It's so pretty."

I smile, happy with their responses. "I'm so glad you like them."

I do not expect the wave of emotion that comes over me. Tears spring to my eyes, and I find it difficult to speak. But I want to say what I've been planning. "You've been good friends all my life," I begin, looking at each one of them. "What would I have done without you? Really? I can't imagine. Thanks for being here for me, thanks for laughter that wouldn't have been possible without you, and thanks for being in my wedding. I hope we'll always be in touch, but when we are separated, look at your bracelet and know I'm somewhere in this world, loving you."

We sit here unable to move until Heidi yells, "Group hug!"

Hugging each other, trying not to cry, communicates what we feel as much as anything else could. Leaving for separate colleges was bad enough, but I am the first to get married and change the dynamic forever. It is time for such change, of course—we know that—but we have loved our time together, and letting it go is even harder than I thought it would be.

Heidi and Caitlin put their bracelets back in their boxes and head across the landing to the guest bedroom and bath, and Jackie and I clean up in mine.

After our showers, Jackie and I stand in our underwear in front of the mirror, putting on makeup, our hair wrapped in fluffy yellow towels. After we've finished our makeup and before we tackle our hair, Jackie asks me to put her bracelet on her. I get it out of the box and clasp it on her wrist. She looks at it and smiles.

"So," I say while we comb tangles from our hair, "what were you and Mother discussing for so long?"

"Just catching up," Jackie says. "I haven't seen her in ages."

"She said you dropped by when you got home from school. That's not so long ago."

"To get my graduation present, and for about a second!"

"What were you laughing about?"

Jackie lays her comb down, puts her hand on her hip. "Good grief!"

"I just wondered what you were talking about; that's all."

"I don't know, Maize. Life."

"It looked important."

"It did?"

I refuse to retreat, and Jackie finally tells me about Sam. We finish getting ready about the same time she finishes her story, and she gives me a kiss on the cheek before she heads across the landing to check on Heidi and Caitlin. This rare tenderness, a flesh-and-blood appearance of her sensitive side, almost does me in.

I don't know why I couldn't let it go. Jackie said she had planned to tell me about finding and falling for Sam when Marcus and I got back from our honeymoon. She told me not to say a word to anyone else about it, that this is my weekend. And I won't. But if Mother knows about Sam, I sure should.

CHAPTER NINE

Kendy

"Don't you look nice."

That's what I hear when I open my eyes and see Paula standing over me. I had almost fallen asleep behind my sunglasses, relaxing on the lounger.

"You think I look nice?" I ask.

"Well, your nails certainly do, all twenty of them."

I hold up my hands and look at the shiny cranberry nail polish, expertly applied.

"You're quite right. That's thanks to Jackie. I told her all of us were getting the works Saturday, but that didn't deter her; she said we needed to look great for the rehearsal too, so after lunch, out she came with the box of manicure supplies."

"Like old times, huh?" Paula asks, pulling up a chair, plopping into it and using my lounger for a footstool.

"It was. When they were in grade school, I don't think the four of them ever spent a night when we didn't play beauty shop. I was usually the nail tech, exhausted and ready for bed after painting eighty little nails."

"One more reason I'm glad I had boys."

"Today they did each other's nails while I watched. But when they were through, Jackie insisted on doing mine too. She tested three colors on my thumbnail before she decided this one was just the thing. She'll be glad you approve."

"The girls about ran over me when I was coming into the house. Where were they off to?"

"They have a final fitting for their dresses. One or two of them are still too long. They're tea length apparently, and Maisey wants to make sure they're just right. Jackie was telling her to relax when they headed inside earlier. Her exact words were, 'I'm getting your meds.' "

"They showed me their bracelets. Quite nice, I must say."

"They are, aren't they? All three of them came out and showed them to me too. Jackie said it was a good thing they did their nails, because they'll be holding out their hands all day long to show off their bracelets."

"It sounds like things went well."

"Very well. I don't know why you've been so worried."

"Oh really?"

Paula is nothing if not observant, and though we've talked little about it, she is borderline angry that I have not so much as seen Maisey's wedding dress and have not been consulted about anything related to the wedding except the menu for the reception dinner and the whereabouts of our checkbook. She said one Saturday in March that it was "awfully nice" of Maisey to finally tell me that her wedding colors were black and white so I could buy a dress. We actually managed to laugh that day.

"The girls enjoyed being together so much," I say. "And Marcus, well, he's an angel."

"He seems like a good guy, all right. Maisey chose well. He's the silver lining in all this, isn't he?"

"Pure gold, as a matter of fact. Every time Marcus comes to visit, I like him more. In fact, I love the boy already. Did I tell you I wrote his mother after they became engaged? I told her I considered Maisey blessed to be marrying her son."

"Do you suppose I'll get one of those letters someday?"

"You should. Your boys are a gift to the world too. As are you."

"Since you feel that way, I'm sure you'll agree to go to Indy with me. I need a dress for the wedding."

"You've got a dress."

"I hate it. I don't know what I was thinking. I look down-right frumpy in it. Why in the world did you let me buy it?"

"You do not look frumpy in it or anything else."

"I do too, and I'm taking it back. I'll embarrass you if I show up in it."

I laugh at the absurd statement. "You're making this up, aren't you?"

"What is it you and Maisey used to say? I'm 'embellishing' a bit. I *am* returning the dress, though; the hem is coming out, and I don't think I should have to put a hem in a brand-new dress. And I have decided to buy something else. You should go with me. It might do you good to get away for a few hours."

"I don't really want to send you off by yourself, but I think I'd better hang around here. I have to fix something for dinner tonight. The kids aren't going to be here long, you know. We have what's left of today and tomorrow. Friday hardly counts, so much will be going on."

"Well, I'm off, then," Paula says, standing up and stretching. "Are you absolutely sure you don't want to come?"

"I'd better not."

"I knew you'd say that."

"And still you came. I don't deserve such a good friend."

"Oh, but you do," she says as she heads around the house to her car. "You really do."

Maybe I should have gone with her. Marcus and Luke went to check on tuxes shortly before the girls left. For one who enjoys blocks of silence, I suddenly feel more lonely than alone. I should have asked someone to find my book and bring it to me before they all disappeared. Instead I sit here, defenseless.

Wouldn't I love it if he were playing in the pool?

Wouldn't I love to hear him shouting, "Mom, watch this dive!"

He would be nine years old now. He might have been in Paula's fourth-grade class next year. I think he'd be pretty gangly at nine, and I imagine him having my dark hair and Luke's brown eyes. I suppose he'd be too old to be a ring bearer in his sister's wedding. But perhaps he could have escorted his mother down the aisle in his new black dress coat and sat beside me, holding my hand, whispering, "Don't cry, Mom."

Maisey

Until he calls my name, I don't see Marcus on the floor of the living room when I walk in.

"What are you doing down there?" I ask.

"Looking at your albums." One is in his lap; another is on the floor beside him. "Kendy was looking at them when your dad and I came home. All three of us sat here and looked at them for a while. I'm not sure where your parents have gone, but I said I'd put them away because I wanted to look through them some more. They're great. I have to say the baby one is very cute. And the basketball one records in amazing detail what a star you were."

"I told you that," I say.

"Yes, and I've seen your prowess with my own eyes, watching you and your dad play. But this album tells the complete story, Most Valuable Player and all. It has some great pictures too. Why haven't you shown these to me?"

"That seems a little narcissistic, don't you think? Do you make me sit down and look at your albums or home videos?"

"If I had some, you'd want to see them. Besides, you *have* looked through our family photo albums, even though everyone had about quit taking pictures by the time I came along."

"Well, that's different."

"I don't see how. In fact, you're the one who stole my second-grade school picture and put it in your billfold, so don't pretend this stuff isn't important."

Marcus slides the albums back into the cabinet, stands up, and stretches.

I change the subject. "Were the tuxes ready?"

"They were, and they're in my room, safe and sound, except for your dad's."

I must look distressed.

"His is safe and sound in *his* room. That's probably where he and your mom are."

"Good."

"Relax, honey. Everything will be fine. You've checked and double-checked every detail."

"Do you know what we're doing for dinner? I thought we could go to a movie and share a tub of popcorn for dinner."

"I think your mom's making a salad."

"They won't mind if we go."

"It's okay with me, but let's see if your parents want to come with us."

"They won't," I say.

Marcus looks at me like I've said something inconceivable. "Let's go up to your room," he says.

"Why?"

"I want to talk to you."

"We're talking."

"Privately. I don't want to be interrupted."

I walk up the stairs with Marcus behind me. As soon as we go into my room and shut the door, his face and body language verify what I suspected downstairs: I am not going to like this private conversation. We walk over to my bed and sit on the edge of it.

"Maisey," he begins. This is the first time his saying my name has made me apprehensive.

"What?"

I suddenly wish Marcus and I were in the kitchen or on the porch talking to Mom and Dad about our fabulous lunch with the girls. I feel like I've been called to the principal's office. I feel the urge to clean my closet or reapply my nail polish, but I make myself sit here and wait for Marcus to explain his weirdness.

He takes my hand. Why would a principal do that? I look into his gorgeous brown eyes and feel slightly better.

"I just want to know what's going on," he says.

That could have been my line.

"What do you mean?" I ask.

"Something's wrong between you and your mom."

I gasp as though he's slapped me.

I can't believe he has uttered those words. Spoken aloud, I can't believe the impact they have on me. Out of the void, he has given form to what should have remained, at most, only a vague suspicion. And I hate it! If I'd known he was going to say such a thing, I would have put my hand over his mouth to stop him. If I could, I would shove the words back into his mouth. My face feels hot, and my heart is racing.

"Are you crazy?" I ask as calmly as I can. I want my hand back, but if I jerk it away, he'll read who knows what into it.

"You know I'm not."

"What has she said?"

"She hasn't said anything."

"What has she done?"

"*She* hasn't done anything. *You* have, Maisey."

Now, there's a bit of irony.

I pull my hand away now—he can make of it what he will.

I get up from the bed and walk over to my windows and look out at the familiar scene: patio, pool, field, woods. I can see, but only because I know it's there, my old tree house on the edge of the tree line. On our first trip here together, I walked with Marcus across the field and showed it to him. I wish I were bewitched like Samantha and could transport myself there now with a twitch of my nose.

Marcus comes up behind me and puts his arms around me. "I don't want to upset you," he says.

"I'm not upset."

"Well, Maisey, we both know that's not true."

I move out of his arms and turn to look at him. "So now you're calling me a liar?"

"Not really. There's a difference between what I said and calling you a liar."

"You think so?"

"I know so. I think you do too. You're avoiding more than you're lying."

This is too much. I thought I was marrying a lawyer, not a psychiatrist.

"I just want to know why you treat your mother like you do."

"This is our wedding weekend, Marcus. If I *had* an answer for you, if I *wanted* to answer your question, I most certainly would not want to go into it now."

"I want to go into it for that very reason. I love you, and I want you to be happy."

"I'm very happy. I'm about to marry the love of my life. I've just started a great job. You know I'm happy. Good grief—I'm absolutely ecstatic!"

"That's true," he says, smiling for the first time since he asked to speak to me privately. "But, Maisey, you're happy and not happy at the same time. You can't be happy treating your mother the way you do."

Even though I'm sure love is motivating Marcus, I'm suddenly as angry as I am agitated. "That ticks me off, Marcus. I treat my parents as well as you treat yours!"

He looks at me and I hear his words again, though they're unspoken this time: *That's not true.*

But it *is* true—as far as Dad's concerned anyway. Him, I adore, which should be obvious. Of course, even in my growing state of delirium, I know this does nothing to build a case for my defense.

Marcus knows it too. "I wouldn't say you deliberately try to hurt your mom, but you shut her out. You all but ignore her most of the time."

"That's ridiculous."

"It's not ridiculous. You fooled around so we couldn't make it for dinner Monday night, and when we finally got here, you hardly spoke to them before you went upstairs to bed."

"You know I was tired."

"I know you slept three of the five hours we were on the road."

My room has been transformed from a safe haven to an arena. I stand frozen in the sand, waiting for the lions to be released.

"Marcus, I don't want to talk about this now. Why are you insisting we talk about this *today*, for goodness' sake?"

"Because I was embarrassed for your mom."

"What are you talking about?"

"I felt sorry for her when you made it clear this morning that you didn't want her to join our team."

"Our team?"

"Our team, in the pool this morning. It would have been fun. I really don't get it. The girls didn't seem to notice. Maybe you do that sort of thing all the time, but I noticed. And Kendy noticed. I saw her face."

"Well, I'm glad you're so concerned for my mother."

"I'm concerned about both of you."

"Don't be."

"I don't know if that's possible. And, Maisey, what's wrong is wrong whether I point it out or not. There are more examples, you know. It has finally occurred to me that you've shut her out of the whole wedding. Why was she sitting here alone looking at your albums this afternoon while you went off with the girls to check on their dresses?"

"How would I know?"

Before Marcus can come up with a response, I grab my purse from the doorknob and stomp out. I feel bad leaving him standing there alone, but I have to get out of here. I will not talk about this any more.

My car is filthy. I need to take it to a car wash. But first I must get down these stairs and out of this house.

And I will, I really will—if I can just keep from dying of sadness.

CHAPTER TEN

Kendy

"Ummm," I say, "that was nice."

"Yes," Luke says, tugging a strand of my hair playfully, "it was *very* nice."

We were simply going to put away Luke's tux, and the next thing I knew he was closing the door and then the shutters, and I was throwing the decorative pillows off the bed and folding back the duvet. We were being wildly impulsive, and didn't it feel good? Impulsive isn't our strong suit. It's been a while since we've made love in the middle of the day. Well, it's almost six, not quite the middle, but still. Not to mention the fact that we have a guest in the house. I should not be smiling!

Luke said no one would miss us and that the important

thing was that *he* was missing me. My goodness, it seems I was missing him too. One of the greatest pleasures of married life is the ability to comfort each other in this tender way. Today, sex provided comfort even more than pleasure or pure relief.

Luke says we'd better get going, but I am not ready to leave this place, and he sees that. "I'll shower first," he says, and I roll over and watch him as he heads to the bathroom. I thank God that this handsome and good man, who has grown into a sensitive and emotionally generous man as well, is my husband.

Poor Mother.

Well, where on earth did that come from?

Until this very moment, I have not once pitied my mother.

I doubt anyone else has ever pitied Carolyn Belk either. Why would they? She has good looks (even now, at her age), class, money, drive, intelligence, and a prestigious position in a respected company.

What she has never had, however, is a husband. And though she has always seemed glad of it, it suddenly strikes me as sad. She made a bad mistake once (enter Kennedy Marie Belk), and she did not intend to make another.

It's quite unfortunate she met my father her first year at the university, worse still that she fell in love with him. Head over heels, as they say. He too was good-looking and intelligent, with the added bonuses of rich and amusing. Too bad she didn't notice he was also full of himself. Mother said if my father had a fan club, he would have been president and CEO. Mother sort of laughed when she said that, but I think she meant it. Mother is confident, but she has never been arrogant or self-absorbed.

She *has* been absorbed by her work, but that may be just one more result of having loved Craig Tanner. He never considered marrying my mother. In fact, by the time she found out she was pregnant with me, he and his deceptive charm had already moved on. When she was completely sure a baby was on the way, she asked him to meet her for lunch at a local café and told him she was pregnant. "Bummer," he said and popped another French fry into his mouth. I'm sure he must have said more, but nothing any more comforting. Mother got up and walked out, leaving him to finish his fries and to pick up the check.

He called a few days later and said he knew of someone who could take care of her little problem, and she told him she'd take care of her "little problem" herself. To my knowledge, she's never spoken to him since.

She did take care of it but not exactly by herself. She gave birth to me the summer between her freshman and sophomore years of college and needed help in order to finish her degree on time and get on with her life. My grandmother had been in her early forties when my mother came along, which was uncommon then. Yet at sixty-two and sixty-five, her parents took the news of Mother's pregnancy well, offering no reproach—"mistakes happen." They wouldn't allow a church baby shower, wanting no controversy, but they welcomed everyone into their home to see the baby when I was born and proudly took me to church when I was a mere five days old. They told Mother they would be happy for us to live with them and happy to help her with me until she could finish her degree, so she moved back home, commuted to a nearby college, and graduated on schedule.

Mother appreciated her parents, and though we did move into an apartment of our own as soon as she graduated and got a job, we did not move from Texas to St. Louis until her parents died within a year of each other when I was in the fourth grade. I was grown before I realized how good it was that Mother understood and appreciated her parents' sacrifice and love, and how good it was that she took a job near them, even though she had many, and perhaps better, offers in distant locations. They had not said "Bummer," and she would not deprive them of their only child and grandchild.

I doubt Mother would have told me most of these things, but I had bugged her once too often about my dad, and on top of that she had just buried her father. She apologized later.

"That was pretty brutal," she said.

"That's okay," I said. And it was okay. Brutal or not, I wanted to know everything I could about my dad, good or bad. However, as upset as she was the day of that conversation, I still didn't get a name out of her.

"When you're older," she said.

"How much older?"

I'd really wanted a dad.

But at least I had had good grandparents. Grandpa used to hide my Hostess Sno-Balls from me, and Grandma used to take me to the park to feed the ducks. Their picture is on a shelf in our living room. Mother rarely visits their graves, though she makes sure they're being cared for. She says their pictures are their memorial, and she visits it every day.

Mother's parents were not good at saying loving, even

positive things; that was not their way, and as old as they were when she was born, they surely weren't the type to play with her or attend any school events. But when she came home, they were always there, keeping her safe and warm. They gave her a stable foundation, which accounts, I think, for the strong qualities that have made her a success in the business world. What would her parents think about her becoming the CFO of such a prestigious company?

Though she has certainly never said so, I think working hard and accomplishing goals was something Mother could control. I heard her say once she never planned on "being stupid" again. Once I was married, I concluded that Mother could work with men well because her job required it, but she never desired another personal relationship with a man. She did not want to be vulnerable again.

So she let ambition victimize her instead.

I was horrified, then, when I realized my husband had an ambition not that different from my mother's. Luke and I weren't married long before his working on Saturday was more the rule than the exception. And worse than that, at least early on, his job included consulting that took him away for days and, on occasion, weeks at a time. The traveling may have been required, but as far as I was concerned, working on Saturdays and until seven many evenings was not.

Luke has a father who enjoys his work, but he is not driven. Where did Luke's ambition and competitiveness come from? Perhaps his playing competitive sports in school and his living and studying with an aggressive group of college friends are responsible; otherwise, I don't know how to account for Luke's determination to be a partner by the time he was forty.

When he was home, he was wonderful. That was never a complaint. He was kind, pleasant, and attentive in the scarce time we had together during those years. But to find myself lonely so often took me back to Saturdays in the condo, waiting for Mother to finally come home, exhausted and ready to chill in front of the gas fireplace with a book until she couldn't keep her eyes open and told me it was time for bed.

My sophomore year I threatened to move in with Margaret and Hugh. Mother started to laugh until she saw my face and realized I meant it. "No you won't, Kennedy. You can visit them all you want, but whether I'm busy or not, this is your home, and I will take care of you."

She didn't get it.

And neither did Luke for a very long time.

I had kept his dinner warm for hours when I ended our last argument about his being gone so much by slamming his plate on the table in front of him and stomping out of the kitchen. I hadn't gone far before I turned around and walked back as far as the kitchen doorway. When Luke finally looked up and saw me, I summed up for him everything I had been trying to say for so long: "Listen to me carefully, Luke—I did not get married to be lonely."

That was my final word on the subject.

Luke comes out of the bathroom now, towel drying his hair, and that confrontation in the kitchen seems eons ago.

"Your turn," he says.

"No," I say in mock defiance. "No, I won't go! You can't make me."

He laughs, and I find his laugh as comforting as his touch.

Maisey

My car hasn't looked so nice since it sat gleaming in the showroom. I have washed it, dried it, vacuumed it, cleaned the inside of every single window, and polished the dashboard. I'm standing here in the bay, having to concede there is nothing else I can possibly do to it.

What now?

Like a beacon in the night, I look up and see the Golden Arches. I slip behind a steering wheel that I have energetically attacked with leather cleaner, drive down the block to McDonald's, run in to get a Coke, and rush back out as quickly as possible to sit in my clean car and watch the highway traffic.

I wish to be as hidden as Waldo.

I have to go home; I don't see any way around it, but Marcus has made that very difficult. In grade school I had a recurring dream that I was walking into the school building in my underwear. When I looked down and realized it, I felt utterly exposed and mortified and didn't have a clue what I should do. Fortunately at that point I always woke up.

I feel like that now, except this is not a dream and I'm not going to wake up. I remain exposed. But I'm not mortified—I'm angry.

Furious.

Marcus doesn't know what he's talking about, and he has no right to interfere. But I'm not just angry with Marcus. I'm angry, period. I've been angry for such a long time now. I'm even angry that I'm angry.

My phone is ringing. I wait until it stops and check for missed calls. *Marcus.* I knew it would be. How can I go home when I don't even want to answer his call?

It was such a nice day until he insisted we go to my room for that private little talk.

The girls love their dresses. I had to talk them into the simple elegance of a black strapless dress with a straight tea-length skirt, but they are all about it now. Jackie's dress is made the same way, but it is a black-and-white floral. She loves that her dress is different. "I'm special," she said when the others weren't listening, and I couldn't disagree.

We left the shop today with everyone's dresses in garment bags, ready for Saturday evening. I was so relieved. And then I walked in and found Marcus sitting in the middle of the floor with my albums.

Why did Mother have to drag them out?

Paula said she was going to try to talk her into going to Indy. Why couldn't Mother just go with her? Marcus was so unfair. Why would Mother have wanted to go to a dress fitting if she hadn't even wanted to go shopping with Paula?

Of course Jackie had asked me much the same thing. "Why don't you ask your mom to come?" But before I had to say something, Paula walked into the house, the perfect answer.

Someone's honking interrupts my thought. How irritating!

I look up and see that the offending honker is Jackie. She has parked next to me and is getting out of her car. My passenger door is locked, and she beats on the window. With the slightest hesitancy, which I hope she does not notice, I unlock the door.

"What are you doing?" she asks, plopping into the seat, leaving the door open.

"Shut the door," I say. "The air-conditioner's running."

"Well, good grief. Let's go in. Stop wasting petrol."

"I'm not in the mood for a crowd. What are *you* doing?"

"Getting salads for Heidi and me. I don't know for sure what you'll be doing the day after your wedding, but Heidi and I will be right here buying a Big Mac and fries the minute we decide to get up. What are you doing at McDonald's by yourself when your mom has a great dinner waiting for you at home?"

"What makes you think so?"

"Marcus called about two minutes ago, asking if I'd seen you. He said something about dinner, and I'm assuming it's great. When isn't it great?"

Oh brother, my mother could serve Jackie a peanut butter and jelly sandwich on a paper napkin and Jackie would call it gourmet.

I ignore what was a rhetorical question. "I'm on my way home. I needed to wash the car." I look over at her car. "You might want to try it."

"Easy, now."

I almost laugh.

"Marcus seemed worried about you."

"What did he say?"

"It wasn't so much *what* he said but how he said it. He sounded worried. What's going on with you two?"

"Nothing."

In response, she just looks at me.

"Nothing's going on," I repeat.

"She doth protest too much, plain and simple."

"Nothing much. I just didn't like defending myself. When I came in a while ago, he wanted to know why Mother didn't come with us to the fitting."

"I thought she was going somewhere with Paula."

"I guess she didn't."

"Well, she *should* have come with us, then! While I was doing her nails, she asked me what the dresses look like, for goodness' sake. What they *look* like? Haven't you shown her a picture or anything? She *should* have come to see them."

"You know what—I don't think I can handle any more interrogations or accusations."

"My gosh, Maisey, I'm not trying to interrogate you or accuse you of anything. What's the matter with you?"

Another conversation I don't want to have.

"Wedding jitters, I guess."

"Are you sure that's all?"

"Yes!"

Jackie shakes her head. She isn't buying it.

"I mean it. Everything's fine. I just needed to get away for a while. It's been a busy day, a busy week."

She smiles sweetly and grabs my hand. Her sensitive side is making a surprise visit. This isn't a good time.

"You look sad, Maisey. I know something's wrong."

"I've got to go, Jackie. I'll talk to you tomorrow. Okay?"

"I guess it'll have to be." She opens the door, gets out, and leans back in for a parting shot. "But something *is* wrong, and I wish you'd tell me what it is."

She shuts the door gently.

The gentleness of the gesture gets me. I want to say, *Get back in the car—I'll tell you what's wrong.* Instead I back out and head for the exit, feeling worse than ever, if that is possible.

Oh, Jackie, you really don't want to know what's wrong. Is that what has kept me from telling you about it all these years?

Jackie and I, along with four other kids and our youth sponsor, were packed into the van that was taking us to a middle-school week of church camp. We had been gone from home at least fifteen minutes when I realized I had left my sheets and towels sitting on my bed. That was mistake number one.

"No problem," Andy had said, turning the van around, "that's the beauty of starting early. We've got plenty of time before we have to meet the others." Mistake number two.

The third was my sneaking into the house to surprise Mom with one last kiss good-bye.

CHAPTER ELEVEN

Kendy

Luke and Marcus sit at the bar, keeping me company while I dice the chicken Luke grilled after finishing with the hamburgers earlier.

"You can take your pick," I say to Marcus. "Santa Fe salad or a Mexican chicken wrap—same ingredients, except for the flour shell."

"I'm getting hungry," he says. "I might have both."

It seems like I've been cutting up chicken for thirty minutes. "Both won't be a problem," I assure him.

"I'm hungry too," Luke says. "Where's Maisey? Let's get this show on the road."

I've been wondering where she is myself. It's almost seven, and Marcus came into the kitchen a few minutes ago looking a bit lost. Luke hops off his barstool and says he'll run up and get her.

"Don't bother, Luke. She's not here," Marcus says.

"Well, my goodness," I say, snapping a lid on a plastic bowl stuffed with chicken, "where has she gone at this time of day?"

Marcus says he doesn't know, which surprises me. The late hour does too—it's past dinnertime. Of course, she didn't make it for dinner Monday night. She may have moved dinners to the bottom of her priority list.

Luke looks concerned. "Should we be worried?" he asks.

"I don't think so," Marcus says. "I made her mad this afternoon, and she took off. Wanted some space, I guess."

We look at him as though he's confessed to armed robbery. We are that stunned. Marcus is so easygoing, we've come to believe he is incapable of conflict, certainly conflict that would result in Maisey's taking off without him. I want to ask him what he could possibly have said or done to make her that mad—it is beyond imagining—but asking would be prying, and I have resolved I will not be a meddlesome mother-in-law. Besides, we all need a certain amount of privacy. I didn't explain to Marcus why Luke and I disappeared earlier, did I?

"Maybe she's at Jackie's," I say.

"I called," Marcus says. "She's not with her."

"And you've called Maisey's cell phone?"

"Several times, but it always goes to her voice mail."

"You're not worried, are you?" I ask.

"Not really," Marcus says.

But he looks worried.

Luke takes his cell phone from his pocket, tries Maisey's number, and gets her voice mail too. I can't quite read his face. Is it worry or agitation I see there?

At seven we set the table and decide to start without Maisey. Luke says if she isn't home when we're finished, we'll take two cars and canvass the area. He says he'd call the police except she hasn't been missing twenty-four hours. We sort of laugh at that, but we aren't really amused. I wonder if they remember that about this time last year a young woman went to fill up her car one evening, and though her car was found, she was never heard from again.

We eat in relative silence, and when we hear a car door slam and footsteps on the porch, we look up with relief. Then Maisey appears in the doorway to the kitchen, dropping her keys into her purse.

"Good," she says. "You started without me."

"We waited until seven," Luke says.

She sits down, grabs the tongs, and begins filling her plate with salad.

"What do you want to drink?" I say, getting up.

"I'm fine," she says.

I retrieve her glass from the counter, pour off water from ice that has melted, and get a Coke out of the refrigerator. This is her drink of choice when she eats anything that remotely resembles Mexican. I pour it, wait for the foam to settle, and pour some more. No one has spoken since I got up.

When I set the glass in front of Maisey, she says, "I *said* I'm fine."

All three of us look at her.

We have no idea what to say or do. I am actually interested

to know who will find the wherewithal to speak next. And what will that person say?

It is Luke who dares to open his mouth. "Is there an explanation for such rudeness, Maisey? The appropriate and obvious response to someone who brings you a drink is 'thank you.' "

"Thank you," she says, staring at her plate, "thank you *so* much."

The sarcasm in her voice is heart-stopping.

"Maisey," Marcus says, "you're mad at me. Don't take it out on your mom."

I take in my breath and steal a look at my daughter. I haven't entirely processed the sarcasm, and now this. I wonder if Maisey has merely misplaced her mask of civility or has intentionally discarded it. I fear the latter. Seething—she is seething. Her anger and disgust are palpable.

Maisey glares at Marcus. "Oh *really?*"

Luke and I look at each other. *What in the world is going on?* Of course no one is eating. The lettuce, grated cheese, and diced chicken heaped on our plates look ridiculous. The routine of life has been suspended.

Maisey pushes back her chair, stands up, and stomps toward the doorway.

"Maisey!" Luke shouts. "Come back here right now. I can't imagine what's wrong with you, young lady, but I do know you owe your mother an apology."

I'm sure an apology is the least of our worries.

Something is terribly wrong, of that I'm certain, and I wish to help Maisey, but no matter how frantically I search my mother's mind and heart for something I can say or do, I find nothing.

"You two," she says, coming back to the table, looking at

Marcus and then her father, "are *so* worried about Mother—dear, sweet Mother."

She does not look at me. She is shaking.

"Here you sit, feeling so bad that I didn't ask her to be on our stupid team this morning, or that I didn't ask her to go with *my* friends to see their stupid dresses, or that I didn't thank her for getting me a stupid Coke I didn't want. I'm so bad, is that it?"

In this moment, we have been struck dumb.

Marcus stands up and finally utters a single word: "Maisey!"

"Leave me alone, Marcus. You seem to think my mother is a saint. Well, she isn't!"

Luke is staring at Maisey like he's never seen her before.

"Oh, Maisey," I say, but she doesn't seem to see me or hear me.

"Okay, everyone, listen up. It was a summer's day nine years ago in this very kitchen that I found my precious mother pressed against my dad's uncle, kissing him like a crazy woman. Mr. Impressive himself, wonderful Clayton Laswell, was all over my mother. It was disgusting. It made me sick, Dad! It *makes* me sick!"

Maisey looks at her dad, tears streaming down her face. "I'm so sorry, Daddy."

Then she turns to look at me, furiously wiping the tears from her face. "I hate you, Mother. Do you hear me? I hate you, hate you, hate you! You *so* deserved to lose the baby! He probably wasn't even Daddy's!"

She runs from the kitchen, and this time Luke doesn't stop her.

"I'm sorry," Marcus says to Luke and me, following her.

"Aren't we all," Luke says to no one in particular before he gets up and walks outside.

Where is he going?

I cannot ask. I have just been stripped of the right to ask even an innocuous question. Perhaps he has gone to the out-building to work on any number of his tools: a tractor, a push mower, a weed eater, a chain saw, a tiller, a leaf blower.

"My dad's a good fixer," Sammy said to me a life-time ago.

"My husband is too," I said.

Or perhaps Luke didn't make it that far. Maybe he's merely sitting on the patio, trying to breathe in the fresh evening air, wishing for twilight to envelop him.

I sit here, my hand over my mouth, looking at the aban-doned dinner table without really seeing it. After a minute, maybe two, I stand up to clear the table. The contents of the plates, I put in the trash; the salad left in the large serving bowl, I store in a sealed container; the ranch dressing bottle, I meticulously wash and place on a shelf in the refrigerator. Then I load the dishwasher, wipe the counters, clean the table and place the crystal bowl of lemons back in the middle of it just so, and deposit the damp towel on the sliding rack.

What to do now?

CHAPTER TWELVE

Maisey

"Go away!" I shout for the fourth time.

Marcus has been out there the fifteen minutes I've been lying here in the dark. I know he will knock again, call my name again. Oh, how I wish he would just go away and leave me in peace.

In peace? Now, that's funny. There will be no peace. There has been no real peace for years.

And now what have I done?

It has made me sick, but I have kept Mother's betrayal to myself for nine long years. I've told no one. *No one*. Why, why, why did I let those words come out of my mouth tonight, after all this time? If I could, I would take them back, just as I wanted to shove Marcus's words back in his mouth this afternoon. How could I have hurt Dad that way? I have protected him all these years, and now, because I could not control myself, I have broken his heart.

I saw his face.

I saw shock on Marcus's face, but I saw desolation on Dad's. Maybe that is what I have feared all these years. Well, the frustration and rage finally erupted, and I don't want to know what the landscape will look like now.

Oh, Clay, I hate you as much as I hate my mother.

Mother taught me never to use the word *hate*, and I have never uttered the merciless word—at least aloud—until tonight. Tonight the dam of restraint has broken, and I seem to be drowning in hate. I'm horrified to think that when I was a little girl, I sometimes felt guilty for loving Clay as much as I loved Dad. He and Rebecca didn't seem like a great-uncle and a great-aunt; they seemed like grandparents, only younger. I thought they were so cool.

But Clay ended up completely ruining what should have been some of my happiest memories. I don't want to remember learning to ride a bike, because I learned in his driveway. He ran behind me for hours, holding on to the back of my banana seat until I could quit wobbling and maintain a steady line. It was his garage I ran into when I foolishly forgot to brake; it was his bushes I fell into when his son, home from college, drove into the driveway and scared me to death; it was the ointment from his medicine cabinet he smeared all over my scraped palms and knees. And it was he who somehow made the scratches disappear from my new bike too. I never knew how he did that.

I rode that bike until the summer before I started middle school. Clay insisted it was much too small and that a new bike would be a great graduation present. He took me to a bicycle shop to pick it out—bigger and fancier but the same cobalt blue—and I rode it until the day I found him with my mother.

As soon as I got home from camp I told Dad I was too old for a bike. He was surprised and said he was going to store it in the garage in case I changed my mind, but I told him to give it to some kid who didn't have one, that I would not change my mind. He said he didn't know a kid who didn't have one, and I said we could take it to the Salvation Army. We donated things to them all the time.

I didn't get on a bike again until last fall, when Marcus wanted us to ride a scenic trail with some of our friends. "I haven't ridden for so long," I said, hoping that would serve as an excuse. He came back with, "You know what they say—it'll come back to you." And it did. It turned out to be a beautiful day and a good way to spend it, and in my heart I blamed Clay for almost missing it.

Until Dad and Mother put in our pool, a gift for the whole family when I graduated from fifth grade into middle school, we spent as much time at Clay and Rebecca's as we did at home. Not only did Clay teach me to swim in their pool, but he also taught me to fish in their pond. We have a picture of me when I was only five years old, holding up a three-pound bass I had just caught. I would remember that day clearly without the picture. I wanted to help fillet my whopper of a fish, but Clay said I'd have to wait for that experience. On another day Clay jumped into that pond after me when I fell off his fishing dock, and on another sunny afternoon, he obliterated a copperhead that crawled too near my tennis shoes while I stood reeling in a perch.

Deciding we should call it a day when he killed the copperhead, he collected all our gear and put me on his shoulders for a ride back to the house. He said I was light as a feather and added, as he did many days, "You're the only baby we've got, you know."

"I'm six; I'm not a baby," I said.

"Comparatively speaking," he said. And that I couldn't argue—Clay's boys were in college, and his daughter and Dad's sister were college graduates, both married less than a year.

I was done with Clay the day I walked into that kitchen and saw him with Mother. Of course, if I wanted to keep what I saw to myself, I had to act pleasant around him, or at least decent. But at that point we didn't see him and Rebecca all that often anyway. They had a grandchild by then and more on the way. I was in middle school and busy with my friends, we had our own pool, and the next year Mom started teaching in another district. It was manageable.

There's another knock on the door, slightly louder than the previous taps. "Maisey," Marcus says, "I'm not going away."

"Please do."

"No."

"Just for a while."

"No."

I walk to the door, unlock it, and stand holding it. "Obviously, I'm not fit company."

"That's not required," he says. He walks across the room and leans a pillow against the headboard and sits on the bed. "Come here," he says. "Let me hold you."

I stand looking at him in the dim light shining into the room from the hallway. "I'm too tired."

He laughs.

I smile.

"Well, truly, I am. I'm done in, too crazy to sit and be held. Will you go buy me some sleeping pills? If you really want to help, go buy me some sleeping pills. I need sleep."

"I might, but come let me hold you first."

He is stubborn. He calls it persistent.

"You started it, you know," I say, crawling over him, propping up my pillow next to his, leaning on his padded shoulder. "Why didn't you leave well enough alone, Marcus?"

I know even as the words are coming out of my mouth that none of this is his fault. My consolation is I know he knows it too.

"I had no idea what you've had bottled up inside you for so long, honey. I thought you might have had a disagreement with your mom about something to do with the wedding and were holding an unreasonable grudge. I swear my mother knows more about this wedding than your mother does. The only person I've seen you involve in the wedding plans to any degree is your grandmother."

"The first wedding I ever went to was my aunt's; have I told you that? Dad's sister. You'll meet her Friday. I was only five when she got married. Dad was a groomsman, and I sat beside Mother, holding her hand, utterly enthralled by the music, the candlelight, the dress. Mother bought me a bride doll that Christmas. I mean, really, how many girls get bride dolls these days? But I was thrilled. I've been thinking about my wedding and the man who would be waiting for me at the end of that center aisle for a very long time. Gram gave me some suggestions, but the truth is I've had this wedding planned for years. There wasn't all that much to do, really."

"But we've got a problem now, wouldn't you say?"

"Wouldn't you say I've had a problem for a long time? Of course now we're all wonderfully aware of it. But we'll just have to work around it. I think we can if you get me those sleeping pills."

"How about some ibuprofen?"

"You're funny."

"I'm serious. When my dad can't sleep, he gets up and takes one and falls right to sleep. It must relax him. You could give it a try later."

"I want something serious."

"When you get ready for bed, you can take an ibuprofen, two even, and let me hold you until you fall asleep. Then I'll take an ibuprofen myself and go to bed. This has been one long day."

"I'm sorry."

"I know you are."

"I shouldn't have said anything."

"You should have said something to someone a long time ago."

"I couldn't."

I explain about the people waiting for me in the van that day and the long week of camp. "I was supposed to come home on Saturday morning, but Dad came to get me Friday evening. Mother had miscarried that morning. Dad was so sad. And Mother, well, she was crazy."

I sit up straight so I can look at him. "I mean, *really* crazy. She didn't come out of her room. Ever since I was old enough to know anything, my mother had taken her shower and made her bed before she fixed breakfast. It was rare for her to spend time in her room until she and Dad went to bed after the news each night. But after she lost the baby, she hardly left her room for six or seven months. Heck, she hardly got out of bed. Or opened her blinds. If I ever got a look in there, the room was always dark. That's how I remember it anyway. When she was herself again, I couldn't imagine telling her what I had seen. I couldn't imagine talking to her about much of anything at that point. I had Dad. I had my friends."

"But maybe you misinterpreted what you saw. You were what? Thirteen?"

I shake my head. "I was quite old enough to understand what I saw."

I stand up and head for my dresser. "I'll get ready for bed. I think there's probably some ibuprofen in the medicine cabinet. It's early, though. Want to play Connect Four? Or gin rummy? Or you could go get your DVD player and we could watch a movie."

"Get ready. I'll keep you company until you're ready to sleep."

"Thanks."

I get the things I need from my dresser and closet, walk into the bathroom, shut the door, and lean against it. I love Marcus. I feel like going out there and asking him to elope with me tonight. But I know I'm too sad for this to be my wedding night.

"Marcus," I say through the closed door, "I'm going to take a quick shower."

I turn on the water and wait for it to get hot. I strip off my clothes and throw them in the hamper, step into the steamy confines of the tiled shower, and let the water "minister" to me.

That's how it feels—like a ministry. I stand with my back to the hot water and let it stream over me and over me and over me. When I have stood here long enough, I begin to experience the slightest measure of relief, and I turn and offer my face to the rush of soothing water and let it wash away the torrent of tears—tears which, without warning, have been sent on a mission of mercy.

"I didn't even tell you, God," I whisper through the water and tears. "You knew, of course, but it seemed like a kind of treason to actually mention it to you. I should have told you anyway. I should have told you."

Kendy

I need to talk to Maisey, and I will talk to her, but not now. She will not want to talk to me tonight. I guess it's fair to say she hasn't really wanted to talk to me for a long time now. Regardless, if talking to her tonight would help her, I would pray for the strength and wisdom to do it, brace myself for the task, knock on her door, and ask, *Maisey, may I come in?*

What a terrifying thought.

Walking to our bedroom, I hear quiet voices in Maisey's room. Marcus must be with her, doing what he can to help. *Please, God, let him help her through this wretched night.*

As for me, I have a plan. There's nothing worse than being without a plan (understatement has always appealed to me). I think I might be able to sleep if I run on the treadmill for thirty minutes minimum, follow that with a nonnegotiable shower, and begin another book I tucked away for after the wedding, one that might engage me more than the one I've been staring at today. I doubt Gabriel García Márquez has won a Nobel Prize for nothing.

I get on the treadmill and do a forty-five-minute cycle of running and walking, and then I take a long, steaming hot bath. It is more relaxing than a shower, and more time-consuming. Next on my agenda, I wrap my exhausted and squeaky-clean self in a robe and lie on the chaise with the new book. When I'm settled in, I'm relieved to see it's ten o'clock, a reasonable time to think about going to sleep before long.

I pick up the Márquez book Paula gave me. She thought I might be able to read the book even though she couldn't drag herself to the end of the first chapter. I begin, but I abandon it by the end of the first page, not because it is tedious but because it begins with death. They say misery loves company, but I really don't think I can handle any more misery tonight. Besides, a phrase in the very first paragraph startled me, and I closed the book, as much as anything, to ponder its aptness: *the torments of memory.*

Ah yes.

I hear the television in the living room. Luke must be watching the news. Will he come to bed when it's over or watch Letterman's monologue? I get up from the chaise and prepare the bed for the night. I've always hated going to bed without Luke, but I get under the covers, turn out the light, close my eyes, and hope sleep will come. Is this becoming a pattern—the wish for sleep?

I open my eyes and stare at the ceiling.

Nancy Ogden comes to my mind. I haven't seen her in years, but here she is invading my thoughts on this horrific night. Not without reason, I suppose. She isn't Ogden anymore. She was on husband number four the last time I saw her, and her latest last name escapes me. It would have been expedient for Nancy to have kept her maiden name all along.

Nancy, Paula, and I usually had the same lunch shift, and we often ate together in the school cafeteria. We spent most of our short lunch break listening to Nancy and her fantastic tales. We called her Wild Woman to her face, and she loved it. There wasn't a teacher in the building who would let her plan a wedding shower, because her idea of entertainment would not include guests taking a three-by-five note card and blessing the bride-to-be with a favorite recipe or a tried-and-true tip for marital bliss. Nancy had the phone number of a male stripper in her billfold, and she wasn't afraid to use it to spice up a ho-hum wedding shower—provided it wasn't being held in a church fellowship hall.

Nancy would never think in terms of "torments of memory," though she apparently had hundreds of memories that should have tormented her. She spent many a weekend barhopping after her marriage ended, and a few before the divorce papers were drawn up. She told Paula and me that by the time she was thirty, she'd had enough experiences, good and bad, to last four women a lifetime. (It is overstatement that appeals to Nancy.)

When Clay Laswell was nothing more to me than Luke's uncle and one of the best superintendents a teacher could have, he was Nancy's fantasy. Between husbands one and two, and two and three, Clay was her main topic of conversation. "There he is," she said the day we really began to notice her fixation. He was walking across the lunchroom with two other official-looking men in nice suits and waved at us as he passed. Nancy picked up her napkin and began fanning herself. "I need me some of that," she said.

I gasped.

Paula said, "Are you *crazy?!*" She had long since forgotten the effect Clay had on her the first time she met him.

In some ways Wild Woman fascinated me—no one else in my life could make me gasp—but she tended to irritate Paula.

I finally found my voice. "Nancy," I said, "Dr. Laswell is a happily married man."

"So?" she said. "I'm not out to marry the guy."

What *was* she out for exactly? Her worldview seriously collided with ours.

"Listen," she told us, "I'm just saying he's hot. You two are too uptight. You're going to be sitting in a nursing home one of these days, wishing you had some outrageous adventures to look back on and savor while you're rocking away on the front porch."

She laughed then, grabbed her tray, and told us she'd see us later.

I hit Paula when she mumbled something I never expected to come out of her mouth: "Not if we see you first."

I reminded her that Nancy could be a lot of fun and that she was a very good teacher, amazingly adept at keeping her private life out of the classroom. Time for chitchat was running out, and we crammed the last of our vanilla ice cream into our mouths before the bell rang us back to fourth-grade students who couldn't wait to get on with their education. That's what I always said to my class when we reconvened after lunch: "You look like a bunch of kids who can't wait to get on with your education." They always laughed.

Grabbing my tray and heading for the stainless-steel

counter to drop it off, I had one last thing to say about our fellow fourth-grade teacher: "Nancy just needs the Lord, Paula!"

"Well, now that's an understatement if I ever heard one."

"No, Paula," I said, hurrying to class, "it really isn't."

"Conversion doesn't seem imminent," she said. "Do you suppose you should warn Clay?"

"No need," I said. "I'm pretty sure he's immune to Nancy's kind of charm."

I was right about that.

But did I know, even then, that he wasn't immune to every temptation? Did I know that most of us, even the admirable, even the converted, are susceptible to one kind of charm or another? I'm not sure I did. That understanding may have come later.

I wonder if Nancy has discovered yet how foolish her words to live by were. I wish beyond what I could possibly say that I had no "outrageous adventures" to look back on. *Savor?* Hardly. What I would give to erase those memories as easily as I erase math problems and story starters off the whiteboard in my classroom.

What I would *like* to look back on is a life marked by integrity and loyalty and faithfulness—no exceptions. How satisfying that would be! I suspect that the "no exceptions" addendum might make such a thing rare, but that suspicion does not help to ease my grief. So, yes, the phrase I just read in the Márquez book shocked me with its familiarity. He has articulated what I have experienced: *torments of memory.*

I hear the door click. Luke is making his way toward the bed in the dark. He stops and slips out of his jeans and T-shirt before pulling back the covers and getting into bed with a minimum of movement. He does not look for me but settles into his side of the bed, turning to face the other way. Was it only a few hours ago that we lay here, touching so tenderly? I long to touch him now, to curl up behind him, feel the heat of his body, and hold him like he has so often held me. But I'm frozen in place, afraid to move, afraid to speak.

"Luke," I finally whisper.

"What?" he answers, and I'm amazed to realize he was almost asleep.

"I'm sorry."

He turns to lie on his back, looking at the ceiling as I have been doing. I hold my breath, wondering if he will say anything else, wondering what it will be.

"From what you told me, Kendy," Luke says, "I knew such a thing had happened." His voice is kind but weary, like a doctor talking to a patient who has received devastating news, a doctor who has known tragedy himself.

"But it's hard to hear it," he adds. "Hard to see it flashed on the screen of my mind, to hear the agony in our daughter's voice, to realize what her undetected discovery has done to all of us."

We lie here, staring at the ceiling as though an answer for what we can do is written there. After a few minutes I reach over and put my hand over his, but only for a moment. Then, because there seems to be nothing else to say, we roll over, face opposite walls, and wait for the panacea of sleep.

The children's prayer comes to my mind. The last line of it has always struck me as macabre. Grandma taught me the prayer and had me recite it as soon as I could talk, and many a night I fell asleep hoping this wasn't the night I was going to die. Granted, I was a strange child, but that was a prayer I never taught Maisey. Still, lying here tonight, wondering if sorrow can be intense enough to kill, I find myself altering the line ever so slightly and praying it for the first time since I was a child: *If we should die before we wake, I pray thee, Lord, our souls to take.*

THURSDAY

CHAPTER THIRTEEN

Kendy

I wish I could apply my makeup without looking in the mirror. On a scale of 1 to 10, I'm about a 2.4 this morning, even for the over-forty demographic. I enjoy my *More* magazines, but if the contributing editors were sitting on the edge of my tub watching me get ready, they'd wonder what has happened to one of their faithful readers. They should not immediately assume the answer is sleep deprivation. I actually ended up getting eight hours' sleep last night, a gift from a merciful God.

I hope Maisey slept.

Luke was gone, his side of the bed cold when I opened my eyes at seven-thirty. I can't say I was unhappy about it. Hiding out here alone all day sounds pretty good to me. But I've had a talk with myself and have called on the Lord this morning, so as soon as I finish getting ready, which seems to be taking longer than usual, I'll find Maisey and ask her to talk with me. I will be kind but firm. It is time.

I have no control over my thoughts this morning, or I would not be sitting here trying to pinpoint when exactly the Clay mess began.

I'd seen approval in his eyes from the moment I walked into his office for an interview. But it was no different from the approval he showed any of his enthusiastic and hardworking teachers and staff. He put together excellent faculties for the schools in his district and took pride in their performance.

I taught only three years before I had Maisey and took a six-year hiatus to stay home and spend as much time as possible with the child I'd thought I might never have. As much as I loved teaching, I loved time with my daughter more. I returned to the classroom when she started first grade, and Clay told me more than once that I should be voted Teacher of the Year. My third year back I did receive that honor. My fourth year back was even more special to me because I had so many of Maisey's friends in class, including Jackie and Heidi. I considered asking Clay to break a rule for me, just once, and let Maisey be in my class too, but I sucked it up, as the kids say, and didn't try to interfere with standard policy. But I did want my daughter in class and was glad when weather kept us inside during recess and the fourth graders could go to any fourth-grade classroom for their free time. Seeing her in my room, mingling with her friends and my students, delighted me.

That same year something happened, a small thing really, that made me almost uncomfortably aware of Clay's approval of me. It seemed different from the norm, moving beyond mere approval to overt and possibly excessive admiration. On a stormy afternoon that spring, Clay was doing a walk-through in the elementary building and stopped by my classroom during an indoor recess period. Maisey and her friends were in the back, playing Twister while other groups of children played quietly together in other parts of the room. This allowed Clay and me to talk about Maisey's spending the night with him and Rebecca that Friday and going with them to Indy on Saturday to see Miller and Anne.

But fourth graders are seldom quiet for long, and Clay and I noticed that three kids playing hangman on the whiteboard seemed to be having some sort of argument. The boy in the middle I didn't know well, but the other two students were mine and not contentious as a rule. The unknown quantity threw down his marker and called my sweet boy stupid.

Both of my students looked at our visitor like he was an alien. "Oh," the girl said, "we don't say that in here."

"Say *what?*" he snapped.

"We don't say *stupid,*" she said. "This room is the *positive* zone."

After this clarification, my two students looked at me and smiled.

"So," Clay said, sitting on the edge of my desk, "this remains the positive zone, does it?"

"It does," I said.

He started to say something else and then stopped himself. But he smiled at me, and his smile lingered long enough that I had to look away.

But it was the wreck a year later, I think, that began the

nearly imperceptible change in our relationship, though all I felt at the time was cared for and grateful.

It was a warm Friday in April during Maisey's fifth-grade year. I remember it well, for hardly a day went by that spring that I didn't realize school days with Maisey were almost over. Counting down the days—something only the overly introspective do—tinged all of them with sadness.

My car was the sole one left in the parking lot when Maisey and I left the building. I unlocked the car with my key fob, and Maisey jumped into the back seat and clicked herself into a seat belt. (She tended to scream if I started the car before she had taken this safety measure.) "Hey, Mom," she said when she was all settled, "can we stop on the way home and get a malt?" We often stayed late on Fridays so that I could get all my work done to facilitate a carefree weekend, and we typically rewarded ourselves in one way or another for such a fine display of discipline. It was also a particularly beautiful Friday, and Luke was out of town, so despite the fact that a chocolate malt probably contains three thousand calories, I told her that was a great idea.

I had just entered an intersection a few miles from school when I noticed in my peripheral vision a car not slowing down for a stop sign. I knew instantly that it was going to hit us broadside, and I made the split-second decision to turn my car sharply to the right, in the direction the renegade car was going, thinking that would minimize the impact. How can one think of so many things in a few seconds? The boy slammed into the left front fender of my car with so much velocity my car spun around and smashed into the back of his car. When both vehicles finally came to a stop, I was frantic to unhook my seat belt so I could see if Maisey was okay.

"Whoa!" she said when I turned and looked at her. She seemed fine, but I was immensely reassured when she added, "Can we still get a malt?"

That's when her door was yanked open and Clay was there, yelling, "Maisey, are you okay?" As soon as he saw that she was, he opened the front passenger door. "Kendy," he said, sitting beside me. "What about you, honey? Are you okay?" He put his hands on either side of my face and looked into my eyes as though that would best tell him what he needed to know.

"I think so," I said, pulling back and gingerly touching my rib cage, hoping everything was where it should be. "My ribs hurt, my left shoulder is aching, but yes, I think I'm okay."

He didn't look convinced. "You could have been killed!"

I would never have imagined that Clay could be so upset, especially when he had seen for himself that we weren't hurt. Nor would I have ever imagined he would, under any circumstances, touch my face.

What a strange thought to have while sirens blared and emergency vehicles began to arrive. Finally I thought to ask him if the other guy was okay.

Clay said he didn't know and didn't much care, but he went to check when I asked him to. Meanwhile EMTs checked on Maisey and me and insisted on taking us to the hospital for a more thorough examination. Clay had returned and said the guy—"driving without a license, by the way"—was in pretty good shape, considering. He also said he'd take care of having my car towed and that he'd come to the hospital and get us when he had tended to everything else.

After Maisey and I had been thoroughly examined and X-rayed, I called the number Luke had given me and told him about the accident and subsequent visit to the hospital. I told him both of us were sore and bruised in a few places but fine otherwise. He was relieved to hear Clay had actually seen the accident, had taken care of the car, and was coming soon to take us home. Luke was thankful we were okay and said he'd get home as quickly as he could wrap things up there. Where was he that week anyway? I couldn't remember.

We were ready to be released when Clay arrived. Maisey ran to him, and he scooped her into his arms and walked over to where I was signing some papers.

"Did you two check out okay?"

I told him what I had told Luke, only I added that I had a killer headache. "But considering how bad the car looked, I'd say we're in great shape."

"We need a malt," Maisey said when Clay deposited her next to me.

The lady behind the discharge counter said everything was in order, and as Clay, Maisey, and I headed for the sliding doors of the emergency room exit, Clay took my daughter's hand and said, "Three chocolate malts, coming right up. Three *large* ones."

Maisey smiled.

I did too. "Thanks, Clay," I said.

"For what?"

Excuse me?

"Well," I said, "for everything."

Maisey

I'm up and almost ready when I knock on Marcus's door and tell him I want to be on the road to Indy by eight. He looks at the clock and then me and says that's ridiculous, that the stores we are going to probably won't even be open when we get there. I tell him Wal-Mart will be and I want to get some things there too.

He looks extremely skeptical—he always has a hard time interesting me in a Wal-Mart run. But without too much prodding he gets up, and in fewer than twenty minutes, he meets me downstairs. I have just come down myself and wonder, as I have many times, how anyone can get ready as quickly as he does.

"You probably even made your bed," I say.

He looks at me like I'm nuts, and I take that for *Are you kidding me?*

I tell Marcus I want to stop and get something to eat on the way, but he walks toward the kitchen, saying something about Raisin Bran. I take that for *I have my rights too.*

He grabs the cereal box, and I make myself two pieces of toast. While we eat, I keep an eye on the clock. Mom usually doesn't come out of her room before eight on summer mornings, but I'm worried about how close we're cutting it. Marcus is finishing his bowl of cereal at seven forty-five, and I'm relieved that my deadline is a possibility until I look up and see Dad coming in from outside.

"You're up and around early," he says.

He sits at the table with us, not bothering to get something to eat first, not even a bowl of cereal or a piece of toast. I ask if he wants some orange juice, and he says he'll get some later. I almost jump up and get it for him anyway, but visions of Mother doing the same thing for me the night before keep me in my seat. I tell Dad that Marcus and I are up early because we're going to return some things in Indy. I add that we'll eat lunch there before we come back home sometime this afternoon.

He looks upset. "Don't you think you should wait and talk to your mother first?"

Marcus looks at me, lifting one of his perfect eyebrows. He said the same thing when I awakened him so abruptly and told him my plan.

"Not yet, Dad," I say, reaching for Marcus's bowl to put it in the dishwasher.

"Hey," Marcus says, "I'm not through."

"Slow down, Maisey," Dad says. "Nothing is pressing today. It's time you talked to your mother."

I stare out the window, wishing we had made our getaway before Dad came in, wanting the impossible. "Why?" I finally mumble.

"I'm sure there are things you need to know."

I pick at the polish on my thumbnail. "I'd say I know too much."

"Yes," he says, "that's true enough. Unfortunately, knowing that much requires knowing more."

I turn to look at Dad. "Actually, Daddy, you're the one who should be talking to Mother." I look down, knowing my statement was presumptuous, knowing my outburst last night might have forced them to talk all night long.

"We talked about this a long time ago, Maisey."

"What? When?"

"After your mom lost the baby."

"I don't remember her talking to anybody after she lost the baby."

"You need to understand you don't know very much at

all about what happened to your mom and me the year after we lost the baby."

That is *so* unfair.

"How could I? This place was a tomb," I say.

"You're right. It was a terrible time for all three of us. Your mom spent a lot of time in her room, and she didn't talk to anyone much for six or seven months. Paula did manage to get a little out of her, but yes, I guess it *was* something of a tomb."

"I don't remember anyone but you in that dark room."

"Do you remember that in the spring she was out of her room more often, sitting on the patio and doing a few things around the house? Do you remember she began attending church with us regularly again on Easter Sunday?"

"I remember she came out at some point. So when did she tell you about Clay?"

"Not long after that Easter. I took some time off, and we talked about a lot of things, including Uncle Clay. That's when I understood her depression had to do with more than losing the baby."

"Then why have you always acted like nothing happened?"

"We didn't know you knew anything about it, or we would have talked to you, honey. What parents talk about such things unless they have no choice? You were thirteen years old! We didn't even consider it. We thought the Clay issue and some of the things that led up to it were just between us."

There shouldn't have been a Clay issue!

"Of course we knew her depression couldn't help but affect you, but we hoped you would be okay when she was herself again."

I sit here, arms crossed, horrified that Marcus has poured another bowl of cereal while Dad has been talking.

"But you can believe this, Maisey: No one involved acted like nothing happened. Plenty changed."

"Like what?"

"Well, for one thing, your mother took a job the following school year in another school district."

"She had to; she had given up her old job to be with the baby."

"Nevertheless, there was an opening in her building the following year, and she would have gladly taken it except she had made the choice to distance herself from Clay. She accepted a job in another district, and while it's been a good job, for a lot of reasons, it wasn't easy to leave her school. It helped that you were in ninth grade by then, but it was still hard. She and Paula had taught together for a long time."

I roll my eyes.

Dad sighs.

"Do you remember Clay and Rebecca changing churches about that time?" he asks.

"They transferred to the new church where their kids and grandkids were going."

"That's true. But my grandparents helped establish our congregation. They were charter members, Maisey. That may not mean much to you, but it means a lot to Dad and Clay. Clay would never have changed churches if he hadn't thought he had to."

"Well, whose fault is that?"

"You just need to know that no one acted like nothing happened. Including me. That's when I moved my office here and started working from home."

"'Cause you had to keep an eye on her."

"Maisey."

I get up and throw my bowl in the sink. "Really, Dad, I don't know why you didn't leave her."

He shakes his head. "Are you serious?"

"Let's not talk about this right now," I say.

Leaving the kitchen, I tell Marcus I'm getting my stuff and will meet him at the car.

But here I stand, lost in my closet, looking for the pink sack containing those ridiculous red-net pajamas that I plan to return today. *Where is it?* The stupid thing couldn't just disappear. I'm making such a mess of this closet.

I hate messes. I'd say the conversation I just had with Dad was a mess—a heck of a mess.

I hear Marcus coming up the stairs. At least I hope it's Marcus.

"There you are," he says, joining me in the closet. "I started for the car, but you weren't there."

"I can't find the darn sack," I say.

"It's not in here, honey; it's on your dresser."

I start to cry, and he puts his arms around me, letting me sob into his Colts T-shirt. "It's okay," he says. "It's okay."

"He should have left her, Marcus."

"I can't see your dad ever doing that. And why should he have left her?"

"You know what she did."

"I know what you saw."

"What does that mean?"

"It means a lot of things, honey. It means you should talk to your mom. Your dad's right: There's a lot you don't know."

I wipe remaining tears off my face with the back of my hand and look at him. "And I don't care."

Marcus seems shocked, but he recovers and looks at me

calmly. "I'd hate to think that's the difference between you and your dad."

I wonder if I've heard him right.

"Your loyalty should *so* be with me, Marcus. It really should!"

He takes the sack from me and removes my purse from the doorknob and hands it to me. Or more accurately, he shoves it at me. "Let's just go if we're going," he snaps.

So, this is Marcus upset.

At the top of the stairs, he stops and makes a final comment: "I think the vows we chose include 'for better or worse.' Do you want to reconsider that demanding little phrase?"

I want to cry, *Objection!* That is so out of context. Anyway, that vow causes me no pause, since there's also a vow about keeping ourselves only unto each other.

I might just tell him that later, but for now I'm ready for all talk to cease. I check to see if my iPod is in my purse, and I follow Marcus down the stairs, thinking that what I might want to reconsider is our wedding.

Kendy

The phones rings just as I'm putting away all the hair paraphernalia. I run to get it when it becomes clear no one else is going to pick up.

"May I speak to Kennedy Laswell?"

The voice is unfamiliar, and I hope it's not some sort of telemarketer. But the voice sounds more official than irritatingly cheerful, so I respond as pleasantly as possible.

"This is she."

The man quickly identifies himself as Phillip Jamison, a

name I recognize. It strikes me as surreal to be standing in my bedroom on a summer morning talking to the president of Mother's company.

"I'm afraid I have some bad news, Kennedy."

These are words no one wants to hear. What follows is necessarily dreadful. I wonder in the space of a few seconds what horrible thing has happened to my mother.

"What is it?" I whisper.

"Your mother had a heart attack in her office this morning."

My mother? Ever efficient, ever in control. Oh, Mother, this was not in your Day Planner. You were going to finish a week's worth of work in four days—performed, as always, at the distinguished level—drive five hours tomorrow to bring Maisey her wedding dress, and sit by your only child on Saturday to watch the marriage of your only grandchild.

But all that has changed, hasn't it?

Dread fills my heart. Tim Russert comes to my mind, sitting at his desk, preparing for Sunday's *Meet the Press*, gone in a moment.

"Is my mother alive, sir?"

Give me the bottom line—Mother would be proud of me.

"Oh yes, dear. I'm sorry; I should have made that clear right away. In fact, tests indicate that damage to her heart was minimal. An angiogram did show a substantial blockage in one of her arteries, and her doctors recommended a balloon catheter. She's just been taken to surgery. Try not to worry; her surgeon assured us it is a routine procedure."

"Routine?"

"That's what he said, and I think it probably is. If all goes as well as everyone anticipates, she'll be resting in her room before noon. So you see, there's good news too."

He pauses, probably anticipating a response at that point, but I am still trying to process everything I have heard in such a few minutes.

Finally I manage one socialized word. "Yes."

Too brief. I try again. "Yes, that's good news."

"I could have waited to call you until the surgery is over—your mother suggested that—but I thought you'd want to know now."

I finally gain a measure of composure. "I'm so glad you called, Mr. Jamison. Of course I'm thankful to know as soon as possible."

He tells me the name of the hospital where Mother is, and I tell him I'll be there as soon as possible. "By three, I hope."

Luke walks in while I stand here with the receiver disconnected but still in my hand. I'm looking out the window—one second, praying; the next, trying to collect my thoughts.

"Who was on the phone?" he asks.

"Mother's boss."

He looks as bewildered as I must have looked when Mr. Jamison was trying to tell me the bad and good news.

"Mother's had a heart attack."

"What?"

"Yes, at the office, shortly after she arrived this morning, I guess. I really don't have many details, except it was a mild attack, she has a blocked artery, and she's having balloon surgery as we speak. I need to go, Luke. I need to see her, and I need to get Maisey's wedding dress. You knew Mother was bringing the dress tomorrow, didn't you? There's no way she'll be able to come to the wedding now. She probably won't be released from the hospital until Sunday. And even if she is released Saturday, she won't be coming to the wedding. I'd like not to bother Maisey about it yet."

"Maisey just left."

"Left?"

"She and Marcus are returning some things in Indy. I suppose we should call her and let her know what's going on."

"No, no. Give the girl some peace. I'll have the dress home and hopefully a good report on Mother before she has a chance to worry about it."

"I have a meeting at the main office this afternoon," Luke says, "but I'll make some calls and have someone else cover it or have it rescheduled. You shouldn't go alone."

"Don't do that. Someone needs to be here when the kids get home. And actually, I think I'd like to be alone today—if you don't mind. The drive will probably do me good. Then I'll see Mother, make sure she's okay, get the dress, and drive back. I should be home by ten or eleven."

He doesn't seem to like that idea much. "Don't you think you should stay there overnight? That's a lot of driving."

Suddenly I really *see* Luke, and I'm amazed at the conversation we're having, so businesslike. It's true I was glad he was gone when I awoke this morning—what could we say to make this day something more than bearable? But in this moment I want very much for him to stretch out on the chaise so that I can lie beside him before I go. I want to feel his strength and warmth, hear his heartbeat, and whisper what my heart repeats when it has nothing else to say: *You are my beloved.*

But there is no time for that, and I'm not sure I would follow through with that lovely impulse if there were time, not *this* day.

Instead I say, "Do you know what tomorrow's going to be like? Oh my goodness, things will be crazy up to and through the rehearsal dinner. I just want to get this done and get home."

I go into my closet and exchange flip-flops for espadrilles and grab a blazer to wear with my T-shirt and jeans. When I return to the bedroom, Luke hands me my purse and my cell phone.

"Thanks," I say.

"You're welcome," he says. "Be careful. I hope everything will be okay."

"I do too."

Luke heads for the shower, and I head for the garage. It goes without saying that I will be careful—our daughter's wedding is two days away. *But how*, I wonder, *can everything possibly be okay?*

CHAPTER FOURTEEN

Maisey

Marcus seems content enough, watching the road and listening to ESPN. I have been listening to my iPod since we left the house. The first fifteen minutes we were on the road, I gave rapt attention to the countryside flying by the passenger window, remembering for some reason that this scenery has charmed my mother for decades. And I must admit, I love it too. Gram cannot grasp the concept. She honestly feels like she's back to nature when she sits on her tenth-story patio balcony among the lights of the city and catches a glimpse of her hanging fern and the pot of red geraniums on the glass table next to her.

I took out my earphones a minute ago, just in time to hear

yet another argument heating up on the radio—more on the steroid issue. How can that be? I gave Marcus a quick smile and returned to my tunes.

I've reclined the seat a little, and I'm hiding behind my eyelids. Marcus will say I slept most of the way to Indy, but he will be wrong. I am not asleep. Far from it.

I'm thinking, and how I wish I weren't, about shopping in Indy with my mother. We used to shop till we dropped in a couple of really cool shopping malls. She and I made the trek to Indy several times a year from the time I started first grade through the seventh. We went when I was in high school too, but then Jackie or someone always shopped with us—the more the merrier.

I'm thinking specifically about a beautiful winter day that seems as long ago and far away as any in a fairy tale. I was in the seventh grade, and Mother and I were looking for a dress for the Valentine's dance. I had confessed to Mother the thrilling fact that one of her favorite former students wanted to meet me in the gym and dance the night away—make that dance away the two hours between six and eight. I thought that was pretty nice of the guy, considering that only two months earlier my dad had refused to let me "date" him simply because that pretty much required holding hands in the halls between classes.

I told Mom I needed to look fantastic, and she understood. That shopping trip was unusually successful. We found a darling dress, grown-up but not too grown-up, and half off half price. Mom said we saved so much money on the dress I could get some shoes to go with it, my first pair with a little heel (which made me a little heel taller than my love interest), and a few accessories—a clip for my hair and a necklace I still have.

Mother said I would look more than fantastic and maybe we could get out of the house before Dad noticed the heels.

Before we left the mall, we ate hamburgers and fries and shared a malt at Johnny Rockets, but the most memorable part of a memorable day was the trip home: Mom had to pull into a Wal-Mart so she could run in and throw up.

"Whoa, Mom," I said outside her stall. "Did you eat too much? Was your hamburger bad?"

She came out looking pretty terrible and went to the sink to rinse out her mouth. She said this was the third time she had thrown up this week.

"I haven't felt like this," she said, wiping her mouth with a damp paper towel, "well, since I was pregnant with you, sweetie."

We just looked at each other in the mirror over the sinks.

"Mom!" I said. "What if you're pregnant?"

"Oh, sweetheart, that's virtually impossible. My doctor said *you* were a miracle."

I smiled. I had always liked thinking of myself as a miracle.

"Maybe you'll have two miracles. It's been thirteen years since the last one."

"True," she said, looking doubtful and hopeful all at the same time.

"Have you missed a period?" I asked.

"I don't really have regular periods."

Better than nothing, I thought while she cleaned the counter with her paper towel. I hadn't had a period yet, and I was awaiting the event with great anticipation. Mother said I shouldn't be so eager, that it really wasn't all that much fun, but all my friends were good to go, and I didn't like being left behind. Though I didn't brag about it, I was more knowledgeable about what Caitlin called "the curse" than any of my friends who had made this rite of passage into womanhood back in, oh, the first or second grade.

So, standing with Mom in the Wal-Mart bathroom, I knew exactly what we should do. Actually, I suppose anyone who watches television would know. "Mom," I said slowly, "we need to get a pregnancy test. We're right here. Let's do it."

"That's silly, Maisey. And a waste of money."

"I'll float you a loan," I said, and she laughed.

Then, with no transition whatsoever, she grabbed my hand, walked out of the ladies' bathroom, and headed straight for the Health and Beauty aisle. We stood there, staring at the vast array of testing options for a few minutes, until she finally grabbed a box. Rolling her eyes, she walked toward a cashier, saying, "The things I let you talk me into!"

Back in the bathroom after paying for our crystal ball, we stood staring at the little window in the plastic wand we had placed on the counter between the last sink and the wall. Mom said a watched pot wouldn't boil, so she leaned against the wall, staring across the room, and I began pacing, circling the small bathroom. Mom said I would have made a good Israelite marching around the walls of Jericho.

A lady came in to wash her toddler's hands and looked at Mom leaning and me pacing and the wand sitting on the counter. "Good luck," she said as she was leaving.

Mom smiled, checked her watch, took a deep breath, and looked at me with wide eyes. "Okay," she said, and we walked over to the counter to discover the verdict.

"Mom!" I yelled, giving her a huge hug. "That's the biggest, brightest plus sign in the history of the world!"

Kendy

They say more women die from heart attacks than men. But still I'm shocked to think my mother could have had one. At sixty-five, she still seems young to me. And she has always seemed invincible. Her company sends her to Mayo to get a thorough physical every other year, and when she turned fifty she began taking advantage of the gym in her building, exercising most days on her lunch hour or before leaving for the day.

I once told her she could get exercise by simply walking to work, but though she won't admit such a thing, I believe she likes her Lexus and the space reserved for her in the parking garage way too much to walk. Plus, I doubt she'd want to be seen on the street in walking shoes. But I imagine the main reason she doesn't walk to the office is her belief, possibly an unconscious one, that the ten minutes it would take would be better spent making herself indispensable to the company.

Over the years that philosophy has paid off. The fall Margaret took me off to college, Mother kissed me good-bye and said she knew I would do well in my studies and that I had the good sense to make wise choices and take good care of myself. She also said she'd miss me, but I doubted that very much. If she missed me at all, the transition was helped immensely when she was named CFO that October, the first woman in the history of the company to hold that position.

Mother is in surgery right now, and I feel panic welling up within me. I want to be there more than I could have imagined, and I want to be there *now*—goodness, someone besides her boss should be there—but nearly five hours of interstate lie between me and the hospital.

Mr. Phillips said the procedure was routine, but sometimes routine goes awry. *Dear God, please don't let Mother die.*

It seems to me she has not begun to live.

That sounds so judgmental, and I, above all people, cannot stand in judgment of anyone else's choices. But I can't help but be sorry Mother gave everything for her job, for however good that job has been, it does not love her. And I wonder, can one pass on a meaningful legacy to a utility company? I don't doubt that my mother has been appreciated or that she will be hard to replace; nevertheless, the company will get along just fine when she packs her things into a cardboard box and turns out the lights in her office.

I wish Mother had diversified her time as she has done her portfolio.

I do find it interesting that she has apparently made so much time for Maisey this past year, helping her find a wedding dress, helping her and Marcus find a good apartment with reasonable rent, and hosting a wedding shower, for goodness' sake.

Of course, Maisey has not minded asking for her help. I wasn't very good at that. When Mother said she didn't see how she'd have time to help me find a wedding dress—"Such short notice, Kennedy"—I told her not to worry about it, Margaret would help me. I was twenty-three and didn't need all that much help anyway. But the thing is, Margaret and I had so much fun the day we found my dress, and it makes me sad Mother missed out on it, as she missed out on so many things.

At the time, I felt sorry for myself. Today I feel terribly sorry for her.

Luke was spared Mother's fate; unfortunately, my breaking his heart provided his reprieve. After I lost the baby and finally told him about Clay and me, his job ceased to be his number-one priority. Out of all the misery, there is this one good thing: He and Maisey have enjoyed each other so much.

I see now that the special bond between them began the minute he picked her up at camp the Friday we lost the baby. She felt the need to protect him, and she compensated, as best she could, for the son he would not have. The months I was lost to them and to myself were not the sole cause of her exclusive devotion to her father, her switch of allegiance—as I have always thought.

I began to come out of that dreadful depression the spring of her eighth-grade year, but the girl I knew so well and loved so deeply was nowhere to be found. I've blamed those debilitating months of seclusion for our breach, but now it seems so obvious they weren't the cause. *My* Maisey would have tiptoed into the dark room of my depression and curled up beside me without saying a word or requiring one. She would have come day after day, week after week, until I could speak again.

I told myself that in the months of my illness several things happened to change everything: She went through the throes of puberty; she began to count on Luke for everything—lunch money, rides, basketball tips, good-night kisses; and she developed a preference for constant company, especially Jackie's. There was little room for me when I returned from the far-off country of my despair, and I have reluctantly tried to accept that as the price of desertion.

Last night at the dinner table, I understood the full extent of what Maisey and I have lost—and why. I wonder if, for me, there could be a worse moment.

I would rather have died when Maisey was a child than to have hurt her so badly.

CHAPTER FIFTEEN

Maisey

We are almost to the door of Victoria's Secret when Marcus says he wants to look for a hat while I exchange my gift. He says he has no desire whatsoever to weave in and out of a store full of merchandise that, as far as he's concerned, should not be publicly displayed. It seems he was traumatized twelve years ago when his mother dragged him through another Victoria's, looking for a pretty something or other for one of her daughters-in-law.

"But don't you want to help me pick out something else?" I ask as we stand near the display windows.

"I trust your taste completely," he says, heading for Lids, a store that doesn't offend his sensibilities. "Call me when you're through," he adds, holding up his cell phone.

Well, it's thirty minutes later, and I'm through. But when I finished my exchange and reached in my purse for my cell phone, I discovered I had left it at home, as I tend to do if I'm not careful. Do pay phones still exist? Will a pleasant stranger lend me her cell? I'm trusting Marcus will figure out what I've done and meet me where he left me.

I'm sitting on one of the couches in the wide hallways near Victoria's Secret, waiting. What else can I do? I scan the crowd, looking for him. I turn and look behind me. Lots of people but no Marcus. I wish he would come. Surely he can find a hat faster than I found something we'll both like. I've put the sack containing my rather skimpy but very tasteful new "sleepwear" on the cushion beside me, warding off any other weary shopper until Marcus arrives.

Soon, I hope.

Circle Centre is remarkably busy for a Thursday morning. That and my lack of attention is why I almost decked my middle school orchestra director when Marcus and I first arrived and rounded the corner by Banana Republic.

"Maisey," she said when we stopped short of body slamming each other, "I'm thrilled to see you, dear."

She looked at Marcus and asked if he was the lucky young man I was going to marry on Saturday, and though I had experienced a moment of doubt this morning, I assured her that he was. She said she'd be there with bells on and that my English teacher for both the seventh and eighth grades was coming with her. "Wouldn't miss it," she said as she walked away, hunting for a cinnamon roll.

I started taking violin in the sixth grade, as soon as I started middle school. Mother thought playing an instrument was a great idea, even though she herself had given up the piano after six years of lessons. She had learned to hold her hands in a way that didn't enrage her fanatical teacher, and she had mastered such classics as Beethoven's "Für Elise," but she knew deep inside that she was never going to be a great pianist.

Skill she could acquire. Skill she *did* acquire. And when the church is in a pinch, she will help out—if the worship minister gives her enough notice. When you hear her play "Amazing Grace," you have to wonder if she was right to give up piano performance for lack of "the spark." She took me to a concert in Indy once and spent most of her time holding her breath or placing a hand over her heart as she watched and listened to the pianist. The woman mesmerized even me as she sat on the edge of the piano bench, erect and regal, her fingers flying over the keyboard with remarkable precision, providing what Mother called "profound interpretation." We just sat there when the curtain fell, and as everyone around us began making their way out of the auditorium, she said, "Now that's spark, Maisey. That is worship."

Although we have a piano, I never really wanted to play it, except when I was a toddler and thought lifting the lid and pounding the keys to be great fun. (There's a picture to verify that in the baby album.) So Mother was glad I expressed an interest in the violin. If I developed the skill, it would be satisfying, and if I found I had the spark, well, that would be exhilarating.

For my part, I was just giving in to Jackie's pleading. She was the third of five children, and her mother insisted that all of them take some kind of music lessons, even though Jackie informed her that child number three, sad to say, had been born without the music gene.

"Please, please, please," Jackie had said the first week of middle school. "*Please* be in the orchestra with me."

"What will I play?" I asked.

And without a moment's hesitation and without ever being able to account for her answer, she said, "The violin!"

So I borrowed a violin from the pool of instruments available at school and began to learn how to draw a bow across those mysterious strings. Mother couldn't believe I didn't go through a screeching stage, and after I had been working at it almost two years, she walked through the room where I sat practicing and said, "I do believe I detect a spark." I had my own violin by then—I got it the Christmas I was in the seventh grade, and I did love playing it. I suppose that's why my teacher loved me so much. Of course she loved all of the students in her fledgling orchestra, even Jackie, who played the cowbell and triangle and was relatively happy about it; Jackie says percussion was her only logical choice.

In the eighth grade I made the decision to switch to the cello. The sound was deeper, richer, even more sensuous, and best of all, more mournful, which appealed to me very much at that point. The instrument was huge, and because I had also begun playing basketball, toting it around seemed like cross-training. I didn't mind the size. I felt at one with this instrument, wrapping myself around it as I played.

During a concert my senior year, I had a solo that moved me to tears whenever I practiced it at home. The night I performed it, I did not cry but closed my eyes as I played, and I heard my mother's words: "That is worship." And when the piece was over and the applause began, I looked into the crowd and caught, by accident, Mother's eyes instead of Dad's. And by accident I smiled, but only for the briefest moment, and then I turned my eyes to my music stand, preparing myself for the next selection.

"Hey!" Marcus says from behind me, and I jump a foot. I have been abruptly jerked from the stage to a couch in the mall.

He laughs. "I thought you were going to call."

"No phone," I say. "Sorry."

"Want a bite?" He holds out that mall delicacy, the cinnamon roll.

Marcus doesn't keep grudges.

He gives me a bite and hands me his coffee while I grab my sack with my free hand and put it in my lap, where it will be safe. I do hold grudges—I tell him he has forfeited his opportunity to see the exchange, at least until we get to Hawaii. He has no problem with that and takes another bite of his cinnamon roll.

"You're going to spoil your lunch," I say.

"When has that ever happened?"

He sits beside me and we share the rest of his cinnamon roll, and since I won't allow him to look in my sack, we talk about my orchestra teacher and Jackie's cowbell and my cello.

He loves to hear me play. I didn't play basketball in college, but I was in the orchestra and I was part of a string quartet that had many opportunities to perform. Gram even arranged for us to perform at her company's Christmas party last year. Marcus says I have to find a way to use my talent now that I'm out of school, and I will try.

Playing my cello has always brought me relief when sadness has threatened to overwhelm me. I sometimes wonder if God in his kindness prodded Jackie to make such a bizarre suggestion all those years ago.

Who can say? But when I play, it is to him I give all my gratitude and praise.

Kendy

I have hit the road again after a bathroom break. I also picked up a large drink, which no doubt will necessitate another break before I leave Illinois. I take my sunglasses off the top of my head and put them back on my face, where they are very much needed. I'm so thankful for a working air-conditioner. I just passed a van full of kids who looked happy enough even though all the windows were down and furnace-hot wind was blowing their hair all over the place and doing nothing for the sweat gleaming on their red faces. I feel rather guilty. I should wave them over and ask if some of them want to ride in my car for a while. They could cool off, and I could take a break from thinking.

Just a short break would be nice.

This much I know—I didn't intend to hurt Maisey or Luke or anyone else. I didn't *intend* anything.

My car was totaled after the wreck, and we didn't buy a new one until a week later, a week and a day later. As a result, Clay gave Maisey and me rides to and from school that whole week, which is what Luke's uncle would naturally do. The only memorable conversation I recall from that week—mainly we chatted about school concerns—took place the day Clay commiserated with me, and Maisey too, about Maisey's impending graduation from elementary school to middle school. He seemed to get how difficult this would be for me especially.

I would not see her at lunch and recess, I would never again look up to see her rushing into my classroom after the final bell rang, and I would no longer have the pleasure of her company as we rode home together after school, chattering away about one thing or another. Those had been blessed years.

That next fall I pulled up to the middle school, let her out of the car on the first day of school, and reminded her she would be riding home on bus eleven. She leaned over and kissed me on the cheek. "Don't cry, Mom," she said. "It'll be okay." I blinked tears away and watched her walk toward a new phase of life with confidence and even excitement.

As for me, despite this trauma I drove away with my own little sense of excitement. I find it difficult to sleep the night before school starts, eager to see the brand-new class that will be waiting for me the following morning.

At the end of that first week, Clay dropped by after school to see how I was managing. I sat at my desk grading a set of papers, laughing.

"What's so funny?" he asked.

"Students!" I said.

"I'm glad you have a good bunch this year," he said, then lingered long enough to read the work of several choice specimens.

He came by again maybe a month later.

"Are you still worried about me?" I asked.

"Not really. You're a trouper. I was in a meeting with your principal and the compensation committee, and since you usually work late on Fridays, I thought I'd see how it's going."

"It's going fine," I said, putting my grade book in my tote bag.

He looked at my bulletin board of assignments and asked

if my students were proving to be as interesting as I had initially thought.

"They are," I said. "Come look." I showed him a bulletin board full of creative new endings for familiar phrases.

Once again Clay remained awhile, studying the board until he declared the winner.

It was not long after that visit that I began to wonder if he'd stop by when I stayed late on any given Friday, and then I began to hope he would. It was much later that year that I found myself looking for his car at the administration building when I drove by on my way home. When had that started? And what was it all about? I suppose I should have recognized that as a subtle indication that all was no longer right in my world.

One Friday the spring of that same year, Clay sat on the edge of my desk, telling me about a mother at the high school basketball game the week before who'd thrown a box of popcorn at a referee.

"What did he do?" I asked, wishing I'd been there.

While he was telling me, I looked up to see Paula standing in the doorway. She sort of did a double take, and when Clay followed my gaze and saw Paula, so did he. Clay said he guessed he had passed on enough local color for one day, stood up, and as he left, told both of us ladies to have a nice weekend.

When he was gone, Paula still stood in the doorway, looking at me, not saying a word—a step up from a pregnant pause.

"What?" I said.

"I don't know, Kendy, honey," she said, finally moving toward my desk, picking up a pencil that had fallen on the floor and handing it to me. "I just don't walk into many classrooms and find the superintendent of schools sitting on the edge of a teacher's desk like that."

"How many teachers are married to his nephew?"

"I'm just saying that it looked—I don't know—strange, I guess."

I was embarrassed for a reason I couldn't quite name, but I was also defensive. "Goodness, Paula, you know Clay is the epitome of decorum."

"I know he always has been."

I had forgotten I was giving Paula a ride home that day, and I slipped a book I needed to read for Monday into my tote with the rest of my things and told her we'd better get going. On the way home we talked about the usual, the kids and what we were going to do over the weekend, but when she got out, she leaned back into the car and said, "Kendy, just be careful."

Be careful?

"Don't worry," I said.

Looking back, I think Paula's early concern, expressed so sweetly, was one of many ways the Holy Spirit tried to intervene, the first of several intervention attempts. But that did not occur to me at the time.

Later, when I knew things were "out of hand" (don't we love euphemisms?), when I crossed first the line of propriety and then the line that separates right from wrong, I pretty much shut her out, which wasn't all that hard to do, we were both so busy with our families and our work. And besides, at first I thought there was nothing behind the door I closed on her. Then, when I was quite sure it was something, I was too horrified to discuss it, and eventually, it was something I wanted to keep to myself, a secret to invigorate my days.

I look back on that woman and can hardly fathom her foolishness.

CHAPTER SIXTEEN

Maisey

Since we are so close, Marcus and I are stopping by the travel agency to see Grandma and Grandpa. I feel a tingle of excitement as we drive up to the shingled building with friendly shutters and a veranda-like porch. When Marcus and I enter the front door, good memories wash over me. Though I haven't come here often since I left Indiana for college, I was a regular before that.

As soon as we walk through the door, I spot my favorite person in the place, not counting my grandparents, of course. I take Marcus's hand and rush him over to the desk of Rowena Presley, my grandparents' able and robust assistant. Rowena thinks she is Elvis Presley's distant cousin and keeps a sign on her desk that says, *Don't be cruel.* She says that's good advice for her and anyone else who approaches her desk.

I start around the desk to give her a hug, but she puts up her hand to stop me. Then she grabs her jar of jelly beans from the top of her desk and puts it in the bottom drawer. I laugh, and she stands up and catches me into a bear hug that lifts me off the floor. She hugs Marcus too, the friendliest introduction he has experienced yet, though she doesn't hoist *him* from the floor. She returns to her chair, retrieves the jelly beans, and offers them to Marcus.

"I always hide them when Maisey comes in," she says, "because when she was two or three she confiscated the jar while those of us who should have been watching her talked about some kind of urgent business—at least we like to think it was urgent. Leave it to that girl to sit under my desk and devour every one of the jelly beans in a jar filled to the brim. We probably would have had her stomach pumped, except she proceeded to throw up all over my favorite shoes."

"True," I say, smiling at Marcus, who chooses just two yellows and a green.

"Kids!" Grandpa shouts. He has spied us through the glass in his office door and is beckoning us in.

Leaving Rowena and her jelly beans to join Grandpa, I tell her I hope to see her Saturday. Her response I could have guessed: "Fire-breathing dragons couldn't keep me away, darlin'!"

Grandpa gives us the bad news that Grandma didn't come in today. "She's having fun doing some last-minute shopping for the big weekend," he explains. "I don't much want to go home and tell her she's missed seeing you two."

We talk about the wedding awhile and look at more pictures

of our accommodations on Maui, and then Marcus asks me to wait for him in the car so he can talk to Grandpa about a little surprise he wants to arrange for me on our honeymoon trip. I tell him I'll just chat with Rowena, but he says he wants me out of the building.

So I'm banished to the car with a bottle of cold water and a promise that Marcus won't be long. He'd better not be, or we'll run out of gas. Even though we're parked in the shade, I have the car running and the air-conditioner blasting away.

I use Marcus's phone to call Gram, but her phone goes to voice mail. She must be in a meeting. I really don't have anything to say, which might have irritated her some. But not too much—she's gotten used to being pretty nice to me. I think Mother is surprised at how much time I've spent with her.

When I made the choice to attend Washington University in St. Louis, I can't think of one person here who was particularly happy about it. Jackie, Heidi, and Caitlin said it did not compute. Jackie waffled between supportive and disgusted and argued with me about it off and on until the day I drove away, leaving her standing in the driveway with my parents. They weren't thrilled either, of course. Dad was vocal in his opposition, saying it was hard enough having his only child leave home without her going across two states. Mom's disapproval—I suppose that's what you'd call it—demonstrated itself in her utter silence on the subject.

One evening the summer after I graduated, I overheard her talking to Dad on the patio about how strange my decision seemed to her. He told Mom that she had made the same strange decision when she chose Butler University, also two states away from her home. But she didn't think her choice was strange at all—she had spent months in Indiana during junior high and high school, and she would be with Paula, her best friend. Besides, Butler was Margaret's alma mater, and Margaret had decided to move to Indiana to be near her sister when Mother came here to college. Mother said her choice had made sense; mine didn't.

Even Gram was surprised. At my high school graduation party, she said the first and only thing that resembled support: She told Mother that she had wanted *her* to go to Washington University.

As long as I can remember, we visited Gram in St. Louis twice a year without fail, and she visited us twice a year unless something made it impossible, which happened a few times. Dad liked to plan our visits to Gram's around ball games, and Mom checked out concert schedules when it was getting close to time for a visit. Our concert tastes were eclectic. We attended the philharmonic orchestra, but we also stood up and jammed with everyone from Garth Brooks to Coldplay.

When we visited St. Louis, Gram usually took us out to eat at very nice places, and she endured most of the concerts and even a few ball games. I liked St. Louis, and I thought going to school there would be an adventure. Plus, I thought Gram needed someone besides fellow employees and something besides work in her life for a change, even if she didn't know it.

But this I know: My mother was the main reason I went to college in St. Louis. I think what Marcus said yesterday is probably true. For the most part, I don't deliberately try to hurt her. But did I get in my car and take myself to a place she had left twenty-five years earlier because I knew how much it would hurt her?

I don't know.

Maybe. And if so, what does that mean?

Marcus might conclude I have appointed myself her prosecutor, judge, and jury. Maybe Dad would say the same thing. I certainly didn't think of it that way, but if that's the case, is that so awful? Would there have been a shred of justice otherwise?

Regardless of my motives, I did like St. Louis and the university, and I'm glad I made that choice. I'm not sure how much I would have seen Gram if I hadn't been so lonely my freshman year. One Saturday I just called her up and asked if she wanted company. When she hesitated, I told her I'd stop and get a movie and a pizza, not thinking that she probably wouldn't want either of them. But finally she said, "That sounds fine, Maize."

After that I went over at least once a month. By my sophomore year, she was letting my college friend Sarah come along on my monthly visits, and by my junior and senior years I came every two or three weeks, sometimes with Marcus, Sarah, and her current boyfriend. When we were all there, Gram generally had reading to do in her bedroom, though one night she played Pictionary with us, staying up long past her bedtime. She stocked her condo with our favorite snacks, and that gesture, along with the flat-screen television mounted over the fireplace, and the view from her patio, kept us coming.

I remember Mother saying she never had friends over when she lived at home and that if Gram had finished the work she brought home and Mom had finished her homework, they capped the night off with store-bought cookies and a good book for each of them. In my opinion, Mother should have been a little more pushy. This year Gram has been downright friendly, getting me the internship with her company and then a job, and helping me find a wedding dress and an apartment.

She actually took me to lunch one of the days we looked for my dress. She seemed sort of sad that day. She said she hadn't had time to help Mom shop for a dress, but she was glad that all these years later she could help her daughter's daughter. I said I was glad too. That day she also mentioned retirement, which apparently isn't that far away, and she gave me the impression that she could think of nothing less desirable. I believe her exact words were, "I think I would prefer death to retirement." And looking at her across the linen tablecloth, I had the awful feeling she wasn't kidding.

And really, what *will* she do? Well, she got me my job, so I'm just going to have to hook her up with some kind of volunteer work before Marcus and I leave St. Louis. She's gone to church with me a few times. That's good. Maybe I can help her see there is life outside of her job. God will have to intervene, though, because as Marcus's mother would say, she'll be a hard nut to crack.

My vision of my grandmother vanishes when Marcus knocks rather loudly on the window. I don't sit in the car without a few precautions: the radio or my iPod blaring, the air-conditioner on—at least in the summer—and the doors safely locked against kidnappers and killers.

"You've been keeping me waiting a lot today," I say when I unlock the door for him.

He settles himself behind the steering wheel. "We're a long way from even!"

I smile at him and give him a quick kiss. You don't hear anyone complaining about my choice of colleges these days. If

I hadn't attended Washington University, I wouldn't have met Marcus Blair, and that's too awful to think about.

Kendy

It is not as sharp, as brutally focused, as it once was, but unfortunately, the summer before Maisey started seventh grade still stands out in my memory. What has made me literally sick is knowing that at that point I had a chance to avert disaster, but I did not take it.

School wasn't out long at all before I became aware that I missed my talks with Clay. That's how I put it to myself. Of course it was Clay himself I missed. Being "seen," being so obviously cared for, being appreciated so thoroughly, these things are exhilarating, and they are addictive. I saw him, as usual, at family get-togethers, but that wasn't the same.

At our annual Fourth-of-July picnic, there was the briefest moment when I felt as though I were alone with him in my classroom again. He happened, along with one of his sons, to be standing across from me at the end of the food line. Clay handed me silverware wrapped in a napkin, which I was about to pick up for myself. That simple gesture, hard as it is to understand, seemed more than a friendly courtesy, even more than warm familiarity. His hand grazed mine in the exchange, and he looked at me so intimately I almost gasped. I looked around, afraid that someone had noticed, but even the son standing beside him had his eyes fixed on a platter of fried chicken, unaware of the mini-drama playing out beside him.

I distanced myself from Clay the rest of the day and into the night when the family gathered to watch fireworks, but I couldn't seem to keep myself from looking his way a ridiculous number of times. I hated that, but at the same time I loved it, because every time I looked at him, he was looking at me. Could it really be that Clay Laswell was as enamored with me as I was with him? For the first time in my career, I was eager for the summer break to end so the school year could begin.

That might have concerned a cognizant woman.

I actually looked forward to the tedious, time-consuming meetings that always precede the first day of school, because Clay would be presiding over many of them. But instead of milling around the meeting room, talking to him comfortably as I had in previous years, I waved from several rows back and left without saying a word. I couldn't think of anything to say that wouldn't sound contrived.

It was a month before Clay dropped by my classroom on a Friday afternoon. After all, Maisey was in her second year of middle school and I had survived the trauma of her leaving these halls well enough. I did not need Clay or anyone else checking on me. I had almost quit looking for him when he appeared one Friday in early October, so handsome, so concerned, asking if I had another good class this year. "I think it might be," I said, hoping my face wasn't flushed. It felt flushed.

Needing something to do, I began erasing the whiteboard behind me. I caught my breath when I realized he was standing just behind me, reaching over me to erase what was nearly out of my reach. I stood there without moving, holding my breath and my eraser, until he finished and moved away. "Thanks," I said, thinking I should make eye contact but finding that impossible. He didn't stay long, but if Paula had been standing in the doorway while we were doing that little dance, there would have been no possible way for me to ease her mind.

It was shortly before the Thanksgiving break when Clay stopped by again after a meeting in the elementary building. "How's it going?" he asked as I sat at my desk entering math scores in my grade book. Instead of coming in and sitting on my desk as he had the year before, he leaned against the wall near the doorway. That's when I realized he was as afraid of me as I was of him, as drawn to me as I was to him. I had the shocking and overwhelming desire to stand up, walk across the room, and kiss him.

"It's going okay," I said.

He didn't say anything. Just watched as I entered the last of the grades.

"I'm about done here," I said, shutting my grade book and putting the lid on my Sharpie. I stood up and stretched. "I need to get home."

That wasn't entirely true. I had spelling tests yet to record and I had nothing to get home for, at least no one was waiting for me there—Maisey was spending the night with Jackie, and Luke had told me that morning he would be working late, not to bother fixing dinner for him. "Just come home and relax," he had said. He knew I liked to chill after my work was done each Friday.

"Okay," Clay said. "I'll walk you to your car."

I should have said, *No, that won't be necessary*, but then he might have turned and left, hearing what he needed to hear in that subtle rejection.

"So," I said on the way to the car, "what are you and Rebecca doing tonight?"

He sort of laughed.

I did a double take. It was such a strange thing for him to do.

"Rebecca and I aren't doing anything tonight," he said. Then he opened my car door after I had unlocked it with my key fob. "How about a ride to the office?" he asked, going around the car and getting in before I had a chance to say anything.

I started the car, and he leaned his head against the back of the seat. "Rebecca's in St. Louis for the weekend," he said. "Another seminar."

"Are you upset?"

"Not really."

"Well, Clay, you sound a little upset."

"Let's just say I've always admired your balance, Kendy. You have a life outside of your job."

"My job allows for balance. Besides, Maisey's still home; balance is a necessity. If I remember right, Rebecca didn't work at all when your kids were home. I guess she was volunteering at the shelter some, but still."

He shrugged.

I pulled up to the empty parking space next to his SUV, trying to remember a time Clay had seemed anything other than upbeat.

"Are you okay?" I asked, turning off the ignition and turning to look at him. "Maybe you can come to the house tomorrow night for dinner? It's been forever since you've come to dinner."

Although I had turned to look at him, he wasn't looking at me but at the console between us, and he didn't seem to be listening. That was very unlike Clay.

"Do you really have to get home?" he asked.

"What do you mean?"

"You're not a good liar. I imagine you've had little practice."

I stared through the windshield, biting the inside of my bottom lip.

"I just doubt you have to get home, that's all," he said.

I could have responded in several ways that would have ignored what he was saying or the intent behind it. Instead I chose a directness that wasn't any wiser, in retrospect, than his question. Don't the magazines and books insist that married men and women should never let someone they've found themselves drawn to know how they feel?

"Well, tell me this, Clay," I said, gripping the steering wheel. "Wouldn't you say I *need* to get home?"

He looked at me sweetly and got out of the car.

Tears burned my eyes as I drove away, and I was still wiping them from my face when I pressed the button on the garage door opener fifteen minutes later. I had wanted to stay with Clay. I had desperately wanted to stay.

After that day, seeing him was unbearable and *not* seeing him was unbearable.

If Luke was late getting home or if he volunteered for an out-of-town trip when I was sure it could not be his turn, I ceased to care. It just gave me more time to think about Clay. I thought about him when Luke was gone, when Maisey was asleep, and even, God forgive me, when I sat in church on Sundays with Luke and Maisey, Miller and Anne, Clay and Rebecca, and any other family members in attendance. I never gave a thought about what or who was ultimately and necessarily being neglected when my thoughts were consumed with

Clay, never thought about what I was missing and would never retrieve because of the time I devoted to him.

I think it's safe to say I was losing my mind; I certainly had forfeited right thinking. I was led by my utterly unreliable emotions, a broken and useless compass. By Christmas it seemed like I did my hair a certain way, or applied my makeup with special care, or wore blue the color of my eyes for only one reason: to please Clay.

It is a sad, stupid, pitifully common story, though the Father of Lies presents it to soul after soul as unique. Luke has always disliked any movie that venerates unfaithfulness. He absolutely hated *The Bridges of Madison County*. I, on the other hand, thought it had some poignant moments.

I no longer think so.

CHAPTER SEVENTEEN

Maisey

I have talked Marcus into taking time for a nice lunch. I scoot into the booth and don't need a menu to know I'm going to order an oriental chicken salad.

"Oh, ease up," Marcus says.

But I remind him that for three months I have been determined to do whatever it takes to fit perfectly into the outrageously expensive dress Dad let me buy.

"Anyway," I say, "I like salads."

"Don't be stealing my fries, then."

We wait for our order a long time, but I don't mind. Our waitress keeps the sodas coming, and Marcus entertains me with sibling stories I haven't heard. He tells about a Friday night he and his parents were coming home late from a friend's card party and noticed a car that had been pulled over by the police. They did a double take and about flipped out when they realized the car belonged to Marcus's sixteen-year-old brother, Max. In the whirling lights of the police car, they saw him walking a chalk line. Max escaped incarceration in the city jail, but the Blair household became his jail cell for two long months, and he didn't get his car keys back for a month after that. The Blairs told Max he had been under the influence of certain friends even more than he had been under the influence of alcohol, and that he had better make wiser choices if he wanted them to respect and trust him.

"So," I ask, "did he reform?"

"He did, but according to Max, that was the only time he had gone out drinking with his buddies. No one, he claimed, could have worse luck than he did. My parents told him the opposite was true: He was lucky, or more likely, blessed."

I ask Marcus if he was ever in serious trouble with his parents.

"I wasn't turned that way," he says, shaking his head. He submitted his kindergarten bear for Exhibit One. On a bulletin board in the front of the room, every five-year-old had a cardboard bear that stood at the starting line of a track that led to Big Trouble. Every time a student got reprimanded for any infraction of the posted rules, the bear moved up a notch on the track. Parents of any student whose bear made it all the way down to Big Trouble were called and asked to come in for a meeting with their child and the teacher. That didn't happen Marcus's year, although several students' bears got precariously close.

"One day," Marcus says, "Mom picked me up after school and asked if my bear had moved yet. I said, 'Are you crazy?' So, to answer your question, no, I didn't get in trouble much. I was sent to my room a few times but not without supper."

"Not eating would have been worse than corporal punishment for you."

"Mom would never have been that cruel," he says. "What about you? I can't imagine your parents ever having to discipline their only child."

"Well, they did," I say, almost offended. "I was put in time-out any number of times and grounded once."

Our food arrives, and we give it our full attention. Chatter practically comes to a halt, and before long our plates have been taken away, Marcus's credit card has been processed, and we have made a quick stop in the relatively clean bathrooms before we start the trip home. Sitting in the car now, full and relaxed, Marcus is listening to ESPN again, and I'm jamming with my iPod, glad the tension that filled the car this morning is gone.

I'm trying not to think about what will happen when we get home. I didn't see *I Know What You Did Last Summer*, but the title I recall—change *last* to *that*, and it is a perfect title for the last nine years of my life. I wish for all our sakes I had kept to myself what I have known for so long. Maybe everyone will choose to worry about it another time, or better yet, agree to go on from here the best we can, no discussion required.

I'm watching the road now, remembering the day my parents grounded me. During the spring of my junior year of high school, Jackie, Heidi, and I spent the night with Caitlin, knowing her parents were out of town for the weekend. Jackie and I had been scandalized when we heard they were leaving Caitlin alone. Later we learned her parents had not left her alone at all but thought she was spending the night with Heidi. After Jackie and I had discussed it for at least a week—we're talking premeditation here—we decided it would be fun. We didn't *exactly* lie to our parents; we just let them assume Caitlin's parents would be home. What we didn't realize is that Caitlin and Heidi had told a couple of people about our plans, and they had told a few more people, and by nine that night half the school had shown up, out of control before they even arrived. When several pieces of the outdoor furniture were thrown into the pool and a window had been broken, Jackie and I flipped a coin to see who would call whose parents. I lost, but at least Mom and Dad picked us up before the police arrived.

After dropping Jackie at her home, my parents told me to sit on the couch, and they proceeded to demand a full explanation, which I eventually gave. Afterward, Dad said I was grounded for a month.

"A month!" I said.

My horror did not faze him. "We can make it two," he said, and I crossed my arms over my chest and crossed my legs and glared at the floor between us.

He told me to look at him, something I did not want to do. My glare immediately turned to tears when he said he was disappointed in the choices I'd made connected with this "little incident."

Mother, who had sat across the room without saying anything, finally came to sit beside me. She took my hand and said, "Maisey, honey, deceit is a terrible thing. We don't want you to take it lightly. It will get you into a lot of trouble. More important, it will hurt your soul."

You should know, Mother.

I almost said that aloud. Instead I pulled my hand away and asked if I could go to my room.

They looked at each other.

"Okay," Dad said.

They didn't make me say I was sorry. I knew they wouldn't. They think an apology should be sincere.

I started up the stairs, still in stomping mode but careful not to truly stomp and get myself in more trouble. At the top of the landing, I stopped and turned. They were standing at the bottom of the stairs, watching me, just as I knew they would be.

I wanted to say *I'm sorry*, but the words wouldn't come out of my mouth.

Kendy

I call Phillip, and he says things have gone well and that Mother is in her room resting comfortably. "Resting comfortably" is a lovely cliché. I'm relieved. The sun is shining brightly, as though nature is celebrating Mother's good report.

But my mind insists on returning to a disastrous snowy day.

Jackie's mother had picked the girls up when school was cancelled at noon, and she called before I left school to ask if Maisey could stay over. Then Luke called to say he'd probably spend the night with his folks in Indy, and Clay dropped by my classroom to take me home. He said the roads were already dangerous. I knew I should have left earlier.

I told him if he was worried, he could just follow me home, but when we got outside and I had to look for my car, already covered with snow, I changed my mind. Luke and I could come for it once the storm was over and the roads were cleared.

Clay had to work on his passenger door to get it open, and he was still there to catch me when I slipped getting into the SUV. "Whoa," I said, sounding like Maisey.

"Can you imagine?" I said when he had gotten in and started his big rig. "This is unbelievable. It's early for a blizzard."

"We're in for a four-day weekend at least," he said.

"But it's beautiful, isn't it?" I said, looking at the snow falling nearly as fast as rain, piling on the fields, the trees, and the roads, shining so brightly that I felt in my purse for sunglasses I had put away months before. "Look, Clay, the flakes are as big as the palm of my hand!"

His Tahoe slid and spun several times before we pulled into my driveway, and I doubted my car and I would have made it all the way home. We estimated the snow was already a foot deep, maybe deeper, and I dreaded getting out of the warm SUV and making my way to the porch. I was glad I wasn't stranded on the side of the road somewhere, glad I had allowed Clay to bring me home.

"Maybe we should have a snowball fight," I said, smiling at my knight in sweater, slacks, and overcoat.

He smiled too, a smile I adored, and turned off the engine.

"Miller and I loved few things more than playing in the snow," he said. "We started hoping for it in October. We made snowmen—or I should say, snow cowboys and Indians—and we built snow forts and had hundreds of rounds of snowball ammunition."

"I rarely went out in the snow when I was a girl. I watched the spectacle from the windows of our condominium. But my best memory of my mother took place when we were stranded at home during a blizzard. Maybe that's why I love snow so much."

I began to shiver. "I should go in," I said, though that was the last thing I wanted to do.

"Don't go," he said, restarting the engine, the heat returning. "You're right—it's beautiful, and this is the perfect place to view it."

"It's true," I said, looking around me. "We're in a snow globe!"

We watched the giant snowflakes dropping daintily now to blanket the hood of Clay's Tahoe, and then he turned to look at me. He seemed to be studying my face. "You're like the snow, Kendy."

"White? Cold? Deep?"

Was I being obtuse? Or coy? Both were unlike me, but isn't that the problem with similes—they can miss the mark? Or did I simply want him to say what wasn't vague at all?

"Beautiful," he said. "You're absolutely beautiful."

I was a thirty-eight-year-old woman, aware, like many women I know, that I was attractive enough, but I couldn't recall the last time I'd heard someone say such a thing. Of course, if it does not occur to your husband to say it, who will? Is it ever appropriate for another man to tell a married woman she is beautiful? And isn't it pathetic to enjoy hearing it so much?

I turned to inspect the landscape outside the passenger window so intently that Clay might have thought I hadn't heard him.

Except he knew I had.

Had he intended to fluster me?

When I turned back around, he was leaning against his door, still looking at me as though he hadn't said something that both embarrassed and ridiculously pleased me. I'm sure I surprised him then; I know I surprised myself. I leaned against my door and looked at him as studiously as he was looking at me, with as much interest, with as much desire. I had never been so audacious, eschewing propriety, forgetting completely the virtue of restraint.

The engine was still running, but he had turned off the windshield wipers, and we could see nothing but snow and each other. For a few brief moments we could imagine we were alone in our snow-globe world. That was the first time I kissed Clay Laswell—gently, and then with a fierceness that comes from months of curiosity and pent-up longing.

Why the fascination with what we cannot have, *should* not have? And why do the doubly blessed so often want more? I really don't understand it, this problem as ancient as Eden. Even now, all these years later, it is a mystery to me.

I finally went into the house that day, thinking, *There, that's done, I'm free.*

But of course I was not free. There were other kisses, other times he held me, other times he did not want me to go. I can hardly bear to think of these generalities, much less the specifics.

Most of that particular brand of madness was confined to a frantic two-month period. The following February in a Wal-Mart bathroom, Maisey by my side, I discovered I was going to have a baby. How could that be? Why would such a miracle be bestowed on me now?

I knew the exact night Luke and I had conceived the child. It was New Year's Eve, when Maisey was celebrating at a church lock-in. Luke decided, of all times, we should cel-ebrate alone rather than with family or friends. But although initially I had wanted to attend a party, had bought a dress at an after-Christmas sale anticipating one, Luke and I ended up having a lovely evening together. We ate in front of the fire, put on our favorite CDs, and actually danced the new year in. He told me he loved me, and I believed him. With a will I thought I no longer possessed, I pushed Clay out of my mind and gave my husband this time, gave him myself like a gift.

But with the morning light, life returned to the normal that had numbed me for so long, except Clay and I didn't see each other every single chance we got as we had been doing. And after I got the amazing news about the baby, we were alone together only twice: the day in my classroom when I told him I was pregnant, and the day I went to his office in April to give him my resignation. He still could hardly believe I was pregnant. I didn't look pregnant.

"Are you sure you want to quit?" he asked.

"I have to," I said. "I was home with Maisey until she started school, and I want to be home with him."

"Him? You already know it's a boy?"

"I haven't had an ultrasound yet. I just think this baby's a he."

"That would be nice."

I looked at my hands folded in my lap. "I have to quit for other reasons too, Clay. You know that."

"This is crazy, Kendy," he said. "Just crazy."

The "this" was vague, which was appropriate, for it could mean so many things. I realized, for instance, that for this meeting I had chosen to wear a cotton sweater the shade of blue he loved me to wear.

"*We* are crazy," I said.

He laughed.

I smiled only faintly, shaking my head slowly back and forth. "You know it's not funny."

"I wouldn't have laughed, except I'm crazy."

"You will regain your senses."

"Do you know how much I love you?" he said.

Words so thrilling to hear. And so awful.

I sat there trying to fathom what he had said, while at the same time recalling the sweet, pure excitement I had felt sitting in this exact spot sixteen years earlier, talking with this charming man about the possibility of being a fourth-grade teacher in his elementary school.

"Well," I said, taking a deep breath and letting it out again, "I'm sorry to say I love you too."

I stood up and walked to the door. With my hand on the doorknob, I turned and looked at him, still sitting at his desk, my resignation in his hand. "You do realize," I said, "that we will have to get over that."

"No other option?"

"None at all. At least, none either one of us would really want to consider."

We didn't see each other again until the July morning he stopped by with tomatoes from his garden. "For Maisey," he said when I let him in the back door. He and Maisey had been cultivating tomatoes together for at least ten summers. I told him she had just left for camp, but we'd take them anyway.

Except for the Fourth-of-July family gathering, I hadn't

seen Clay since school had let out. I couldn't believe he was sitting at my kitchen table, looking so healthy with his summer tan. I had thought of him every day. I hadn't stopped loving him yet.

"You look good," he said.

"I feel good."

I asked him if he had hired someone to take my place, and he said he didn't want to talk about that. I leaned against the counter and closed my eyes. He shouldn't have gotten up, he shouldn't have put his arms around me, he shouldn't have kissed me one last time, and I shouldn't have kissed him back.

Then Maisey wouldn't have tiptoed into the kitchen and found us that way. Then she wouldn't have walked quietly away from a mother capable of such unfaithfulness.

CHAPTER EIGHTEEN

Maisey

"Was she a good mother?" Marcus asks when we aren't far from home.

"Well, yes," I say, "I guess I'd have to say she was overall."

Then I put in my earphones and stare out the window again. I don't feel like proving my assertion with details, though Mother taught me to do that when I was a mere child.

"It's a beautiful day," I'd say.

"What's beautiful about it?" she'd ask, wanting me to observe the day's specific glory, wanting, she said, to benefit from my perspective.

The trip to Indy has done a number on my nice clean car. Marcus is getting quarters out of the change machine to wash it again. He doesn't believe in drive-through car washes, and if he can find a do-it-yourself car wash with unlimited time, or at least a ridiculous amount of time, he is in heaven. Today I'm glad he has found this bliss. I'd like to have a few minutes to myself. The inside of the car is still spotless, so I have the luxury of just sitting here, staring through a windshield slathered with soap and drenched with water.

I've been thinking about my culinary ability—rather unusual, I think, for one my age. Jackie's specialties are frozen pizza and instant pudding. I can make a coconut crème pie with a flaky crust. I can make lots of cookies, including our favorites—chocolate chip and peanut butter. I can make at least six kinds of soup from scratch. I can make stuffed peppers and cashew chicken. I got on a cooking kick when I was in the fifth grade, and Mother taught me how to make these things and more. By the time I was in the seventh grade I could make everything but the cashew chicken by myself. Our apartment has a great kitchen, and I am stocking it with everything I need to make Marcus happy he's married a chef.

Mother taught me to cook. That was good.

It is also good that my parents were very nearly omnipresent. When I looked into a crowd at a ball game or a concert, I would find them there, clapping wildly at a concert, hollering with the best of them at a ball game. That wasn't true for all of my friends. Some parents weren't interested enough. Some were too busy. Even Jackie's parents couldn't always be there, since they were trying to keep track of five children.

My parents' commitment is just one more reason Jackie

quite lovingly calls me Spoiley Girl. Besides orchestra and basketball, I held an office in the Honor Society, wrote for the school newspaper, and attended church activities without end. Dad called me well-rounded; Mother called me busy. But they came to games and concerts, inductions and award ceremonies. Mother cut out my newspaper articles and hung them on the refrigerator.

"I'm not in first grade," I'd say.

"No first grader could write like this," Mom would say, securing each new article with a daisy magnet.

I became Activities Queen, with a full schedule of games and concerts when I started eighth grade, a month or two after my mother lost the baby and temporarily dropped out of life. That hiatus changed everything. In my opinion she might as well have been in Outer Mongolia. She was that absent from our lives.

That was the first Halloween the girls didn't sleep over since the four of us were in third grade, something we'd done even when Halloween was on a school night. "Your poor mom" was their take on it. I just stuffed my things into my duffle bag and huffed out the door to spend the night with Jackie. It was the end of October, for goodness' sake!

That Thanksgiving Dad and I showed up at my grand-parents' without Mom. She had actually planned on going, but at the last minute said she just couldn't do it. Not yet.

That ticked me off. "Do what?" I asked Dad in the car on the way to Indy. "Can't eat Thanksgiving dinner? She didn't even have to bring anything."

Dad said she wasn't ready to attend a social function. I said dinner at the grandparents' didn't exactly qualify as a social function. When he sighed, I let it go. But I distinctly recall looking out the window and thinking, *Who the heck cares?*

Dad explained more than once that Mother was depressed, something about an "episode." Only the episode was lasting longer than even he expected. "She's just so sad, Maisey. Just keep praying, and your mom will be okay one of these days."

Dad didn't know I wasn't talking to God about Mom.

I felt sorry for him when the Christmas season arrived, Mother's favorite, and she still wasn't okay. She went to the Christmas Eve service with us, sitting there like a zombie, but Dad and I put up the tree and did the Christmas shopping and wrapped the gifts. She watched us open our gifts Christmas morning, pleased with everything I opened, which had been purchased, I found out later, by either Dad or Paula.

On Christmas Eve, when we open one gift, Mother handed me a tiny box that she brought from her bedroom. This one, apparently, she had bought before catastrophe struck. "I hope you like this, honey," she said, tears brimming in her eyes. "I should have given it to you for your thirteenth birthday," she said. "But you know how I love Christmas, so I saved it for your thirteenth Christmas."

"Thanks," I said, opening the package and finding a pinky ring, a band full of tiny diamonds. I gasped, slipped it on my finger, and without thinking, walked over to Mother's chair and held out my hand to show it to her. She smiled. "It's beautiful," I added before I remembered seeing her in Clay's arms on that disgusting day in July. Instantly, pleasure was replaced with irritation. I began helping Dad gather wrapping paper and followed him into the kitchen to load the dishwasher. She came in, kissed Dad and me, and told us good-night before she headed back to her dark room.

That spring things were finally fairly normal, and one evening the following summer while we were eating dinner on the patio, she looked across the table at me and said, "I'm sorry I missed so much of your life last year, Maisey."

I stood up and said, "No problem," before I rushed into the house to get more ice. I like my drinks to have plenty of ice.

From the eighth grade on, my friends seemed to live at our house, especially Jackie. Mother continued taking me to Indy to shop three or four times a year, only now Jackie went too, and sometimes Heidi and Caitlin. They were always asking when we were going again. She was the mother who took us to concerts during the winter and amusement parks each summer. During those years, Mother always had to have a five-passenger vehicle—at least.

In the summer when the girls came over to swim, everyone took a turn sitting on a lounger by Mother, telling her a good story or asking her advice about something or other. She listened to them, and they listened to her. She was forever their teacher and friend. Sometimes I felt like telling them to go home, she was my mom—but then I'd remember what she had done, and I was glad someone was there to divert her attention from her only child.

My friends, my dad, and my activities were a buffer between my mother and me, and when I graduated from high school, a university two states away took over where they left off. But today, watching the water pour in sheets over the windshield, this thought has occurred to me: If I were dying and my life flashed before my eyes, the first thing I would see, and the last, is my mother.

Kendy

I do hope that's the last pit stop before I get to the hospital. I'm making good time, despite two stops, and I should be at the hospital by three. I haven't even turned on the radio or listened to CDs. I've hardly been aware of time passing, of miles covered.

I am aware, however, of the time travel I've been doing since I pulled onto the interstate. Now I've landed in my dark bedroom, where much of a year was lost to me.

I have looked at it another way as well: During those many months, *I* was lost. I wandered in "a far country," not really wanting to find my way back home. Home was too painful. Home was where I had betrayed my husband; home was where I had lost our baby boy.

I lost him on a Friday morning, the week Maisey was at camp. Luke had not yet left for work when the cramping and bleeding started. I was doing nothing more strenuous than making our bed. It didn't matter that the chances of my becoming pregnant were so slim I never bothered with any type of birth control, and it didn't matter that my doctor had said the chances of carrying the baby to term were minimal. I had seen my son's heart beating on the ultrasound monitor, I had felt him moving inside of me, and I had already imagined Miller Luke's chubby arms encircling my neck.

"Luke!" I called that morning, holding my stomach with both hands, as if that could keep our son safely in my womb.

We were at the hospital in less than an hour, but though I've heard of incredibly premature babies surviving, our son did not. He lived only long enough for Luke and me to see him, to hold for the briefest minutes his tiny form wrapped in a warm blanket, to say, "We love you, sweet boy." To say good-bye.

If only I could have kept him safe inside of me a little longer. If only I had been restricted to my bed sooner. I must have repeated those *if only*'s ten times on the way home that afternoon, each time Luke nodding as though he had just heard it. I barely remember standing in the cemetery that Monday morning with Luke, Maisey, Miller, and Anne—all five of us crying, Maisey standing beside her dad, squeezing his hand. I stood between Luke and Miller, already beginning my journey to a place where I hoped no one could find me.

I hardly got out of bed the first month. Luke asked Miller and Anne to let Maisey stay with them until school started, not wanting her to see me so devastated. He told Maisey that I wasn't myself, that I needed time to get over losing her baby brother. Luke had never seen me in such a state or anything remotely close to it. Most evenings he would come in and lie beside me and try to engage me in simple conversation about his day or Maisey's. I'd lie there with my arm crooked over my eyes and try to listen, and then I'd turn toward him and listen to the sound of his voice with my eyes closed. I remember his hand on my shoulder, his kiss on my forehead.

I got up, of course. I had to go to the bathroom. I also showered some days but quickly and without fooling with my hair or applying makeup. When Luke came in from work, he'd check on me, ask if I'd eaten anything, insist I have something for dinner. I knew I had to cooperate to an extent or he would snatch me out of my hiding place and take me to a doctor or the hospital. I began to eat some of whatever he brought: soup, a sandwich, a salad, even a piece of fruit, if he would just let me be. "Thank you," I'd say.

He studied as much as he could about depression. He decided I was having a major depressive episode, combined with postpartum depression (wouldn't that be magnified if a mother didn't bring her baby home?), and when winter set in, seasonal affective disorder. He sensed the effect gloomy weather might have on me even before he read about it. By the end of September he opened the blinds before he left for work, knowing how much I love the sunshine, and turned on the lamp by my chaise longue, hoping, I'm sure, that the light would beckon me that far from my bed. He continued to do these things long after he realized I shut the blinds and turned off the light as soon as he left.

He was also tenacious about asking me to let Paula visit. She had stopped by many times, bringing me flowers, books, notes from my former students. For weeks I was asleep when she came, or pretended to be. When Luke begged me to see her, I finally relented. Like Luke, she came in and lay beside me. "I'm sorry, Kendy," she'd say. Eventually she began to say more than that on her weekly visits, and eventually I half listened as long as she talked about nothing that mattered.

By sometime in October, I put on one of my two sweat suits after my shower and gathered my hair into a wild ponytail. I'd pull the bedspread up and lie on top of it, covering myself with a throw. I hoped Luke would call this progress. I still wished to sleep constantly; that's all I had energy for.

"I feel like a balloon that's losing its air," I said once, trying to explain to Luke how very weary I felt. It was a rather bad simile, but it was the best I could do. When I did wake up, I wanted to sleep again and found myself taking a sleeping pill even though I had already slept for hours.

When Luke complained of how many bottles of sleeping

pills I was consuming, I told him they were over the counter and much milder than prescription sleeping pills. "Still," he said.

So I began alternating sleeping pills with allergy pills, which contained the same ingredients but in smaller doses. Sleep served as Novocain to deaden the pain of guilt and regret and sadness, and it allowed me to spend my days wandering in the darkness, far away from home.

I tried to go to Miller and Anne's for Thanksgiving, I really did, but as I told Luke and Maisey after I had dressed for the occasion and actually put on makeup, I just couldn't do it, not yet. I had managed to go to church once before Thanksgiving, but the mere act of greeting people and trying to assure them I was better overwhelmed me. I told Luke I was sorry but to please tell anyone who asked that I'd be back as soon as I was comfortable in public again. "I'm just indisposed," I said. "Tell them I'm indisposed." Somehow he covered for me.

When December arrived, Luke broached the subject of decorating the tree. The task seemed insurmountable, and just thinking of it made me laugh. So the following week, having graduated to holding a book in my lap as I lay on the bedspread with a throw over me, I heard Luke and Maisey putting up the tree, the requisite Christmas carols playing on the stereo. Tears spilled down my face when I heard through my closed door the strains of "O Holy Night" and remembered what life had been like when I had loved living.

Maisey spent New Year's Eve at church again and went to Jackie's when the party was over. I heard her telling Luke rather tentatively to have a happy new year, and I got out of bed and came into the living room as she was collecting her things to leave.

"Maisey," I said.

"Jackie's mom is waiting, Mother."

"I just want you to know I love you."

"Okay," she said, heading for the door.

"And, honey," I said, exhausted by the effort of speaking to my darling child, "I hope you have a good new year."

"Thanks," she said, and she was gone.

Luke lay beside me that night. "We conceived our son a year ago tonight," I whispered.

"I know," he said.

I rolled over and soaked my pillow with tears. Luke curled up behind me, holding me, until I finally felt myself slipping into sleep, relieved that the worst year of my life was coming to an end.

"Better?" Luke asked the next morning.

"I hope," I said.

I showered and stayed up much of the day. I even ate at the table with Luke and Maisey that night, listening to Maisey's reports about the party the night before and about Jackie's bursting into her parents' room when they got home from it, clanging two pans together and shouting, "Happy New Year!" Luke said it was no wonder they agreed to let Jackie stay with us so often.

But it was February before I dressed every morning, tried to do a small load of wash every afternoon, and even fixed something for dinner several nights a week, if you call grilled cheese sandwiches dinner. Spring came early, and I put on a jacket and began to sit on the deck, soaking up the sun. I realized sometime in March that I wasn't taking sleeping pills anymore, and when Paula stopped by, I joined in the conversation, at least asking questions and smiling when smiling was called for.

One day during Paula's spring break, she asked if I was going to try to teach the following year.

"I deserved to lose the baby, Paula."

"What?" she asked.

"I deserved to lose the baby."

"What do you mean, honey?"

"Nothing."

Before too many more weeks passed, swearing her to secrecy, I gave her a summary of my time with Clay. "I thought I loved him," I said, a summary of my summary.

"I don't think losing your baby and crossing the line with Clay are related, Kendy. Could you give yourself that much of a break?"

"Maybe," I said. "I've started back to church. I've been listening to my worship music. I don't think I'm well, but I'm better. In the last few weeks, a vivid image has comforted me from the time I wake up in the morning until I fall asleep at the end of the day: Ragged and weary, I'm caught up in the embrace of a tender Father who's been watching for me, longing for me to come home."

Paula's eyes filled with tears. She got up from her chair to sit beside me on the glider, holding my hand until Luke came home and asked what we were up to.

"Girl stuff," Paula said.

I smiled, but how I dreaded the day I would have much the same conversation with him.

Maisey

I hold my breath when we walk into a house that is eerily quiet. I hold it again when we enter the kitchen. I see a note on the kitchen table, my name scrawled on the envelope in Dad's handwriting. Tearing it open, I read that Mom is running an errand and won't be back for quite a while. Dad is at a meeting and should be back by five.

So the house is empty. What a relief.

I pour a soda and walk out on the patio, sit in the sun, and pray that everything can go on as usual, at least until the wedding is over. Marcus is returning phone calls and grabbing a book from his room before he comes out to chill awhile with me. These may be the last hours we'll have to ourselves before we rush to my car and leave for our first night as husband and wife.

I wonder where Mother is. Maybe she's avoiding me as I have been avoiding her.

That is very unlikely. She's always been one to confront— me or anyone else in her "sphere of influence." That would be one of her favorite phrases. Maybe it's the teacher in her. When we were still in elementary school, maybe fifth grade, Heidi, Caitlin, Jackie, and I were out here dancing on the patio with Mother. She was trying to show Jackie another move besides the sprinkler.

"Girls," she said, stopping her demonstration and walking over to our CD player. "Come here!" The four of us gathered around quickly; Mother seldom gave commands. She pushed Repeat and listened to a few lines, stopped the CD, skipped back again, and listened one more time. "Do you hear that?" We looked at each other and then at her. "Do you really think we need to be listening to these lyrics? This is trash. Really. And you're not going to fill your minds with it on my watch."

Jackie ran to her purse and pulled out another CD. "How about this one?"

We put it on and were relieved that one of our favorites received unqualified approval from the most important censor in our lives.

Of course the worst confrontation took place the night she came to my room after Dad tucked me in, wanting to discuss the "distance" that had come between us during the months she went on sabbatical in her room.

By the time Mother had returned to the land of the living, I was able to look at her without throwing up, but everything had changed, and by that summer I think she began to realize it. That fall she was teaching in another district and got home later than she had before, and I had started high school and was involved in so many activities I usually got home even later than she did. That seemed a good enough explanation for the "distance," but when she sat on my bed that night in November and brushed the hair out of my eyes, I realized it wasn't completely adequate.

"I miss you," she said.

Not to worry, I thought, *you have stupid Clay.* Of course I never saw them alone together after that day in the kitchen, but that didn't mean anything; I hadn't seen them alone together *before* that day either.

I didn't say any of that, of course. Mother's the confronter, not me.

"I'm right here," I said.

She looked at me. Or maybe she was looking *for* me. "I know you are," she said, trying to smile. "But it seems like I woke up and my little girl was gone."

"She *is*, Mother. I'm a big girl now, practically an adult."

She smiled again, but tears brimmed in her eyes.

For a moment I felt bad. But she had brought this on

herself. As far as I was concerned, she was lucky to have Dad and me at all.

"I'm sorry," she said.

My heart stopped.

"For what?"

"Well, honey, I've told you this before, but I'm sorry I disappeared on you last year. It was an important year for you—so much was going on in your life. And while your father and I lost a son, you lost your little brother, and I wasn't there to help you through it."

Now, that was an understatement.

"Dad was here," I said.

"I know. And I've been so grateful for that."

Please.

"He's good at tucking me in too," I said. "He said he didn't know what he'd been missing."

"Well, that's the upside, isn't it?"

"I'm tired, Mother," I said.

"I love you, Maisey, more than anything in this world."

"Thanks," I said, which was more of an insult than it sounds. I knew she wanted to hear something else, something I had said thousands of times before the catastrophic event that changed our world forever: *I love you too.* That I could not say, but when I heard the door click and her footsteps on the stairs, I cried myself to sleep, completely forgetting I was a big girl now, practically an adult.

I've been tempted, especially at first, to tell my friends about what I saw—their adoration can be sickening—but something's kept me from it. I do sometimes wonder what they would have said. All these years, and I told no one until yesterday. I almost told Marcus after our engagement became official, but by then I knew him well, and I could just hear him saying, *Don't you think you've made her pay for her sins?*

If so, I'd say I've paid for them too.

CHAPTER NINETEEN

Kendy

Ah, the Mississippi River. I am close. This trip, one I've made hundreds of times, has seemed much longer than five hours. I wish I could have been here earlier, and I wish I could be home the minute I leave Mother's room. But, what is it Luke says? If wishes were horses, then beggars would ride?

Well, as a matter of fact, I wish beggars *could* ride. And I might as well go whole hog and wish there were no beggars. Too much sadness in this world. Some of it I have caused.

With the distance that years bring, I have wondered what kind of deficiency accounts for what I allowed to happen. Surely there must be one. Possibly more than one. Isn't there someone or something I can blame besides myself? Or along with myself? It wouldn't make it better, but it would make it at least comprehensible.

I'd like to blame my birth father, a deficiency if there ever was one. If I had told Mother of my incredible indiscretion (such an innocuous term for falling in love with my husband's uncle), she might have been generous enough to let me place some of the blame on my father's neglect, though strangely, she herself blamed him for nothing. She did say once, however, that he was useless.

I of course didn't quite believe that. How could I believe that of a man whose name I did not know, but who must have wanted so much to know me, despite his indifference in his youth? That was one thing I did pursue: I nagged and nagged Mother to tell me who he was, and finally she said she'd tell me the name of the "sperm donor" when I turned eighteen. "Mother!" I had said. Not a nice thing for a child to hear, but I'm sure frustration had gotten the best of her.

"Okay," I said when she gave me my present the evening of my eighteenth birthday. We had just come home that Friday evening from the dinner Margaret had prepared in my honor.

"Okay?" she had asked.

I felt bad. She thought that was my response to the gift I hadn't even opened yet.

I laughed and told her I was thinking about something else, and then I opened my present and saw, resting on plush black velvet, a stunning pair of diamond stud earrings. I rushed to the mirror and put them in. She stood behind me and said they looked perfect. "They are," I said. And I didn't have the heart, when she had bought me such a thoughtful and expensive keepsake for this special birthday, to broach the subject of my father that night.

"I'm being lazy today," she said when I came to the breakfast table the next day, "taking the morning off."

She smiled when I acted like I was about to faint.

She looked across the table as I sat down with my bowl of cornflakes and said, "Okay."

I held on to my spoon for support.

She said she had been in bed for quite a while last night before she finally understood what I had meant by "Okay."

I put down my spoon and told her I was sorry my dad's name had dominated my thoughts even while I held her unopened birthday present in my hand. "Such a wonderful present," I said, touching an earlobe, still trying to fathom my mother's unprecedented attention to this particular passage, especially nice since we had had several unpleasant discussions about my choice of universities during that year. No, I hadn't expected such a generous and special gift.

She told me there was no need to apologize, that I had been waiting a long time to know my father's identity.

She got up, retied her robe, and walked to the refrigerator to get both of us some orange juice. I sensed how badly she did not want to say his name inside the walls we inhabited. I know now he had nothing whatsoever to do with us, but that was something I would have to find out for myself. I know now how much Mother dreaded that for me.

"Your father's name," she said, putting the pitcher and two juice glasses on the table and sitting across from me again, "is Craig Tanner."

I repeated it, amazed I finally knew his name. I don't know how many times I repeated it in my mind after that moment at the breakfast table, and I puzzled even myself when I waited more than a year to contact him. I didn't ask my mother to help me locate him, but at some point during my freshman year of college, Margaret tracked him down for me in Denver, Colorado.

I picked up the phone to call him several times until finally stress alone caused me to stay on the line to hear his voice and to say, "Hello?"

"My name is Kennedy," I added seconds later. He didn't reply but seemed to be waiting for something else. I realized I needed to add one detail. "Kennedy *Belk*." Still nothing. "Your daughter."

He of course was very surprised to hear from me, or perhaps *horrified* is a better word. For some reason in those first minutes, he told me, among other things, that he had been married a couple of times but had no children.

"No *other* children," I replied, surprising myself. I thought he might be glad he had an offspring in the world, but if tone and words are any indication, he was far from elated. I said I'd like to see him, and he took my phone number and said he'd get back to me.

"I can come to Denver when school's out," I said before he hung up.

He didn't call for weeks, but finally the phone rang, and instead of Paula saying she'd be late or some guy asking for a date or my history notes, it was my father on the end of the line. He didn't want me to come to Denver, but he said if I wanted to meet him, he'd fly to St. Louis the next time I was there. I did not intend to let this opportunity get away from me. I told him I'd be home the next Friday.

"That'll work," he said.

He didn't even get a hotel to spend the night the Saturday

I met him. He fit me in for a long lunch between his flights in and out of St. Louis. We met at a restaurant near the airport. I told the hostess I was meeting Craig Tanner, and she led me to a luxuriously padded booth where a handsome man with my sky-blue eyes sat drinking a glass of wine and perusing a menu. He stood up and put his hands on my shoulders, as close to intimate as we would ever be. "Well," he said, looking into my face, "there you are."

We ordered (I have no recollection of eating whatever was put before me), and he looked at me across the linen tablecloth. "I do believe you favor my mother," he said.

"I wouldn't know," I said. "Do you have any pictures of her or my grandfather? Do I have aunts and uncles? Do I have cousins?" Seeing him had been my focus all these years, the family that came with him not even in my peripheral imaginings. Suddenly I longed to know them.

"Not with me," he said. "Maybe I can send you some."

He had no trouble chatting. I learned his family knew nothing about me. I think I might have winced when he said that, though he didn't notice. It made me terribly sad, because I knew I wasn't the one to tell them such a thing and doubted very much that he ever would. I was glad my grandparents had other grandchildren from an aunt and uncle I'd never know either. My father repeated what he had said on the phone: that he had been divorced twice ("Not a bit good at the marriage thing") and that he had no *other* children (his voice implying "Thank God"). He added that he was dating a woman a mere five years older than his recently discovered daughter. How about that?

He did accomplish one important thing with that two-hour lunch: He made sure I understood a relationship wasn't going to happen, though he was "certainly glad" we could meet.

Like an idiot I hugged him when we parted and said, "Thanks for coming."

"I wish I had more time," he said, hurrying outside to grab a shuttle, though I had offered to drop him off at the terminal. "You take care of yourself now."

No doubt I'd have to. Or if someone contributed to my care, it most definitely would not be Mr. Cliché. I drove back to the condo, disappointed that my "father" was so unbelievably self-absorbed. He was a flat character in the play of life, a most reprehensible type. I summed up my impression to try out on Paula when I returned to Indy: "As deep as a thimble."

Still, I couldn't say I was sorry we'd met. My curiosity was satisfied and my silly illusion that my father was impatiently waiting to meet me and love me was irrevocably shattered—far beyond the help of Super Glue and a steady hand. I had also learned about my grandfather's serious hypertension and my grandmother's bout with breast cancer. Those are important things to know.

"You were right, Mother," I said when she got home that evening. "My father is useless."

She put down her briefcase and walked over to the couch, where I was sitting with a book in my lap. Then, to my great surprise, she cupped her hand under my chin and kissed the top of my head. As far as memories of my mother go, that kiss is right up there with the blizzard.

Maisey

Marcus is walking outside, holding a cell phone to his ear. He pivots the phone away from his mouth and whispers, "Blair emergency."

My heart stops. And I must look like I need resuscitating,

because he holds up a hand to stop my imagination in its tracks and quickly adds, "*Minor* emergency."

He speaks into the phone now. "Don't worry, Mom, I'm sure we can work out something."

He snaps the phone shut, pulls a chair up beside me, and squeezes my hand. "My calm and capable mother is uncharacteristically freaked."

"What's wrong?"

"Pete."

"Pete? Do I know a Pete?"

"Pete the dog?"

"Oh, *Pete*!"

"Yes, Pete the ten-year-old dog, as cherished as any one of us sons. Mom likes to say he's caused her a good deal less trouble, has not had any use for higher education that would continue bankrupting them, and has never strayed farther than the yard."

"Is he sick?"

"No, but his regular sitter had to go to Wisconsin this morning. Her daughter had her baby early."

"How rude."

"Very. Mom said she's pretty disgusted with the whole lot of them."

"Can't Pete stay in a kennel?"

"Excuse me?"

I laugh.

"I believe she'd miss the wedding first—or rent Pete a tux."

"Well, Marcus, your mom really has no problem. We have an empty pen. Pete can stay right out there." I point at a pen beside Dad's outbuilding, one long side of it being the building itself.

"He's a house dog, honey."

"The outdoor pen is on a concrete slab and there merely for his enjoyment of nature. There's a hole cut into the side of the building, an entrance into lovely quarters. If those accommodations were fit for my darling dog, Lady, they're fit enough for Pete, trust me. You've seen it, haven't you, when you were out there with Dad? Believe me, we've allowed few people to see such excess. There's even a fan on the wall, pointing straight at the unreasonably luxurious doggie bed. Honestly, it will do. I'll put a rug in there if that will make your mom happy. We can go right now and buy a carpet remnant so you can tell her the outbuilding is a guesthouse."

Because Marcus hasn't paid all that much attention to the dog pen on any excursions to the outbuilding, we walk out so I can show him I do not exaggerate. After the inspection, we return to the patio, where he calls his mother to convince her Pete will be fine in the "guesthouse" and that the Laswells will be glad to have him occupy it for the weekend.

I head into the house to get us sodas. I fill glasses with ice and conjure up my dog, Lady, as she was—so lively, so loyal. It's been a while since I've thought about her, which surprises me. There was a time I was sure I'd look for her every day of my life.

I loved her a lot.

She was the best dog a girl could have. She was officially Dad's dog, but from the time I could toddle to the pen, she was really mine. Dad had bought the beautiful yellow Lab the year before I was born, choosing her out of a litter of ten. He bought her to hunt with, but he didn't get around to taking her hunting more than two or three times a year, if that. Grandpa and Clay hunted with her more often than

Dad did, mostly out of pity, I think. They didn't need to bother; Lady was a companion much more than a hunter. I rarely spent the night with my grandparents or Clay and Rebecca without taking Lady. She especially liked to be at Clay's, because she could run all over his twenty acres and swim in his pond.

Most of the time, Lady sat on our patio, waiting for me to come out. Mom could have the loungers; I preferred to put cushions on the concrete to lie on, using Lady for a pillow. With this dog, my pillow and willing listener, I shared my considerable joys and occasional sorrows. Or we just lay there quietly, looking for cloud sculptures in the blue of the afternoon sky or clusters of stars at night. She had looked up with interest the day I exclaimed I had found a cloud that looked exactly like her. Mother said I was lucky to have such a good dog, that when she was a girl living in the condo, she couldn't have anything but a fish. She said there was absolutely no comparison—try laying your head on a fish!

Lady, fourteen by then and old for a Lab, died the fall of my seventh-grade year. Could the timing have been worse? She had cancer. Inoperable cancer. Dad would have spent a fortune if it would have helped.

When she was too sick to wobble to the fencing, he said, "We need to put her down, Maize."

"No, Dad," I said. "She might get well."

When she could no longer eat and couldn't even get up to greet us when we came out to check on her, Dad refused to put it off any longer. "She's a dog, honey, and suffering too much. We've got to let her go."

He let me sleep in the outbuilding with her that night before taking her to the vet the next morning. I've always believed Lady spared me that agony, though I had been slow to spare her. I woke up as the sun began to rise and reached over to pet her. When she opened her eyes and looked at me, I kissed her furry head and watched in wonder as she took her last breath and slipped away.

I must have scratched her gently behind her ears and whispered, "I love you, girl," ten times before I went inside to get Mom and Dad. He wrapped Lady in a white blanket Mom contributed and buried her close to the pen. *Lady*, I wrote with green latex paint on the marker we had made for her, trying to keep my hand steady, *my best friend*.

Dad patted me from time to time as we worked, and when we were finished and returned to the house, Mom brought a cold washcloth for my swollen face and held me while I sobbed.

My parents helped me get through that awful loss, and the next summer when the three of us went through a different kind of trauma, one I could never have imagined, Mom and Dad went to their room, and I gathered blankets and pillows and spent a lot of time in the outbuilding next to Lady's pen, wishing she were there to lie beside me and help me through the utter misery of loss upon loss.

Kendy

Mother is sleeping.

Her nurse said the procedure went very well but that she would be asleep for a while. She is paraphernalia free, except for one bag of fluid hanging from a hook, an intravenous drip that had better be doing something terribly helpful for her, because when she awakens, Superwoman won't like looking down and seeing a needle embedded in her arm. She can't handle needles. When I was a child and immunized for one thing or another, *she* was the one who squeezed her eyes shut, and *she* was the one who needed reassuring. It was a strange role reversal: I always reached out and grabbed her hand and said everything would be fine.

Her private room is shadowed and cool with the curtains drawn to block the afternoon sun. I stopped in the gift shop and bought the nicest vase of flowers in the cooler. I've placed them on the bedside table nearest the windows, so she can see them as soon as she opens her eyes. Even before I saw her, I felt the need to do whatever I could in the short time I have today to make her feel cared for. Sitting here, I'm shocked at how vulnerable she looks. I prepared myself for the worst, and she looks better than I thought she would, yet I did not anticipate this vulnerability, this smallness.

Maybe a heart attack, since it was a mild one, will turn out to be a good thing for Mother. She isn't wired for introspection. But perhaps this will force her to ponder the years ahead and quit dreading the idea of retirement and look forward to what life has to offer outside of the four walls of her office—or an equivalent. During one of our semiannual trips to St. Louis a few years ago, I got up in the middle of the night to get a drink and found my mother sitting at her desk, working away on some sort of report.

"Mother!" I said, "you and your computer have got to quit meeting like this!" On my way back to bed a minute later, I bit back a snide question: *Is that computer your best friend?*

I can't say Mother's obsession with work hasn't given her satisfaction, but I've been sitting here praying that from now on Mother's life will be filled with wonder and joy. Satisfaction is good, but joy and wonder are better.

"Kennedy?"

She has opened her eyes, and I walk over and stand beside her bed. "I was saying a prayer for you."

"Well, that's good," she says, trying to smile.

I nod at the table on the other side of her bed. "I brought you flowers."

She turns and sees them in all their glory. "Oh," she says quite spontaneously, and I'm glad I bought the prettiest flowers the gift shop had to offer.

I look around her room. "Can you see them there? I want them where you can see them. They're absolutely the only cheer in this room, Mother."

"Well, that's just not true."

I looked at her doubtfully.

"*You're* here," she says, her voice hardly more than a whisper.

Excuse me? What's in that IV? What have they done with my mother?

I smile. "Yes, I'm here. And after the wedding, I'll come back and stay with you for a few days. Someone needs to make sure you recover properly."

"Oh, Kennedy," she says. "The wedding. I wanted to be there. I wanted it very much."

"I know you did, but you don't need to worry about that right now. The wedding will be recorded. You can watch the DVD with the kids when they return from Hawaii."

"But the dress."

"I'll pick up the dress when I leave here."

"I said I'd bring it."

"And you would have except for a little technicality called a heart attack. I'm just so glad that I can go home and tell Maisey you're going to be fine."

I hear the door open and turn to see Mother's boss standing in the doorway. So she wasn't completely alone. I'm relieved.

"You're awake," he says, smiling at her.

"Phillip," she says, "what are you still doing here?"

He comes into the room and sits down like this is his place. He smiles at me and tells Mother that she can just get used to it, he isn't going anywhere. I look from one to the other and try to process this display of loyalty. Phillip must see something resembling consternation on my face.

"You probably don't know this, Kennedy," he says, "but your mother has been a great friend to me since my wife died three years ago. I'm not sure what I would have done without her friendship."

He shifts his gaze to Mother. "So, Carolyn, you're stuck with me."

"You need to get to the office," she says.

"You're not the boss," he replies. "Besides, the office will get along just fine without us. Weren't we just talking about that last weekend?"

While I listen to their exchange, I notice an envelope on the floor, halfway under her bed. "What's this?" I ask, bending over to get it.

Mother reaches for it. "That's nothing, Kennedy."

I turn it over, surprised to see my name written across the front of it in Mother's neat handwriting. "Well, my goodness, it's *something*, and it has my name on it."

"I wrote you a note in case anything went wrong, but as you can see, it didn't."

"What does it say?"

Mother closes her eyes and sighs. Phillip says he's going to step outside and make a few calls.

"I'm just curious," I say, clutching the envelope, unwilling to relinquish it. So unlike me, to push my mother.

"Open it if you want, Kennedy," she says, fidgeting with the hem of the sheet that covers her.

"I do want." I sit in the chair Phillip has just vacated, slip the note out of the envelope, and unfold it.

> *My dearest Kennedy~*
>
> *I have only a few minutes before I'm taken to surgery. They say I'll be fine, but in case things don't go well after all, I need to tell you something that has been dominating my thoughts these last months: I'm sorry I didn't take you shopping for your wedding dress. I'm sorry for many things we missed. Maybe I failed you as much as your father did, but I hope you believe that I love you, that I have always loved you. You have made my life worthwhile, Kennedy. You are everything I know of joy.*
>
> *Mother*

I am holding a treasure.

I am thankful to be here, thankful I thought to bring lovely flowers, thankful beyond what I can say that my mother has actually written the words *I love you.*

When I gather the courage to look at her, she appears to have fallen back asleep. I stand up and walk over to her bed. Slipping my hand into hers, I bend over and kiss her forehead. "Thank you for this note, Mother. I love you too."

She doesn't open her eyes, but she squeezes my hand,

and I see tears slipping from under her eyelids, dampening her temples.

I reach for a Kleenex and blot her tears. "I'm going to get the dress now," I say. "You rest. I'll see you on Monday."

CHAPTER TWENTY

Maisey

Marcus and I are relaxing after the Dottie and Pete crisis has been taken care of, at least to the extent I *can* relax, knowing that any minute, Mother will surely be home.

Instead it is Dad who opens one of the French doors leading from the kitchen and comes out on the porch. I am relieved until I get a look at his face and know something is terribly wrong.

"I have some bad news," he says.

I hope the bad news is along the lines of Dottie's bad news, relatively easy to fix, but I'm pretty sure it isn't. I'm horrified when he says Gram has had a heart attack. Sheer panic fills me, and I look at Marcus as though he can make it not so. But Dad has good news too. The damage to Gram's heart is minimal and she should recover completely. He consoles us so much that, for one brief, naïve moment, I think she might be able to make it to the wedding after all. But Dad says there is no way that will happen.

Since she is apparently out of danger but unable to come to the wedding, my next concern is my wedding dress, hanging in one of her closets. I need that dress! My mind is racing.

"Dad, if Marcus and I leave for St. Louis right now, we can get the dress and still make it back before everyone starts arriving tomorrow—if you can pick up Sarah in the morning."

"Hold it," Dad says. "That's under control. Your mother has gone to see your gram and to get your dress."

So *that's* where she's been all day.

"When did she go?" I ask.

"She left shortly after you and Marcus left for Indy this morning. She should be back tonight by ten or eleven."

"We could have gone. Why didn't you call us?"

"She wouldn't let me. She wanted you to have a nice day, a calm day. She didn't want you to worry."

"Well, *I* should have gone to see Gram."

Dad looks at me like he can't comprehend my simple sentence. He shakes his head, and for the second time today he seems exasperated with me.

Marcus stands up and walks over to Dad. "Have you heard from Kendy lately?" he asks. "Carolyn is really okay?"

"Yes. Kendy called after she left the hospital and said her mother was doing very well, better than they hoped for."

"That's great," Marcus says.

"When I spoke to Kendy, she was on her way to get the wedding dress. She should be on the road soon."

I sit here while they talk, thinking things are going to be okay: Gram is recovering, my dress is on the way, and Mother will be in so late, I won't have to talk to her. And of course we'll be too busy tomorrow.

Then Dad snatches away the piece of hope I have just picked up and brushed off. He pulls up a chair and sits across from me with a look of resolve on his face that makes it plain this will not be a cheerful chat.

"Your mother will be in late," he says, "but however late it is, you need to be ready to talk to her."

"Good grief, Dad. She'll be exhausted! We can talk after Marcus and I get back from Hawaii. If we even need to. Let's just forget it."

"Like you've forgotten it all these years?"

What is he doing?

I'm not ready to discuss my mother and what I saw in the kitchen so long ago, not with anyone, including him, but here he is, his knees nearly touching mine, and I know there will be no escaping this confrontation. I want to shoot myself for losing it last night. Marcus probably wants to shoot me too. He is heading for the kitchen, but Dad asks him to come back and sit with us. He says that unfortunately Marcus has been made part of this family crisis.

Unable to look at either of them, I study my hands, clasped tightly in my lap.

Dad, I know, is studying *me*, not saying a word—waiting, I finally realize, for the answer to the question he has asked. I had hoped it was rhetorical. Marcus, no doubt about it, will be a mere spectator. He cannot come to my rescue; this is between Dad and me.

Finally I look at my father and answer his question with a question: "Could *you* forget such a thing?"

"No, Maisey, I couldn't. Not in the traditional sense of 'forgetting.' But your mother and I dealt with what happened and then we agreed not to rehearse it. That helped us forget."

"What do you mean?"

"We forgot in the sense that we don't dwell on it or refer to it. We put it out of our minds so it didn't ruin what we had left, which was quite a lot. But what helped most were the verses we memorized from Psalm 103. We rehearsed those truths about God until they became such a part of us that a researcher might be able to isolate them in our DNA."

I begin peeling polish off one of my thumbnails, but he lifts my chin, looks into my eyes, and to my amazement, quotes words not totally unfamiliar to me:

> "For as high as the heavens are above the earth, so great is his love for those who fear him; as far as the east is from the west, so far has he removed our transgressions from us. As a father has compassion on his children, so the Lord has compassion on those who fear him; for he knows how we are formed, he remembers that we are dust."

"Children of dust, Maisey, children of dust. That's not an insult to the human race; it's just a fact. Making mistakes is unavoidable; we are the *created*, not the Creator. But it's also a fact that God loves us, despite our frailty. And it's a fact that life is good when we too choose love and forgiveness."

I close my eyes against his words.

Dad puts his hands over mine and I dare to look at him.

"These are things worth remembering, Maisey—they really are."

I study his strong hands covering mine and say nothing.

"I wish you had told us what you saw," he says, sitting back in his chair.

I'm glad for a little space.

"I wish you had been *able* to tell us," he continues while I return to chipping my nail polish. "Then we could have asked for your forgiveness, and you could have rehearsed this Scripture with us and eventually let go of what hurt you so badly. I really believe that you too would have been able to 'forget.' "

"Wait a minute," I say, looking at him. "Did you say *we*? Hello, Dad, *you* didn't do anything."

"I wasn't without blame."

"Don't say that," I snap. "Really, Dad, just don't say that."

"Both your mom and I have regrets, Maisey. There are many ways to be unfaithful. I also say *we* because your mother and I are 'one.' Just as I hope you and Marcus will be. Even when things aren't perfect."

I roll my eyes.

He leans toward me and grabs my arms. "Stop that! I mean it, Maisey, I don't ever want to see you do that again."

My father has never raised his voice to me. Tears spring to my eyes and slide down my cheeks.

"I'm sorry for yelling at you, honey. I understand you've been hurt, but it kills me to see what the pain has done to your heart, at least as far as your mother is concerned. If you've never heard Psalm 103 before now, I still don't know how it's possible you grew up in this house without learning the necessity of forgiveness. It is the most basic tenet of life in God. He is merciful and desires for us to be. Your mother and I brag on your kindness to others, but why is it you have not extended that kindness to the one who gave you life at great cost and has loved you always—deeply and completely?"

"Always?"

I push back my chair, stand up, and look past him at the field beyond the pool. In the dusk, I fix my gaze on the tree line in the distance, trying to isolate the oak that holds the tree house he once built me.

He stands up too and gathers me in his arms. "Maisey, Maisey, what have you done?"

What have *I* done? *Maize is a-maz-ing,* he used to say.

I can't take any more. Pulling away from him, I run to my room.

I hardly realize I'm grabbing a bathing suit from my dresser drawer when Marcus comes in, asking if I'm okay.

"What do you think?" I say.

"Your dad is going to get a pizza; he insists on feeding me. Do you want to come?"

"Are you kidding? I'm going to swim until I sink. But please, you go. I want you to."

I begin swimming laps before they leave. I don't stop until I have only enough energy to pull myself up the steps and collapse in this lounger. Shortly after I dove in, Marcus brought out my pink chenille robe. In my peripheral vision I saw him put it on the table. "You might need this," I think he said. It has been a hot day, and needing that robe seemed a long shot, but I'm finding it terribly comforting at the moment. I hope they're gone awhile. For the first time in my life I don't want to see my dad.

Sitting here, wrapped in a fluffy, warm robe, I think of

Mother driving home alone from St. Louis with my wedding dress. I'm sure it was nice of her to go, but I would have gone. I would rather have been driving home from St. Louis than listening to Dad's sermon. It was so crazy to hear him ask *me* what I've been silently asking my mother for so many years: *What have you done?*

I know why people say they want to drop off the face of the earth.

And I'd figure out a way to do just that, for maybe a year or two, except there's a wedding in two days and I cannot stand up a man who brings me a robe to wrap up in on a warm July evening. Or would I be doing him a favor? Maybe on their drive to town, Dad's telling Marcus to pack up and head for the hills this very minute, that he'll handle the almost insurmountable problems associated with canceling a wedding at this late date.

Oh, dear God, help us.

I need to get inside and up the stairs before Marcus and Dad come home. I want to hide for a while.

When I was a girl, Mother taught me to call God by many names. All of them have come to my aid through the years, but some of them seem perfect for what I need most tonight: Refuge, Rock, Shield—a Hiding Place.

They used to sing an old hymn in the "big" church when I was in Wee Church and came upstairs to sit with Mom and Dad on family Sundays. We usually sang all the verses, and even though when I was so young I didn't know what some of the lines meant, I loved to hear the congregation sing the song, especially the chorus:

> *He hideth my soul in the cleft of the rock*
> *That shadows a dry, thirsty land;*

He hideth my life in the depths of his love,
And covers me there with his hand,
And covers me there with his hand.

I lean my head against the back of the lounger and look up into a darkening sky. "Please, God, would you hide me in the depths of your love? Would you cover me with your hand?"

I close my eyes, and from somewhere in the night, I think I hear, *I will.*

Kendy

What happened to the sun? And are those drops of rain on the windshield?

I look into the rearview mirror for the tenth time. It is such a relief to see Maisey's dress hanging securely on a hook, spread across the back seat.

It's coming, Maisey.

She's right. The dress is beautiful.

So was my wedding dress, of course, but a contrast to hers, tight only in the waist with a skirt full, light, and billowy. I loved it as much as Maisey loves hers. When I slipped the dress on the evening of my wedding and swished down the aisle, it was beyond imagining that I would ever betray my husband. Wouldn't it be nice if this Saturday were my wedding day, instead of Maisey's? Wouldn't it be nice to begin again and somehow avoid any heartbreaking mistakes?

Beginning again wouldn't interest Luke. He likes where we are now, or maybe I should say, *who* we are, what we have. He says mistakes are part of living. "Children of dust," he calls us quite tenderly, whether he's dropped one of my china plates or has told me about an employee arrested for embezzlement. His favorite hymn is "O Worship the King." I remember standing and singing that anthem the Sunday I could finally believe emotional and spiritual healing were a possibility. A poet had given us words to express our thoughts, including the last verse:

> *Frail children of dust, and feeble as frail,*
> *In thee do we trust, nor find thee to fail;*
> *Thy mercies how tender, how firm to the end!*
> *Our Maker, Defender, Redeemer, and Friend.*

One of my favorite Christian artists has an updated version of this hymn with a contemporary chorus added. I like it, but I was surprised this last verse didn't include "frail children of dust." I was rather disappointed and wondered why other words were chosen to replace these. Were the original words too archaic? The alternate words speak of God's "ineffable love" and are certainly beautiful, perhaps part of the original poem. But I've wondered if even we Christians are pluralistic at times—knowing we need a savior but refusing to believe or say we are truly needy; willing to be God's beloved children but unwilling to admit we are children with much to learn— and not the omnipotent, all-knowing Father.

At least the last lines are intact. His mercies *are* tender and firm to the end. And don't I love those names for God? Maker, Defender, Redeemer, Friend. I was restored to emotional and spiritual health because he is those things and more.

Which came first? Confessing to my husband or repenting before the Lord? I'm not sure I can remember. They seem rather interwoven. Both took place on the patio in the spring sunshine that was tending me.

But it is logical that repentance came first.

On Easter Sunday I had returned to church, not as an obligation but as an act of worship. The following Sunday our minister began a series of four sermons on the book of Psalms. I don't doubt the timing was a gift from a good and generous God.

The sermon on David's psalms of repentance resonated so deeply within me that for weeks I devoured those psalms and the others David wrote, as well as the books that record David's life. Reading them was a balm for my wounded heart.

David adored God, but he was still capable of committing terrible sins. Even before my crisis, I had read Psalm 51 and wondered why David had said to God, "Against you, you only, have I sinned." He had obviously sinned against Bathsheba and Uriah too. But during this quest for understanding, I began to make sense of his statement. Bathsheba and Uriah weren't his Creator and Sustainer; they had not protected and honored and loved him; they were not the subjects of countless pleas and as many outbursts of praise in David's poetry.

The psalms of repentance are full of lament. It seems to me that people respond in a variety of ways to sin and the suffering that comes with it. But only one who loves deeply wrote Psalms 6, 32, 38, and 51. And I like to think that only one who loves deeply can be so affected by them.

I do not look back with regret on the afternoon I sat on my lounger with my Bible in my lap and became vulnerable before God, like David, sharing intimately and honestly, because I no longer doubted he would hear me in his "unfailing love."

Those were good days.

But bad days were not over.

I was ready to think about returning to work, and Luke

came home one day, excited to tell me that he had run into Clay and that he had told him a third-grade position had opened up at my former elementary school. My hesitation puzzled Luke. He was further confused when I told him I had already applied at two districts farther away and had interviews at both schools scheduled for the next week.

"Well, sweetheart, you can cancel them," he said.

Without any warning, the moment had come to break his heart.

"Sit down, Luke," I said.

He pulled a chair over and slid into it, his legs stretched out in front of him.

"What?" he asked. He couldn't have been more unsuspecting. I'm sure he thought the worst days were behind us.

Nothing, I wanted to say. *Nothing at all*. But I could not escape saying a terrible something.

"I would give anything if I didn't have to tell you this," I said.

I took a deep breath. What words would be sufficient for this hateful work? And even if they came to me, how could I possibly utter them aloud?

He jerked out of his slouch and sat up straight. "Good grief, Kendy. Just say it. What could be so difficult?"

Can laughter be both logical and also utterly insane? *Be calm*, I told myself. *Hysteria will not help*.

"My depression," I began, "or desperation, as I've come to think of it, didn't happen just because I lost our baby boy, though that was certainly the catalyst for it. But something else contributed to it."

I paused and took another deep breath. "Just say it," Luke had said.

"I can't return to my old school because I became *much* too close to Clay."

That's how I put it. I looked at him when I said it, and I said it slowly and deliberately. I wanted him to understand what I was saying, but I very much wanted not to say it any more specifically, not unless he made me. I so hoped my few words and my eyes had said all he needed to know.

"What do you mean? What's *too* close, Kendy?"

I put my head down. I searched for words, but there were none I could possibly say.

Luke grabbed my hand. "Look at me. Tell me."

From somewhere came an answer to an unspoken prayer—I was given the ability to look up and meet his eyes, the ability to speak. "We spent a lot of time together, Luke. A lot of time alone."

I wondered for a moment if he understood what I was implying, and then I saw in his face that he did. He stood up and turned away from me, studying the field he had mowed only yesterday, when he thought he had a faithful wife, incapable of any kind of disloyalty. He looked away from me while the full impact of my words finally detonated, destroying the world he had known. Then he sat back down again, or I suppose it is more accurate to say he collapsed.

"We mainly talked," I said.

"Mainly."

"Yes."

"And what does that mean?"

Mercy.

I took a deep breath and let it out again.

"It means he's kissed me. We've kissed each other. I guess

you could say we've made out—which sounds so stupid. It *was* stupid."

He sat on the edge of his chair, elbows on his knees, hands clasped. He looked at his hands, not me.

"Made out?" He was incredulous.

"We didn't have sex—technically—if that matters. But I thought I loved him, Luke, and I know what a betrayal that is. I loved you too, or I like to think that. But of course I wasn't thinking of you at all during that time, or it wouldn't have happened."

He closed his eyes. Was he trying to make everything I'd said go away? To make *me* go away?

"What I allowed makes me sick," I said, "because I *do* love you. I'm so sorry it happened. And I'm sorry that saying so helps so little."

Did we sit there with tears brimming in our eyes for days? Or was it only minutes until he finally got up and walked into the house, leaving me with the task of trying to breathe, leaving me with only a plea in my heart that God would somehow help my husband.

Nine years later, thinking about it still makes me sick. Can I rate the worst moments of my life? I do believe I could come up with a top ten list. Until Maisey's anguish erupted so violently at the dinner table last night, the number-one worst moment of my life by far was the afternoon I told Luke I had been unfaithful.

I'm in the middle of Illinois, driving farther and farther into what is now a horrible storm. Frightening black clouds met me when I drove across the Illinois state line, and now my windshield wipers can't keep up with the torrents of rain. Unable to see the lines on the road, I pull over and park under an overpass, hazard lights blinking. I stare out my windshield at the apt image. Nature, smiling with me earlier at Mother's good news, is now weeping with me. She is sobbing.

I dig in my purse for a Kleenex and press number two on my speed dial, hoping for a connection.

"Hello," Luke says.

"It's me," I say. "I'm driving through terrible weather."

"I can barely hear you."

I move the phone closer to my mouth, but I can't do anything about the downpour and the rumble of thunder. "Is this better?"

"Some. There are tornado warnings all over Illinois, Kendy. Marcus and I have been watching the Weather Channel. It's beginning to get bad here too. You need to get off the road."

"I suppose. I'm tired anyway. Really tired. I saw a sign for Effingham just before I pulled over. I'll stop there for the night."

"Be careful, and call when you're in a room."

"I will."

"Are you crying? You sound like you're crying."

"It's just . . . I'm so close, Luke. I want to come home. I could have been there in two hours."

"I know, but it really is too dangerous."

"Okay. I'm just being silly."

"Call me when you are in a room," he says.

I slide my phone into a pocket in my purse and tell myself there's nothing to cry about.

But last night Luke and I lay in the same bed with too much distance between us, and tonight this storm has caused a literal separation.

My memories have made that unbearable.

CHAPTER TWENTY-ONE

Maisey

Marcus has gone to bed, so the knock on my door is probably Dad.

He opens the door and peeks in.

"You're not asleep, are you?" he asks, though he can see perfectly well that my light is on and that I'm sitting up in bed looking at a *People* magazine.

"Your mom has run into bad weather," he says, "and she's spending the night in Effingham, Illinois. She and your dress won't be here until sometime tomorrow morning."

"Okay," I say.

He turns to leave, and in spite of the reprieve I've just been granted, my heart is heavy.

"I'm sorry, Dad," I say, stopping him before he makes it to the door.

"Sorry for what, Maize?"

"Sorry I've disappointed you."

He smiles. "I'm quite sure your mother would like to have made the same apology to you. We all disappoint those we love at some point, don't you think?"

"Children of dust?" I say, wanting to assure him I heard his lecture, even if I hadn't exactly appreciated it.

"All of us." He comes back to my bed and kisses my forehead. "Sleep in peace, honey."

He is gone, but the words remain.

Sleep in peace. He has borrowed the phrase from Mother. One of the most memorable times she used it was the night of Caitlin's party. After my parents had told me I was grounded for an entire month, Mother came to my bedroom.

"Asleep?" she asked.

I didn't say anything, hoping she'd think I was, but she came in despite my silence, sat beside me on the bed, and brushed my hair away from my forehead. "You know," she said, as though she had no doubt I was awake, "I have a favorite wish for you, Maisey. Actually, it's a prayer. I pray that you'll live each day so that you can always sleep in peace."

She sat there a minute before she stood up, kissed the top of my head, walked to my door, and shut it quietly behind her. That was the night I almost told her what had been bothering me for so long. I had the perfect opening: *Have you always slept in peace, Mother?*

I wonder what she would have said.

I set the magazine on my bedside table. I'd really like to go to sleep so that this day can be over. This is a night for visiting weird places, and I don't like it.

I get up, walk across the hall, and tap on Marcus's door. Nothing. I open the door and hear his soft, even breathing. At least someone is sleeping in peace.

I return to my bed, already heading for another weird place. Next stop, the third grade, when a girl at church accused me of stealing her purse.

I wonder if she has quit making groundless accusations. After she had involved our teacher and every kid in junior church in the stolen purse caper, she found her pink patent leather purse sitting on a bookshelf where movies were kept. My theory is she put it there while she was playing foosball after our Bible lesson was over. But instead of apologizing for her slander, she said I stashed it there when I realized I'd been caught.

From the first false accusation until the last, I cried tears of anger, frustration, and embarrassment. Mother took one look at me when I came upstairs to the main auditorium and said I looked mad enough to spit nails.

Dad was on a business trip that weekend, so while Mother and I hurried to the car, I gave her a blow-by-blow account of what had happened in the church basement. "It was so unfair, Mom!" I wailed as we buckled ourselves in. I said this before I remembered that my mother had forbidden me ever to say the all-purpose phrase "That's not fair!" She always said, "A good many things in life aren't fair, so deal with it!"

But this time, as she pulled her car into the street, she let it go, which shocked me. She shocked me even more when she said she didn't blame me for being so mad, and she absolutely astounded me when she drove around the block like an Indy race-car driver, shouting, "Hold on to your seat, Maisey. I'm gonna find that girl and run right over the little liar!" That made me scream and laugh all at the same time, because my mother wouldn't run over anyone or anything. She cringed and cried the day she hit a squirrel that ran in front of her car, even though it jumped up and staggered away.

But of course my accuser was nowhere to be found, and Mother wasn't really looking for her at all; she was looking for a parking place. This talk couldn't wait until we got home. She parked under a shade tree in an empty parking lot, slipped off her seat belt, and turned to smile at me. Her smile, along with all the craziness, calmed me somewhat.

"I know what happened was unfair, honey," she said. "And borderline cruel. But I doubt anyone really thought you stole the girl's purse. Regardless, you need to forgive her. You need to forgive her for your sake, because bitterness will eat you alive. You need to forgive her for the sake, because she needs absolving and Jesus has shown us the glory of that. And you need to forgive her for the sake of the kids in Junior Church, because one of the last things Jesus prayed for was unity. We can't be divisive, Maisey. We just can't."

I could almost hear angels singing in the background, and I knew Mother was right. What I didn't know was how I was ever going to be able to forgive a girl who would make such an accusation.

I asked Mother if she had ever had to forgive something hard. That's when she told me about her dad. "So," I said when she started the car again and headed for home, "if he ever calls you and wants to see you, will you let him?"

"I don't think that's going to happen, Maisey, but if it does, yes, I'll see him. Actually, I wish something would transform his heart so drastically that he would want to do such a thing—for his sake."

"Have you ever had to forgive anything else that was hard?"

"Not really," she said.

We drove in silence a few minutes before she said, "Well, that's not exactly true. I've had to forgive your gram for a few things."

"Like what?"

"Like not going with me to pick out my wedding dress."

"Oh my," I said, sitting beside her that day.

Tonight, Dad's question won't leave me alone: "What have you done?"

Something terrible, I suppose. One of the worst things I've done may be this: buying my wedding dress without Mother.

What other horrible places must I visit before sleep will come?

No need to ask—I know exactly where I'm going.

When Mother lost the baby and went to her room, part of me was glad I didn't have to see her, but it comes to me now that part of me was destitute. I remember the snowy afternoon Dad and I watched a show on the National Geographic Channel about moose. They can stand six feet at the shoulder and weigh as much as eighteen hundred pounds, and those antlers should be one of the wonders of the world. I wanted Dad to take me to Yellowstone or Alaska to see one until the documentary explained what happens to a one-year-old moose. It seems like a moose has a baby every year, and when the female gets pregnant with the new baby, she drives away the one still by her side. Sometimes she does this quite forcefully. We watched as the yearling tried to come back to his mother, and I stood up in horror when she chased him back across the creek again. He was left to face the world alone. I wanted to cry for the poor thing. All he wanted was his mother back, but all the wanting in the world wasn't going to make it happen—a new baby was on the way.

I understood his longing.

I wanted my mother back too. Oh, how I wanted her back. But so much was in the way. Her disloyalty to Dad infuriated me, and her betrayal of our code of ethics sickened me. And now I have to wonder if I was both infuriated and sickened when she abandoned me for a baby who had died before he lived.

So, I'm sorry, Dad. I'm sure I did grow up knowing the necessity of forgiveness, but I have just not been willing to forgive these things hidden so long and so deep in my heart.

What *have* I done?

Is it my mother's sin I have paid for? Or is it my own?

Kendy

Neon *No Vacancy* signs fill the night sky.

I finally find a place to stay, but by the time I make it from the parking lot to my room, I am drenched. This is why I have left Maisey's dress locked in the car. I fervently hope there isn't a size 6 woman out in the storm, gripping a crowbar and looking in car windows for the perfect wedding dress.

I'm grateful the young man at the desk gave me a toothbrush and a tiny tube of toothpaste. I hope the flimsy thing will make it through two brushings. I towel dry my hair and hang my jeans, blazer, and bra on the shower rod, asking them to be dry by seven o'clock tomorrow morning, eight at the latest. My damp T-shirt is subbing for sleepwear—call me uncomfortable.

After checking in with Luke per instructions, I read Psalm 103, using it as a prayer, really. I often begin my prayers like the psalmist: "Praise the Lord, O my soul; all my inmost being, praise his holy name."

Then the thanksgiving begins. "Thank you for removing our sins as far as the east is from the west. Thank you for healing me, for crowning me with love and compassion, for giving me so many good things, for renewing my strength like the eagle's."

After praise and thanksgiving come petitions, of course. Mother needs physical healing, Maisey needs emotional healing, I need strength and wisdom, and Luke . . . what does Luke need? Comfort? What else? Well, I'm not quite sure, but God knows. I have many petitions before my prayer time is over. Needy, that's what the lot of us are. But I'm trying to remember what God has shown me time and time again: He is able to provide. We have this recurring dialogue: *I can't*, I say. He says, *But I can*.

I close my little Bible, snap it, and put it back in my purse. Then, knowing what an incredibly busy and stressful day tomorrow will be, I turn out the light, anxious to get to sleep.

When I called Luke earlier, I told him again how exhausted I am, and he told me to get a good night's sleep. I said I'd like to, that I need to, but the prospect seemed unlikely.

Those words were a self-fulfilling prophecy. Here I lie—eyes burning, body weary, soul aching, and wide-awake. Call me wretched.

I suppose that's a slight exaggeration.

Wretched is more fitting for how I felt the days after I told Luke about Clay and me. When I finally went into the house, he had left a note on the kitchen table saying he was going back to Indy to help his dad. I hadn't heard him leave. Help his dad with what? I didn't dare call and ask.

Whatever they were doing, it was so late when they finished that he spent the night with his parents. When he got home from work the following day, we talked to Maisey but not to each other and hoped Maisey didn't notice.

When it was time for bed, I asked him if he'd like me to sleep in the guest room.

"Yes," he said, "I think I would. But we don't have that luxury."

He said Maisey had been through enough in the last year; she didn't need any more worries. So for her sake, we slept in the same bed, but we didn't touch each other, not once. Luke's pain and my fear made sure of it.

This went on for two wretched weeks.

Then he came home early one afternoon and walked outside, where I lay stretched out on the lounger, dozing behind my sunglasses.

"Okay," he said, and I stirred.

"Here's the deal," he added.

"*Okay?*" I asked, removing my sunglasses and placing them on top of my head. I couldn't quite comprehend that Luke was standing beside me on this weekday afternoon speaking to me at all, much less saying, "Okay, here's the deal."

"You're changing schools, so I'm making some changes too."

He pulled a chair up and sat down facing me. "I'm moving home."

"What?"

"I'm moving my office to the house and going into the Indy

office once or twice a week. Partners have their privileges. I have a lot of clients on this side of Indy anyway. But that's not the point. The point is I've missed out on too much. That's going to stop."

I was stunned.

"I hate what's happened, Kendy, hate it. But I love you."

I couldn't believe what I was hearing.

"I've been doing a lot of thinking, and I've concluded you've had every right to think I love my job more than I love you."

This I wouldn't listen to.

"Don't, Luke. Don't even think about taking any blame for this."

"I'm not justifying what you've done. But I am saying I've made choices that have hurt you too."

I closed my eyes and asked a silent question: *Did you leave me for a snow globe world?*

He stood up, scooted me over, and sat beside me on the lounger. "Now," he said, "I'm going over to see Clay. I'm going to tell him you won't be taking the third-grade job opening in his district, and I'm going to tell him why. Are you okay with that?"

"Yes. But what about Rebecca?"

"Rebecca's working. This is between Clay and me."

He was gone for over an hour, and when he returned, he began turning the study into a home office, and by Tuesday of the following week it was completed. That night he made love to me for the first time since my horrible confession, and when he did, he made it undeniably clear that I was his and he was mine.

He never told me what he and Clay said to each another. But Clay and Rebecca changed churches and had a series of obligations that kept them from the next few family gatherings. The following summer, however, Luke called and asked Clay and Rebecca to come to the party we were hosting for Miller and Anne's fortieth anniversary. They shouldn't miss that, he said.

We've had more than our share of happiness since the day he came home early and showed me restoration is possible not only with God but with mere mortals as well, at least with those who belong to and listen to and rely on God.

Did last night jeopardize restoration and the happiness that accompanies it? I hope we can survive Maisey's pain and outrage.

The storm has subsided, for which I am grateful. I look at the clock, see it is midnight, plump my pillow, and roll over, determined to sleep.

I'm not making any progress when I hear a knock on the door.

"Kendy!"

I know that voice. He has braved the storm though he didn't want me to. Throwing back the covers, I run to the door.

"Nice outfit," Luke says when I let him in.

He's carrying a small suitcase and an overnight bag. "I thought you might need some things."

He has brought a nightgown, clean clothes for tomorrow, a hair dryer and straightening iron, and my makeup down to the three kinds of eye shadows I tend to use.

I tell him I'm thrilled with everything.

He picks me up and takes me to the bed, saying he has no idea why he bothered packing the nightgown.

FRIDAY

CHAPTER TWENTY-TWO

Kendy

Fueled up and ready to go. That would be both the car and me.

I wanted to grab a cup of coffee and a doughnut at the convenience store where we got gas, but Luke insisted on a sit-down breakfast fit for two lumberjacks instead of two people marching down an aisle to give away a daughter tomorrow. Once the stack of buttermilk pancakes and three lovely strips of crisp bacon were placed in front of me, however, I put all hesitancy aside, drenched them in butter and syrup, and ate every bite. Luke said he was glad to see it. Both of us knew why: This day will require an inordinate amount of energy.

For this same reason, he didn't set the alarm last night, which allowed us to sleep much later than I intended.

We have just started for home in our separate vehicles when Paula calls at ten, saying she tried to time her call just right—after we had time to get ready and eat a decent breakfast, but before everyone began arriving. She tried the house for fifteen minutes before giving up and calling my cell.

"You had to call my cell," I say, "because I'm almost two hours away from home. And I'm glad you called. Would you mind going over to the house to wait for any Blairs who show up early while Maisey retrieves Sarah from the airport?"

"Okay, what's going on?" she says, sounding a tad miffed.

"Plenty," I say.

"What?"

"You really don't have to go to the house. I doubt Marcus went with Maisey to pick up Sarah; he probably hasn't gone far. Besides, the Blair gang shouldn't begin arriving before lunch; at least that's the plan. And they won't be at the house long. According to Luke, they're dropping off a dog—long story—getting Marcus, and heading to the inn."

"Where are you? This is just crazy."

"You have no idea," I say.

So as I-70 stretches out in front of me, I tell Paula about Mother and then give her a summarized version of what happened with Maisey. Several things that have upset Paula through the years should make a little more sense now.

"I can't believe it," she says.

"It's really too horrible, Paula, to take understatement to the absurd."

"Why didn't you call me?"

"I didn't have time."

"Kendy, you had the five-hour trip to St. Louis and the three hours back to Effingham."

"True. Maybe what I didn't have was the wherewithal. The weather was horrendous on the trip home, which is why I stopped in Effingham, and as far as the drive *to* St. Louis—I was lost in a time warp. Since Wednesday night I think I've relived every traumatic experience I've had since birth—I even dragged my father into it before I was through. You know?"

"I can imagine. I wish you had called before you left yesterday so I could have gone with you."

"I didn't have time to think it through; I just had to get there. I think I needed to be alone for a while anyway. Besides, when Luke showed up last night, I was quite glad no one else was there. No offense."

"Fortunately for you, I'm not easily offended."

"Just one reason I love you so much."

"So, what can I do to help you through this day?"

"Pray."

"Count on it. What else?"

"That should do it."

"Listen," she says, "if you have time to kill before the rehearsal dinner, I'm there on the patio with my hat and sunglasses, soaking up some last-minute sun with you."

She makes me smile.

After we disconnect, I call Mother. Phillip answers and says Mother's doing fine. The doctors are in the room talking with her, so I ask Phillip to tell her I'll be thinking of her even during the wedding rush and that I'll be at her apartment Monday afternoon.

The one person I can't call right now is Maisey. And while that makes me sad, I'm trying to remember that I have a lot to feel good about this morning: Paula is a friend who sticks closer than the brother or sister I never had; Mother is doing well, and a letter tucked in the outside pocket of my purse says in black-and-white that she loves me, that I am her *joy*, for goodness' sake; and despite the convoy of semitrucks on the road today, I have a tenacious husband following me so closely I can see him, along with Maisey's wedding dress, every time I look in my rearview mirror.

These things and almost nonstop prayers have given me courage. I need courage. Luke has talked to Maisey, and I'm glad, but now she and I must talk, and too many things can keep that from happening. I'm quite sure Maisey will jump at any chance to avoid speaking with me.

Dear God, that's what she's been doing for years, isn't it? And now, at long last, I finally know the real reason why. I'm not surprised Maisey blew up Wednesday night. Did we really expect her to come into my dark bedroom nine years ago, curl up beside me in my comatose state, and sweetly ask, "Why were you kissing Uncle Clay last week?" And when would have been a good time to say something? What words could she have used to tell me what she saw and how she felt about it?

She finally found some Wednesday night, didn't she?

"I *hate* you!"

It is quite tempting to relegate to my subconscious her hurtful words and the look of contempt and rage on her beautiful face when she shrieked them at me. But I have no time for that. Instead I've been taking them out and looking at them from all angles. I've been asking God to help me think right. I've been asking him to finally let me hear what has been so hard for my daughter to say.

Maisey

"Wake up—it's your last full day to be Maisey Anne Laswell!"

I cannot believe it! Jackie has jumped into the middle of my bed, shouting this command with no restraint whatsoever.

Using both hands, I jerk the pillow from beneath my head and cover my face with it, a shield from her enthusiasm.

"Hey," she says, grabbing the pillow and holding it out of my reach, "aren't you glad to see me?"

"I can't see *anything*," I say, squinting in her direction. "What are you doing here?"

"I told you. We're having a moment. One I didn't exactly plan. But when I woke up this morning, I just knew I should get over here so we could have this special time together. After today, our lives will never be the same, Maize. That's a big deal and—surprise, surprise—I'm aware of it!"

"How'd you get in here?"

"Well, your house is practically deserted. No one came to the door when I rang the bell, so I used the keypad on the garage to let myself in."

Big mistake, giving her that code.

She jumps up and opens the blinds, flooding the room with light.

"Maybe you'd like to throw cold water on me while you're at it," I groan.

"Don't even try to act like you're not touched by this grand gesture," she says.

The time for sleeping is beyond retrieving, so I get up to wash my face and brush my teeth. When I return to the bedroom, she is sitting on the bed, waiting impatiently for me. She wants to know what I did yesterday, and I join her on the bed, sitting cross-legged as I fill her in, leaving out the parts about my fight with everyone Wednesday night and the talks with Dad yesterday. But I do tell her about Gram's heart attack and Mother's being somewhere in Illinois with my dress.

"Wait a minute!" she says. "If your gram isn't coming, does that mean my bedroom will be vacant tonight?"

I don't follow.

"*My* bedroom," she says, pointing across the landing.

"Oh, I guess it will."

"So, Sarah and I can stay here instead of the apartment. Is that not perfect?"

Marcus comes through the open door then, looking as sleep-logged and dumbfounded as I must have looked when Jackie landed on my bed a few minutes earlier.

"Hey, big boy, don't look so disappointed to see me," Jackie says, glancing in his direction. "I know you didn't come in here to spoil your record with only one night to go."

I knock her off my bed.

Marcus helps her up, saying he is glad to see her and that I talk too much. Then the three of us traipse downstairs to find something to eat, surprised that Dad isn't already stirring up something. The kitchen is eerily empty. "Where do you suppose Dad is?" I ask even as Marcus reaches for an envelope leaning against the bowl of lemons on the table. He hands it to me.

"This is becoming a habit," I say. I read the short note aloud: " 'I've gone to be with your mom. We should be back by noon tomorrow. Have a good morning. Love you—Dad.' "

"Well, that's good for your mom," Jackie says, "but bad for us."

"We're college graduates," Marcus says. "We'll come up with something to eat."

"No problem," Jackie says, "Maisey's a chef."

Marcus looks at me. "True."

Chef or no chef, I allow Marcus to fry the bacon, and that, along with cereal and fruit, constitutes breakfast. Then Marcus sends Jackie and me upstairs. "Chat," he says, "while I clean the kitchen so well Kendy will think we went out for breakfast."

Jackie and I have almost two hours together before I have to leave for the airport.

"Come with me," I say as we stand by my car in the driveway.

"No can do," Jackie says. "I have things to do. You've had a shower; I haven't. I've got to do something with myself. One of my good friends is having a wedding rehearsal and dinner tonight, you know."

"Oh, well, get on it, then."

"Besides, the drive from Indy may be the only time you have to spend with Sarah one-on-one."

"You're sweet," I say. "Really sweet."

"Tell me something I don't know," she says, waving and heading for her car.

I get in my own car, thinking how glad I am Jackie showed up so early this morning. She startled me awake before the daisies around my window frame could mock me with their cheerfulness. Or worse, rebuke me with their mere presence.

"Here's what I envision," Mom said a month before my twelfth birthday. She had finished tucking me in, but instead of turning out the light, she had scooted me over to lie beside me.

To envision something sounded rather exciting.

I sat up and looked at her. "What?"

"We probably should have done it before now. Last year at least, when you started fifth grade."

"What?"

She patted my pillow so I would lie down again. "Don't you think it's past time for the teddy bears to go?"

I'd always liked the border—groups of bears in their pastel frocks, dancing in a conga line. But I was rather tired of pink, and now that Mom mentioned it, I *was* ready for something more grown-up.

"So what do you 'envision'?" I asked.

"Golden yellow walls," she said. "*Maize* yellow, to be exact."

"Like bananas?"

"Like the sun."

"Like yield signs?"

"And the tassels topping a field of ripened corn."

"And school buses."

"Like the center of a daisy," she said, kissing the tip of my nose.

With that one, she won.

"That, in fact, is part of my plan," she said. "If you approve, of course."

Several weeks later she had gathered everything she needed for the transformation. "It'll be done for your birthday," she said.

We moved the furniture to the center of the room, taped off the woodwork and ceiling, and laid down plastic tarps on the carpet. Mom did the bulk of the painting, especially the trim, but I rolled the middle of the walls, and we agreed the golden yellow paint was much more suitable than pink paint and teddy bears for a girl only one year away from becoming a teenager.

"Yet it's cheerful," Mom said. "Perfect for your personality."

What made it really pretty, though, were the daisies. Jackie said they were "just too much," the exact thing she would expect for Spoiley Girl's room. We sat on my bed all morning and watched Mom stencil the white daisies with their green stems and leaves all around the white frames of my two windows. When she was finished we took a lunch break before she went upstairs and put up my white valances and handed me pillows to put on my white bedspread—two square yellow ones and a green one shaped like an *M* and sprinkled with yellow polka dots.

"Finally," Mom said, pulling something huge from under my bed, "the *pièce de résistance*!"

"The what?"

"The main and best thing," Mom said. "Well, of course I think the daisies are the *best* thing, but, Maisey, I think you'll enjoy these." On the wall where the door is, she hung two big bulletin boards, long rectangles trimmed with white frames. "You can put up whatever you want—posters, pictures, memorabilia."

"Mem-o-ra-bilia?" Jackie mouthed when Mom looked away to straighten one of the boards.

"There," Mom said when everything was finished. "What do you think?"

"I love it," I said.

That night when she turned out my light and said, "Sleep tight, don't let the bedbugs bite," I told her the bedbugs said they hadn't appreciated all the commotion, but they thought my room was adorable, a perfect place to hang out.

And in the morning when I woke up, I saw the daisies and remembered Mom rocking me when I was little, singing in her soft, soothing voice, "My sweet girl Maisey is more darling than a daisy."

Kendy

Marcus has gone to the store and picked up ingredients for a chef's salad and has it ready when we pull into the driveway just after noon. None of us wants more than that, knowing Dottie has planned quite a nice dinner at the inn for after the rehearsal.

"Maisey picked up Sarah at eleven," Marcus says. "They stopped to eat at a Chinese place in Indy. Apparently Sarah was starving."

We are sitting at the kitchen table, which is a little awkward. We haven't gathered here since Wednesday night, when the four of us were caught in the whirlwind of Maisey's pain.

While we eat, Luke and I fill Marcus in on the events of the last twenty-four hours, and now we are sitting here for no other reason than we don't want to get up. After a short, silent prayer for courage, I broach the subject of Wednesday night, or at least allude to it.

"I hope I get a chance to talk to Maisey today."

Luke collects our plates and puts them in the sink, refills our glasses.

"I do too, Kendy," Marcus says.

"But *you're* here now," I say, reaching over to pat his hand. "So let me tell you how sorry I am that you have been drawn into this family crisis. I'm sorrier, of course, for the poor choices I made nine years ago that have led to it. But by God's grace,

Luke and I have moved past that sad chapter of our lives. Unfortunately, we had no idea what Maisey had seen, no idea what she has been dealing with all these years."

Marcus leans over and kisses my cheek. "Things will be better now, Kendy."

This thoughtful gesture takes me by surprise, and I tear up and smile at the same time. "I hope so, Marcus, I really hope so."

I send Luke and Marcus out to shoot baskets, saying it will be a good way for them to pass the time while they wait for the other members of the Blair clan to show up. Marcus says he needs the practice. Meanwhile, I clean up the kitchen, my specialty. The effects of Marcus's kiss linger, delighting me, comforting me, and imbuing my solitary task with grace. I am happy, even in my distress, because whatever else happens, Maisey is marrying a man overflowing with admirable qualities, not the least of which is mercy. Once again I count Marcus among my best blessings.

I barely finish in the kitchen and unpack the two little bags Luke carried in from my car when the first Blair brother arrives. By two o'clock they are all here, and Pete the dog is safely deposited in the "guesthouse." I'm not sure Dottie is entirely happy with the accommodations, but Doug, Marcus's dad, assures her the dog will be fine, and she puts a smile on her face, gives Pete three dog biscuits, and tells him she'll see him soon. Doug shakes his head, and Marcus laughs.

They're here short of an hour when Maisey and Sarah arrive. Marcus, coming downstairs with his things, puts everything down and hugs Sarah and then Maisey.

"Are you going already?" she asks.

Then because Maisey has arrived, everyone congregates

back on the porch with another round of sodas and tea and discusses the matters at hand for Marcus and Maisey: the rehearsal, the dinner, the wedding ceremony, the honeymoon, and their immediate plans on their return. But before long, Dottie stands up and says they need to get settled in the inn so that she can make necessary preparations in the room reserved for the rehearsal dinner.

We stand in the driveway, waving, saying we'll see them at the church at six. When the five cars pull out of the driveway, silence seems to fill the earth, or at least our five acres of it.

Maisey breaks the silence.

"Do you mind if I take Sarah over to Jackie's for a while?"

"Don't you want to check on your dress first?" I ask. The first thing I did when we arrived home was to take it upstairs and hang it in her closet.

"We won't be gone long," she says. "I'm sure my dress is fine. You and Gram made certain of that. Thanks for going to get it, Mother. But I left Sarah's dress at Jackie's, and I really do want to make sure the hem is right on it. Jackie's mom said she could take care of any last-minute alterations if I got it to her today."

What can I say, especially with Sarah standing here?

"Fine. Tell Jackie hi. Be safe."

And they are off.

Luke is too, cleaning up e-mails and returning calls during this lull. Not much left to do before we meet at the church. I, having chosen the patio over the chaise in my room, am sitting here trying not to brood. I don't know when I thought Maisey and I would have time to talk.

"Hey," Paula says. "I took a chance."

I look up and see her standing beside me, wearing her sunglasses and hat and holding a water bottle.

"I'm glad you did," I say. "Perfect timing, in fact."

"What is *that*!" she asks, looking toward the pen where Pete is sitting—wondering, I'm sure, what he did to be banished to the netherworld.

"That's Pete, the Blairs' dog. Not pretty, is he? I thought Marcus was Dottie's youngest child, but I was wrong; Pete is, by twelve years. Dottie's crazy about that dog, hard as it is to imagine, so would you please pray nothing happens to him out there?"

"Well, I can tell you that will be way down on my prayer list."

"Move it up, will you? Honestly, I have visions of Dottie driving up Sunday and Luke running out to meet her with Pete's collar and an apology."

"What are the chances?"

"The way things are going? Probably fifty-fifty."

"Come now," she says.

"He's not a pup."

"I predict he'll be fine. I'm in a positive mood, mainly because of the dress I found for the wedding. It's perfect."

"I'm glad something is."

"I take it you haven't talked to Maisey."

"No, but she did thank me for bringing her dress. And without a trace of sarcasm."

"That's good, isn't it?"

"Beats 'I hate you' by quite a lot."

"Do you want me to come to the rehearsal after all? Moral support?"

"No, you were right. I need to give my attention to the

Blair bunch. Goodness, there are a lot of them. Maisey really is marrying into a wonderful family."

"It would be so good for both you and Maisey if you can talk to her before the wedding."

"I just have to, Paula. Maybe there will be time tonight. The kids are doing it the old-fashioned way. Marcus won't be seeing Maisey tomorrow until she walks down the aisle. Since Mother isn't here, the three of us should be alone at some point tonight. That is if she doesn't tell me at the rehearsal dinner she's spending the night at Jackie's. Now that Mother won't be here to distract us, I wouldn't be surprised. I know she doesn't want to talk to me about what she saw or what she said."

"And you do?"

"Can you imagine anything worse?"

"There's genocide."

"Well, yes, there's that."

Paula walks over to the edge of the pool with her empty water bottle and dips it under the water. Back in her chair, she dribbles water on her arms and legs and hands the bottle to me.

"I don't know how much a talk the night before her wedding can accomplish," I say, trickling the rest of the water on my arms, "but I want to at least tell my daughter how sorry I am. Then tomorrow, if she lets me catch her eye when she's walking down the aisle, there can be truth and a measure of peace between us. I'd like to accomplish that much—for her sake. And for the sake of the wedding she has looked forward to since she dressed her bride doll with such care and hopped her down our staircase, humming a perfectly pitched 'Wedding March.' "

Paula reaches over and squeezes my hand. "That will be

first on my prayer list, then," she says. "But don't worry—Pete will be second."

We sit here, staring across the field, comfortable in silent camaraderie, until Luke comes out and asks if we want something to drink.

"Bring your wife something," Paula says. "I should go. I have errands to run before dinner."

I tell Luke not to bother, that I'll come get something as soon as Paula leaves.

She has been gone awhile now, though, and here I sit, close to lethargic. I should go in. Miller and Anne will be here any minute. If they said five, they'll be here at five.

I recall the words of Paula's favorite philosopher, Mary Engelbreit. These words have been emblazoned on a sign in Paula's kitchen for I don't know how long: *Snap out of it!*

I get out of my chair and head into the house. *I'll try, Mary, I'll try.*

CHAPTER TWENTY-THREE

Maisey

Jackie, Sarah, and I drive up just behind my grandparents. The girls insist on previewing my dress now that it's safe in my closet. We run in to see it while Mom and Dad sit in the kitchen, chatting with Grandpa and Grandma. I unzip the bag, lift the dress out carefully, and lay it across my bed so they can get the full effect. It's even more beautiful than I remembered.

"Put it on," Jackie says, and though we hardly have time, I can't resist.

"Oh!" Jackie says after she gets me zipped and buttoned. For Jackie, such exclamation is the highest praise.

"Let's go down and show everyone," she says.

"We can't. We're going to be late," I say.

Jackie looks at her watch. "Come on. You have time."

And I do, if I hurry.

Jackie runs downstairs and gathers the parents and grand-parents in the living room for a private showing of the dress. I suddenly find myself apprehensive about walking down the stairs, but the expectation is there, so I can hardly change my mind. I relax a little when I come out of my room at the top of the stairs and hear Jackie telling everyone she'd play the "Wedding March" if she hadn't left her triangle at home.

As I come down the stairs, everyone is smiling, even Mother. "It's beautiful," they all say at once, but it is Mother's voice I hear most clearly, it is her eyes I see brimming with tears, her hand covering her mouth, and I can hardly catch my breath.

"I should have bought it here," I whisper when I reach the bottom of the stairs. "I should have, and I'm sorry."

Everyone else is focusing on the dress, but Mother has heard what I said.

"Don't be," she says, circling me, looking at the dress from every angle. "It couldn't be more beautiful. It's perfect."

"It *is* perfect," Dad says, "but you'd better change. We have to go."

I turn and steal a look at Mother. She's still looking at me and the dress. She seems enthralled.

"Go!" Dad says, pointing to the stairs.

Fifteen minutes later car doors are slamming, and the seven of us—Mom and Dad in their car, Grandma and Grandpa in theirs, and Sarah and Jackie in mine—take off for the church.

The rehearsal goes off without a hitch. I have handed out all sorts of warnings and assignments. I told Marcus he'd better not faint when I walk down the aisle. That's one of the disasters I've read about. And I asked Max, Marcus's brother and best man, to help take care of their five-year-old nephew, who is all about being "ring boy." It will be up to Jackie to watch out for the flower girl, the ring bearer's four-year-old sister. Even with their parents nearby, I don't trust ring bearers and flower girls, and I would drop these two from the program in a minute if they hadn't been on board and focused during the rehearsal. I don't trust candle lighters either, which is why the candles will be lit *before* the service begins.

If I can keep my veil from catching on fire—I've heard of that too—the wedding will be wonderful. I realize, of course, that any number of things can go wrong, even for the totally prepared, and believe me, I fit into that category. I overheard Jackie's aunt, the unofficial wedding coordinator, telling Mother that I've made her job quite easy.

In slightly over an hour, we have gone through everything twice, every question anyone could think of has been answered, and the crowd moves from the church to the inn. Ring Boy and Flower Girl beg to ride with Marcus and me, and the consensus on the church steps and in the parking lot is that Marcus and I will make great parents. Marcus lifts the ring bearer onto his shoulders. "Someday," he says, galloping with a shrieking little boy all the way to the car.

Dottie has gone to so much trouble preparing for the rehearsal dinner that I worry the event might be a bit uptight. But apparently the Blairs don't do uptight, and I don't know how a rehearsal dinner could be nicer. I'm glad I didn't bother to worry about the parents getting along, because they seem to be enjoying each other no end. I heard Mother saying something to Dottie about Pete wanting to stay in the guesthouse for the summer, and whatever Dottie said in reply made them laugh.

After dessert everyone gets up and mingles, talking to people who haven't been at their table. That's when I see Jackie taking Mother aside. I'm pretty sure why. And I'm right. I might look like I'm listening to Marcus's grandmother, but I hear Jackie telling Mother that she and Sarah are going to spend the night at the house now that Marcus is finally out of her room.

"Aren't you happy?" Jackie asks. I turn in time to see Mother smile at Jackie and give her a hug, which Jackie, no doubt, will take for "I'm thrilled!" But when I make the mistake of looking into Mother's eyes, it is sadness I see there, not happiness.

And I feel guilty.

I don't know why. I didn't *ask* Jackie to come.

That's pretty much what I tell Marcus as we sit on the couch in his room. We have the luxury of these few minutes together because the parents and the attendants are downstairs removing the decorations and collecting centerpieces, and Dottie insisted that Marcus and I have a little time to ourselves.

He is massaging my back as we talk.

"Why do you feel guilty?" he asks.

"I don't know."

"I'm sure you do."

That kind of remark would have infuriated me yesterday, but tonight I turn around and look at him, my spirit hushed or maybe defeated—I can't say which.

"I guess I do," I say.

"So what are you going to do about it?"

I do the only thing I can.

I go downstairs and break the news to Jackie that I really think I shouldn't have company on this particular night.

"You're kidding!" she says. I'm sure in her mind the party has just begun.

"Jackie! Think about it. Will I be fresh as a daisy tomorrow if you and Sarah spend the night?"

"We'll get you to bed at a decent hour. We're not talking an all-nighter here."

She isn't buying my objection, so I am forced to take a more honest approach. "I've been thinking I should spend this last night with just my parents."

"Why?"

Good grief.

"Actually," I say, "you gave me the idea."

"Bull."

"Watch your mouth. Besides, you did."

I feel like the Spirit has come to my rescue. If anything would help right now, reminding Jackie of her grand gesture this morning would.

"I shared the morning with *you*. And that was so nice. It made me think I should share this last night with them, just the three of us."

"Oh, okay," she says. "Fine."

"Fine," I say, hugging her.

Then I hug Sarah, who doesn't care where she spends the night. She has been planning to stay with Jackie all along, until Jackie takes her to the airport on Sunday. "No problem," she says.

When I take them home, they insist I come in "for a few minutes." But a few minutes turns out to be more than an hour, and it is late by the time I get away from the apartment.

There isn't a light on in the house, which is a relief, but when I creep inside and start up the stairs, I somehow detect Mother sitting in the living room, alone in the dark.

"Mother!" I say. "You scared me."

She reaches over and turns on the lamp by her chair. Marcus would have said she looks beautiful in the soft light.

"I thought the girls were coming home with you," she says.

"They changed their minds."

"That surprises me."

"It wasn't their idea, actually. I told them I should be alone with my parents the night before my wedding."

"That was thoughtful of you."

"Well, I knew you were disappointed when Jackie said she and Sarah were staying here. I knew it when I saw your face at the dinner. For that matter, I knew you would be when I told Jackie they could stay."

"Because we need to talk."

Which is worse? Guilt or fear? I really cannot bear to talk.

"I don't want to talk, Mother. Can't it be enough that I came home by myself? Isn't it nice that you've seen my dress? And Dad has talked to me already. I'm fine. Really."

"I need to tell you some things, Maisey."

"Please, let's just go to bed. We need a good night's sleep."

I turn and run up the steps, and at the top of the landing I don't stop and look back. Chances are too good that she will be standing there, watching me go.

I've been lying here an hour now, and I doubt I'll get a good night's sleep. Which is upsetting—I want to be rested, refreshed, relaxed for tomorrow.

I actually got up a few minutes ago, tiptoed down the stairs, and tapped lightly on Mom and Dad's door. I thought if I could just say one thing, I might be able to sleep. But when I turned the handle without a sound and peeked in, the terror I had subdued enough to get that far charged again, and I couldn't go any farther. Instead I shut the door as quietly as I had opened it and rushed back to my room.

Two or three times I've had the experience of hearing a song in my head nonstop, all its nuances as clear as if I were listening to it with my iPod set on Repeat. Something like that happened as I hurried up the stairs. What I had wanted to say when I opened Mother's door played in my mind again and again.

I hear it still.

I stare out my window at the night sky and say it aloud so at least the bedbugs and the daisies and the moonlight can hear it.

"I don't hate you."

Kendy

Poor Maisey.

That's what my heart keeps repeating.

And I don't know if I'm thinking of the twenty-two-year-old Maisey who is about to be married or the thirteen-year-old Maisey who stood in a kitchen doorway and learned the meaning of disillusionment. How terrible to disappoint one's child so completely. How terrible to be the source of her pain.

I hear something. I sit up, listening more intently.

"Did you hear that, Luke?" I whisper.

"What?"

He is all but asleep. Sleep is his gift. "Nothing," I say. Why should both of us be awake?

I was probably hearing things. Maybe Maisey's right. Luke *has* talked to her. And her anger *has* subsided. Maybe we should just go on from here. Maybe, but I don't think so.

I get up and splash water on my face, trying to clear my head. I don't think I was hearing things. That was Maisey at the door; I'm sure of it. And even if it wasn't, I'm not going to sleep tonight until this is done.

I make my way out of the bedroom, into the living room, and look up the staircase to the room where my daughter could be sleeping right now. But I doubt it.

I ascend the stairs slowly, wondering what I will say. I have no script, just some general things I want her to know. *But, dear God, what does she need to hear? Please help me say what she needs to hear.*

I stand before her door as I believe she stood before mine a few minutes ago, but I will not turn back.

I knock.

"Maisey," I whisper.

Nothing.

I open the door, and because she has not shut her blinds, the moonlight is illuminating her room. I can make out Maisey in the shadows; she is facing her window, curled up in the fetal position. I call her name again.

Nothing.

She is asleep. No—she is pretending to be asleep.

I walk over to her bed, pull back the covers, and slip in beside her. I curl up behind her and dare to put my arm over her, dare to pull her to me.

"Did you come to our room a while ago?" I ask.

She is silent, but I can feel she is awake. I wait. I can wait; just having her in my arms begins to fill a place that has been empty and aching for so long.

She says something.

"What, honey? I didn't hear you."

"I said—I don't hate you."

I wonder if she can feel my heart pounding. I find her hand and cover it with mine.

"I didn't think you did, Maisey. But I understand why you said it."

I think of sitting up, of turning on the light, but I'm not inclined to move.

"I know you've talked to your dad, but I have to tell you myself how sorry I am, Maisey. Sorry about so many things."

I take a deep breath. She seems to be listening, and I will take this chance to tell her what I've been wanting to say since Wednesday night.

"I'm sorry that I crossed the line with Clay—if you'll allow me to say it that way."

She says nothing, but she pulls her hand from mine and sits up on the edge of her bed, staring into the night sky, her back to me.

I sit up too, determined to get this said. "I'm sorry about Clay for a lot of reasons. You loved him, and you loved Rebecca, and your relationship with them virtually ended when you came into the kitchen that day and saw us like that."

She shakes her head back and forth, as though she's trying to fend off something terrible. But I have more to say.

"I'm sorry that what Clay and I shared, what we *stole*, hurt your father. It was disloyal, and it diminished your father and me during that time. And I'm sorry for how unkind all of it was to Rebecca, even if she didn't know the extent of our involvement."

She is crying now, blotting her tears with the edge of her sheet. Tears stream down my face too. I hate that Maisey has reaped what I have sown.

"I'm sorry about Clay because it was wrong, and I knew it."

She throws herself back on the bed, burying her face in her pillow.

I wish I were through tormenting her with my regrets, but I'm not.

"I'm also sorry I shut down when we lost the baby. I didn't mean to, Maisey, but though I was only as far as my room, I might as well have moved to another universe. I'm sure you felt like I had abandoned you."

"I missed you," she whispers. "Even when I was so mad, I missed you so much."

I touch her hair, and I am shocked at how violently she pulls away.

"Don't!" She has spit the word at me. She jerks herself up, holding her pillow as a barrier between us, and she glares at me through her tears. "You *left* me! How could you leave me? How could you *do* that?"

I'm horrified that this is how she has interpreted my months of depression. But she has, and I have to understand that. I have to accept it.

My answer is unsatisfactory, but the only answer I have.

"I didn't think I *was* leaving you, honey," I say, looking past her, past the windows and the daisies that surround them, into the darkness beyond. "As far as *how* I could do any of the things I did, I can't say with any certainty. But whatever the reason, it wasn't good enough."

"No, it wasn't! You *did* leave me, Mother. You left me for Clay, and then you left me for the baby. And I couldn't do anything about it."

"Then, Maisey," I say, looking at her again and lifting the pillow from her lap and setting it beside us, "of all the things I'm sorry for, I'm most sorry for that."

I put my hand on her warm, wet cheek and look into her eyes, eyes I have loved since she blinked them open for the first time and looked up at me, pleased, or so it seemed, to be wrapped snuggly in a soft blanket and held in the arms of a woman who so obviously adored her.

And now, another miracle, Maisey allows my hand to remain on her face, and she does not turn away.

But she is tired. She is nine years tired.

She gets up and goes into her bathroom. I lie here while she washes her face and blows her nose. I wonder if she'll choose to stay in the bathroom, but the door is opening and she comes back to the bed. I sit up now and put a pillow against the headboard. I put her pillow against the headboard too, taking a chance that she'll sit with me. I'm so happy that she chooses to plop down, her shoulder brushing against mine.

"I would have asked for your forgiveness long before now, Maisey, if I'd only known what you saw."

She turns and looks out her window. This is what we are choosing when we cannot look at each other.

"I *couldn't* tell you," she says.

"I'm sure you couldn't."

"I couldn't tell anyone."

Now I am silent, unsure of what to say.

"Oh, I wanted to sometimes," she says. "There really were times I wanted to tell Jackie and the others. But I couldn't."

She turns and looks at me in the dark. "Why do you think I couldn't?"

The question is not a riddle or a challenge. Her face indicates she is genuinely puzzled. I brush away a piece of hair that has fallen into her eyes. Without mulling it over at all, I think I have the answer for her question.

"Because you love me."

"Yes," she says, wonder in her voice. "I guess that's it." She sounds as though she has stumbled on a remarkable truth.

I take her hand. "I need you to know something, Maisey, because after tonight, I hope we won't ever have to speak of this again."

"Okay," she says.

"The baby we lost was your dad's. Anything else was impossible. Do you understand?"

"I embellished?"

"Well, that's easy to do."

Tears slip down her face again. She wipes them away with the back of her hands. I get up and retrieve a box of Kleenex from the bathroom.

"I'm not through with my litany of regrets yet," I say, holding up the box. I sit down on her bed again, Maisey on my left, the Kleenex box on my right.

"I'm sorry for what we've missed the last nine years."

"Well, I have to share the blame for that, don't I?"

She starts to cry again.

I pull out Kleenexes and hand some to her.

"I pushed you away!" she says, dabbing her face with the tissues. "Maybe I was trying to hurt you for what you had done to Dad and to me. Maybe I left you because I thought you had left me. I don't really know, but I do know I wouldn't forgive you. I wouldn't. I chose above anything and everything else to remember that afternoon in the kitchen, and I'm sorry. I'm so sorry."

I hold her then and pat her back and stroke her hair. "It's okay, honey," I say. "It's okay." And finally her tears subside and her breathing returns to normal.

I go into the bathroom and get both of us cold washcloths to soothe our hot, puffy faces, and Maisey stands up to pull her bottom sheet taut and straighten the top sheet and blanket.

"The bed's a mess," she says, fluffing the pillows and laying them on the bed again.

"*We're* a mess," I say.

We pull back the covers on a bed that looks quite inviting now and lie down again, side by side, with the cold washcloths folded across our eyes.

"Here's what I think, Maisey."

"What?"

"I think we should try not to fret about what we've missed during the last nine years. What good will that do? Let's just think about what we had, because we had a lot. Your dad and I loved going to your ball games and concerts. And you and I did most of the things we would have done—we just had plenty of company."

I'm not sure, but I think Maisey laughed at that.

"You spent precious time with your dad, time you might not have spent if things had been different. And chances are you wouldn't have gone to college in St. Louis if you hadn't been so upset with me. And while it hurt to have you so far away, I can't think of anything that could have been more wonderful for my mother. And of course there's Marcus."

"There's Marcus," she says, and I hear the smile in her voice.

"And there's this, Maisey: No one can take the splendor of your first thirteen years from us. No one."

"That's true. These last two days I have learned and realized and remembered so much. Yesterday Marcus asked me if you were a good mother. I said yes."

She lifts the washcloth off my eyes and takes it with hers into her bathroom and hangs them side by side on a towel rack. On the way back to bed, she stops to shut her blinds.

"Let's go to sleep," she says, "I'm absolutely exhausted."

"Me too," I say.

She climbs back into bed and turns to face her window. She reaches for my hand and draws my arm over her.

"Good night, Mom."

"Good night, Maisey."

She yawns, which makes me yawn.

It feels so good to lie here beside my daughter, to know that this night she will finally sleep in peace.

"I love you, Mom," she says.

I pull her close and kiss the soft skin of her shoulder, remembering the apple smell of her hair. In my heart I pray my psalm: *Praise the Lord, O my soul.*

Aloud I say, "I love you too, my sweet girl, Maisey."

She's almost asleep, but I hear, "More darling than a daisy."

Yes.

SATURDAY

CHAPTER TWENTY-FOUR

Kendy

"Okay, girls," Luke says, standing in Maisey's doorway, "you've slept long enough! Breakfast is on the table."

He informs us that he awoke at seven, wondered where I was, finally found me asleep in Maisey's room, checked on us again at eight, and decided he'd let us sleep until nine. Sleeping so soundly and being awakened by Luke announcing breakfast is a most excellent way to start a day.

We get up with no argument and follow him downstairs.

"French toast!" Maisey and I say in unison when we come into the kitchen, where the table is set and abounds with everything an outstanding breakfast requires. My husband has been busy while we slept.

"Goodness, Luke," I say, sitting down and taking a sip of my juice.

Both Maisey and I eat three pieces of French toast and split the last piece left on the platter. Overindulging for sure, but we agree we'll eat only a salad for lunch on our way to meet the girls at the salon at two. The wedding party and families are meeting at the church at five to get ready and to have as many pictures taken as possible—any, that is, that don't require both the bride and groom.

"So," Maisey says, looking at her dad and then at me as she cuts her French toast, "Marcus and I will come by to pick up our wedding gifts when we get back from Hawaii. We can open them then if that's okay with you."

"That will be fine," I say, "but I'm going to Mother's on Monday to spend a few days. I could take them to her condo, or I could even drop them by your apartment."

"We'll come home."

Such lovely words. Luke and I look at each other. We have just heard words to cherish. They will vie with her first word, prized for twenty-one years now, as most memorable.

Maisey stabs another piece of toast and reaches for the syrup. "I *want* to come home," she says.

Winner and champion.

"And have I told you—Dad, hand me the bacon—that Marcus is going to try to get a job in Indy when he finishes law school? Gram and St. Louis have us for a few more years; then we're coming home for good. At least that's our plan."

"That's great," Luke says.

"We'd love it," I say.

She looks at us and smiles. "So would I."

As soon as we finish eating, Luke sends Maisey and me to

take showers and otherwise prepare for the day. I tell him he is outdoing himself, making breakfast *and* cleaning it up.

"I'm just a nice guy," he says.

Maisey gives him a kiss on the way out of the kitchen and says, "That's for sure."

After she leaves the room, Luke looks at me and smiles. "So," he says, "you and Maisey finally talked."

I throw my arms around his neck. "We did! We had a wonderful talk."

If Luke and I were a picture on the front page of the newspaper, we'd surely look like a couple reunited after escaping some tragedy, a tornado maybe, or a devastating fire. I could remain in his arms all morning, but he, having a penchant for the practical, says I need to get ready and he has a kitchen to clean.

It isn't long before Luke comes into the bathroom and finds me sitting at my vanity, having barely gotten out of the shower. "Kitchen's clean," he says.

"I'm not moving very fast," I say. "I've been thinking about how talkative Maisey was at breakfast. She seems happy, doesn't she?"

"Very," he says.

Luke has come in wanting the scoop about last night. I'm surprised by his curiosity. I really thought his seeing us in her bed together this morning might have said it all. That, and my confirmation in the kitchen that we had a good talk. But he sits on the side of the whirlpool tub, awaiting the details, and I'm glad to tell him what happened from the time I thought I heard her at our bedroom door until I put my arms around her and we whispered good night, her childhood rhyme a benediction.

"Well, that's good," he says when I finish. "It's like an infected wound has been cleansed, medicated, and bandaged. I know it was painful, but I predict a healing beyond what we can 'ask or imagine.' "

"My ever-positive, Ephesians 3 husband."

He smiles, guilty as charged.

"Our daughter has wanted her mom back for a long time," he says. "I'm not surprised she's so happy this morning."

"It's in her chatter, in her smile and eyes, isn't it?" I say. "I'm going to help her pack when I finish getting ready. She wants to show me the things she got at her shower and some other things too. Isn't it wonderful? Such simple things are just too wonderful."

"Get with it, then," he says, heading for the door. "I'll be outside when you and Maisey need help carrying stuff out."

He leaves and I get out the hair dryer and straightening iron, thinking that the morning has been as nice as last night was, minus the trauma. Maisey's wedding *will* be perfect—even if the ring bearer and flower girl exchange fire walking down the aisle, their weapons of choice a pillow and a basket.

At breakfast Maisey was no longer just a daddy's girl. She was *our* girl. That fills me with pleasure.

Maisey

I call Marcus as soon as I come upstairs. I don't even wait until I take my shower. I want him to hear me happy. Completely happy.

He can't believe Mom slept with me.

"Well, we just fell asleep," I say. "We were so tired, but I'm rested now. Dad let us sleep late, and I ate a huge breakfast."

"Finally hungry?"

"Starved."

"I'm glad you're rested. We have a wedding, a reception, and a wedding night ahead of us."

"I'm good to go," I say. "Can't wait. But thank goodness our flight tomorrow isn't at the crack of dawn."

"Your grandpa's idea."

"Isn't he smart?"

"Good at his job," Marcus says. "Now, tell me about last night."

I tell him to put his feet up, because I want to tell him everything. I even tell him about going down to Mom and Dad's room and turning back at the last minute. "But Mom didn't turn back," I say. "She came in and crawled right into bed beside me. I needed that so much, Marcus, and finally I was ready for it."

"I'm glad you got things settled. You sound happy. You sound free."

"Yes! That's how I feel. Free. And I can't seem to quit smiling. Things are going to be all right, Marcus. And I have you to thank for that—at least you deserve a lot of the credit. Honestly, if you hadn't confronted me Wednesday, the anger would still be there, pushing Mom away. You were right; that has taken the edge off my happiness, and for a long time now."

"You can show me your appreciation tonight."

I laugh. "I plan on it. You can be glad Dad was here watching out for your interests, letting me sleep late, calling me to the kitchen to energize me with thousands of calories. But really, can you believe I slept until nine?"

"Can you believe my brother had me up at seven to run three miles?"

"Which one?"

"Max. He's a fanatic. Rain or shine or my wedding day—every morning must start with a run."

"Did you keep up with him?"

"Sort of."

"Are you recovered?"

"Reasonably."

"Good," I say. "I need a *big* favor."

I tell him what I want him to do, carefully explaining it. He asks questions and clarifies details, and I know I can count on him to take care of things.

"Go as many places as you have to," I say. "As many as you have time for anyway. I want this to be outrageous!"

"I will. Max will help; he owes me big time. But this is going to take a while, so I've got to get going."

"Okay," I say, "but do you realize that the next time I talk to you, we'll be exchanging our vows? Unless you stand me up. Then I'll never speak to you again."

"You know something? I'll bet you would. But we'll never know, because I won't be standing you up. I have loved you since you hand-mixed concrete under a Mexican sun, no makeup, a bandanna tied around your forehead, sweat drenching your entire body."

I assure him that's when I began loving him too. And then he is off, running an errand I can't, doing for me what I can't possibly do myself, not today. And I'm off to the shower. I hurry because Mom is coming up to help me pack when she finishes getting ready. I have a lot of things to show her before we leave this afternoon, my suitcases in the trunk of my car. Dottie will transfer Marcus's suitcases there when they get to the church.

This is too, too exciting.

I look at the clock on my bedside table. Only a few hours now, and I'll be Maize Anne Laswell Blair—Maisey Blair for short.

After taking a shower and getting ready in record time, I grab one of the suitcases I need out of the closet and open it on my bed just as Mom appears in the doorway, looking refreshed.

"Ready?" she asks.

I smile, so happy to see her standing there.

"Ready."

CHAPTER TWENTY-FIVE

Kendy

It is done.

Maisey and Marcus are married at last.

Whatever we paid for Maisey's dress was worth it. She took my breath away. It was a delight to see that she took Marcus's breath away too. I was enchanted by everything else as well: the fabulously dressed wedding party, the string quartet, the abundance of candles and flowers, the minister's words, chosen with love for just the two of them. Because I knew so little of what Maisey had planned, I experienced the full impact of it all, and I understood why the audience broke out in spontaneous applause when the bride and groom were introduced as "Mr. and Mrs. Marcus and Maisey Blair."

As I walked up the aisle with one of the handsome ushers, I saw smiling people everywhere I looked. And the reception was as delightful: tasteful décor, a wonderful variety of music, delicious food. The atmosphere—whether people sat at tables, clustered in small groups to talk, or crowded the dance floor—was joyous.

The festivities started with dinner and ended with a dance. As Luke and I took to the floor and danced beside Maisey and Marcus, tears of gratitude hovered, threatening to spoil my makeup. I blinked them away, though; I had replaced my makeup after the wedding ceremony and didn't intend to do it again. Eventually most everyone was on the dance floor: couples as diverse as Jackie and Sam, recent college graduates, and Miller and Anne, on the brink of retirement.

Maisey and Marcus, after beginning their married life enjoying their family and friends, kissed all of us good-bye and left for Indy around eleven. We all stood in the parking lot, throwing birdseed and waving them on their way. The party began breaking up shortly after that. Jackie and Sam stayed until they could catch Luke and me alone so that Sam could make his presentation. As he put a John Deere tractor in my hand, Jackie looked a lot like Maisey did when she first came home and told us about Marcus.

"Are you asleep?" Luke asks from the driver's seat.

"Just resting my eyes," I say. I open them to see where we are. Familiar landmarks tell me we are ten minutes from home. "I was thinking about the tractor in my purse."

"Jackie may be the next one down the aisle."

"I wouldn't be surprised."

"To change the subject," Luke says, "Dottie said she's coming by the house to see Pete."

"*Tonight?* It's midnight, Luke!"

"Well, she *said* she was, but Doug said they were going straight to their hotel room."

"Doug Blair is a dear and prudent man. They both seemed glad to marry off son number five, didn't they? And they seem to love Maisey as much as we love Marcus."

"I think they do."

"Maybe Maisey will enjoy her mother- and father-in-law as much as I enjoy mine," I say, patting Luke's leg. "It's so nice when that happens."

"Dottie and Doug are good people. By the way, you did hear they're meeting us at church tomorrow, didn't you? They will probably go out to eat with us, but Dottie wants to retrieve Pete and be on the road by three."

"Good, we'll have some time to ourselves before I head for St. Louis Monday morning."

"Want me to take some days off and come with you?"

"I don't think so. I'd like to have some girl time with Mother . . . as much as Phillip will allow anyway."

"Phillip?"

"It's only a suspicion, but I do believe Mother has found a man she actually enjoys."

"Her boss?" Luke seems shocked.

"Wouldn't that be something?" I say. "I'll take a DVD of wedding pictures to show Mother while I'm there. She'll be glad to see how nicely everything turned out. I hope to be home by Thursday, since the kids will be back here Saturday. I may go back to Mom's a few days after that. Then I'll have a week or so before school starts. Pardon me while I rest my eyes again."

I think I might have actually dozed off, because we are

pulling into the garage. We come into the kitchen and turn on the light.

"What in the world!" I say.

The sight is glorious.

"Did you do this, Luke?"

"Don't look at me!"

On the bar are two large vases filled with daisies. There is another vase on the kitchen table. I walk over and look for a card, but none of the vases has one.

"I can't believe it," I say.

Luke has turned on a light in the living room and is calling for me. I walk in, and the living room and the dining room have been transformed. Vases of daisies are everywhere. Three sit on the piano, two are on the large coffee table, and every other table in the room boasts a vase full of the darling daisies. Another vase graces the dining room table, and two more are reflected in the mirror over the sideboard.

"They're amazing," I say.

I check each vase for a card, finding nothing. But of course I know who is responsible for this daisy wonderland, and overwhelmed by this offering, I sit on the couch, my face in my hands, and sob.

Our daughter has done a wondrous thing.

Luke sits beside me and dries my tears with one of the Kleenexes he had neatly folded and put in his jacket pocket for emergencies.

He smiles, and I smile back.

"Come on," he says, and he takes my hand and we go into the bedroom, where daisies overflow vases on the dresser, our bedside tables, and the table by the chaise longue. I can even see a vase on my vanity in the bathroom. It is propped against this final vase that I find a card.

It is one of Maisey's gold-embossed thank-you cards. I read it, smiling through the tears once again gathering in my eyes.

I hand the note to Luke and he reads it while I walk through the house once more, looking at this astonishing display of forgiveness and honor and love. I examine the flowers, wondering how Maisey could have orchestrated such a thing, how she could have found so many flawless flowers so quickly, how she could have afforded such extravagance.

Luke says that this gift was obviously a collaboration between Maisey and Marcus. And I know he's right.

"Let's go to bed, babe," he says.

"I don't want this day to end."

Of course I know it must, so I take myself into our bathroom and begin the routine—from the sublime to the mundane. Except tonight, as I exchange my dress for a gown, wash my face, brush my teeth, and take my vitamin and calcium pills, daisies keep me company.

"Done," I say, returning to the bedroom, "but I hate to turn out the light."

"The house will still be full of daisies tomorrow," Luke says.

"That's true."

I sit on the edge of the bed and read my card one more time before I place it against the vase on my bedside table, turn out the light, and nestle close to my husband, throwing my arm across him as I did Maisey last night.

I know he's practically asleep, but he turns to kiss me, an absolute necessity on such a momentous night. "Good night, Kendy."

"Good night, honey."

A *very* good night!

My smile lingers even in the dark, and I thank God that Maisey's wedding was as wonderful as we hoped it would be when she was a child.

I'll probably read Maisey's note again tomorrow before I put it, along with Mother's note, into my memory box for safekeeping. But when I read it in the future, it'll only be for the pure joy of seeing her familiar handwriting, for what she has said will be forever engraved on my heart:

> Mom~
>
> The bedbugs want you to have these daisies. (The bedbugs are talking again, making up for lost time.) They say to share these flowers with Dad. They say your daughter loves you both very much. They say it is you, Mom, who is more darling than a daisy. Though daisies are lovely, aren't they?
>
> ~Maisey

NOVELS BY JACKINA STARK

Tender Grace
Things Worth Remembering

For reading group discussion questions
and additional book club resources,
please visit

www.bethanyhouse.com/anopenbook.

JACKINA (pronounced with a long "i" to rhyme with China) STARK recently retired from teaching English at Ozark Christian College to spend more time writing and traveling. During the twenty-eight years she taught at OCC, she traveled nationally and internationally to speak and teach, and wrote many articles for denominational magazines. She has been married to her husband, Tony, for forty-two years. They live in Carl Junction, Missouri, and have two daughters and six grandchildren.

More From
Jackina Stark

Sometimes it's not the destination but the *journey* that brings healing. But can Audrey embrace the unexpected graces that guide her journey?

Tender Grace by Jackina Stark

IF YOU ENJOYED *THINGS WORTH REMEMBERING*, YOU MAY ALSO LIKE:

She's lost one son. And telling the truth means she might lose the other. How can a mother choose?

Leaving Yesterday by Kathryn Cushman

Sarah Graham is living life hard and fast until it comes to a screeching halt. Now, the only way to find her future is to make peace with her past.

Home Another Way by Christa Parrish

Stay Up-to-Date on Your Favorite Books and Authors!

Be the first to know about new releases, meet your favorite authors, read book excerpts and more with our free e-newsletters.

Go to www.bethanyhouse.com to sign up today!

Calling All Book Groups!

Read exclusive author interviews, get the inside scoop on books, sign up for the free e-newsletter—and more—at **www.bethanyhouse.com/AnOpenBook**.

An Open Book: A Book Club Resources Exchange